SOUL OF MEMPHIS

SABRA WALDFOGEL

CONTENTS

1

NOT IN MY RIGHT MIND

Post-divorce, I wasn't in my right mind, as all my friends were glad to tell me. After eight years and two miscarriages, my husband had traded me in for a younger model, Jewish on both sides and demonstrably fertile. When he asked me for a divorce, he said, "She's pregnant." I didn't hasten the proceedings because he wanted his child to be born legitimate. I hastened them because I was too hurt and angry to be married to him anymore.

I agreed to put the condo on the market. I quit my job at Sotheby's. I'd been there for almost fifteen years, starting as an intern and becoming an expert in early American furniture and decorative arts. And then I left New York. I went back to Memphis.

It wasn't an impulsive decision. Even though I'd lived in New York since I started at Columbia University, even though I presented myself as Natalie Raskin, a Jew who happened to grow up in Memphis, I'd never lost my Southern accent. New Yorkers never lost their habit of assuming I was a redneck because of it. In my work, I

1

dealt in the small distinctions that made the difference between an eighteenth-century rarity and a worthless contemporary copy. It made me crazy that no one in New York heard the nuance in my speech. I wasn't a redneck. On my father's side, I was descended from Russian Jews who had landed in the Mississippi Delta in 1900 and moved to Memphis in 1920. But on my mother's side, the Beardsley side, I was descended from a family that had settled in western Tennessee a few years after it opened up, in the 1820s. They were cotton planters and cotton brokers and, I regret to say, slaveowners. But they were patricians. Even my mother, so far removed from those origins, lived up to them.

After the divorce and all the losses it brought in its wake, I admitted to myself that the persona of Nat Raskin, New York Jew who happened to grow up in Memphis, was a dress that no longer fit me. I was Natalie Minerva Beardsley Raskin, and I was going home.

I settled back into the house I'd grown up in. I moved into the bedroom I'd left at eighteen, swearing I'd never live in Memphis again, and I felt the full misery of my situation. I had the money to move. After the personal wreckage, my ex-husband was decent about dividing our assets. He was glad to sell the condo. After all, he was moving into her apartment, a better address and a better place than we'd ever been able to afford. I left New York with my half, more than a million dollars. But I was too flattened to do anything about it. I was all right for money, but I wasn't all right in my soul, as Mavis, the housekeeper of my childhood, would have put it.

I didn't miss New York, but I missed my job at Sotheby's. I'd always loved old things. One of my earliest memories is of being in my Grandmother Beardsley's house, transfixed by a Limoges vase painted with violets. I knew better than to touch anything at Grandmother's, but my mother swears I pointed at it, saying, "Pretty. So pretty!"

At Sotheby's, my Southern accent helped to pigeonhole me into American decorative art, and I found myself learning to research and evaluate the objects I'd loved as a little girl. They spoke to the adult in a different way. One of the joys of working for an auction house was that I could touch anything I wanted, as long as I handled it carefully. Objects had histories and secrets, as people did. And I'd learned how to unearth them.

I'D BEEN BACK for a week when my mother invited the rest of the Raskins for a Sunday barbecue. My brother, Josh, his wife, Celia, and their two kids, a girl of eight and a boy of five, arrived in a burst of noise and activity. The kids ran to my mother and father, their grandparents, for hugs, shrieking their greetings.

"Kids, kids," my sister-in-law said. "Don't maul your grandmother like that. You're no better than the dog!"

"Arf, arf," my nephew said, grabbing my mother's leg.

My mother tousled his hair with one hand while squeezing his sister close with her free arm. Laughing, she said, "It's all right. Puppies or kids, I'll take it."

My niece said, "He's a dog! I'm not!"

Josh laughed. "It's no worse than what I get when I

come home." Josh was a lawyer, working for a firm that specialized in handling estates, and he worked long hours while my sister-in-law kept the home fires burning. I suspected she wasn't completely happy about it, but she had never complained to me.

I stood aside, feeling out of place.

My nephew pointed at me. "Who's that?"

"Don't point!" my mother said.

Celia admonished my mother with a look. *Let me handle this.* "That's your Aunt Nat, who used to live in New York and who's come back to Memphis."

He shook his head.

My mother said to my niece, "Give your aunt a hug, too." My niece detached herself from my mother's embrace, but she didn't run to me, either.

My last visit to Memphis had been for my grandfather's funeral four years ago. Of course they didn't remember me. "It's all right," I said. "I'll be around, and you'll see a lot more of me. We'll get to know each other."

Losing interest, my nephew asked, "Can we go downstairs and watch videos?"

Before my mother could say anything, Celia said, "I'll get them settled." As they ran downstairs, she rolled her eyes and said to me, "They're a handful." But her comment was full of affection.

After the second miscarriage, I'd developed a pain in the spot where the baby had sat, so severe that I visited my gynecologist for relief. She told me it was caused by emotion, not physical damage, and gently suggested that I talk to a therapist. Now I felt it again, and I pressed my hand against the spot that hurt so much.

"Are you feeling all right?" Celia asked.

"Just a little cramp. It's nothing."

Celia went downstairs.

The doorbell rang. It was Nana. Four years ago, when I'd been back to sit shiva for my grandfather, Nana had looked small and frail. Now she was restored to her usual sturdy self, her face filled out again and her eyes bright. After Grandpa died, she'd stopped coloring her hair, and it was now a peppery gray, carefully cut and styled around her face. Like all the Raskins, she cared about clothes, and she was chic again—not just for nearly eighty but by any standard.

Before she took off her coat, she made a beeline for me and hugged me close, enveloping me in her familiar smell, eau de cologne and fresh babka. "It's so good to see you," she said. She laid her hand on my cheek. "I'm so sorry about your divorce."

I covered her hand with my own. "So am I."

"We'll talk later. Just the two of us."

That was a promise she'd keep. Since I'd been my niece's age, I'd been confiding and she'd been listening. The pain in my midsection ebbed.

As the adults arranged themselves in the living room, my mother offered drinks and brought in cheese and crackers. My mother liked changing the décor, but she hadn't turned the house into something I no longer recognized. A new sofa, some new pillows, new pictures on the walls: this was still home, just a bit refreshed.

As we noshed, my brother said, "We're glad to see you back, Nat, but we're all a little surprised, too."

"You won't hold me to something stupid I said when I was eighteen, I hope."

"Oh, I remember hearing it again when you were twenty-one and then again when you were thirty."

He was teasing me, but it bothered me. "I've got to say, I'm surprised, too."

"Are you planning to stay in Memphis?" Celia asked.

"I think so."

"What are you thinking about doing?"

I picked up my wineglass and swirled the liquid in the bowl. "Maybe I'll open a branch for Sotheby's down here," I said.

Nana said, "Don't hock her. Of course she doesn't know yet. How long have you been back? A week?"

Suddenly everything hurt again, and I needed some air. I excused myself to go outside. I stood on the deck and stayed there for so long that I began to shiver, even though it was fifty degrees out, the equivalent of spring in New York.

The door opened. "Hey, Nat?" It was Josh. "Are you okay?"

"Sort of."

Josh and I had been close as children but had gone our separate ways as adolescents. As adults, we'd been able to recapture our childhood warmth. He'd called me when he heard about the divorce. "I am so sorry about your divorce. Again."

"Me too." I was shivering in earnest now.

He put his arm around my shoulders and hugged me close. "Let me know if you need any help."

"Legal help?" I said, trying to keep the emotion at bay.

"More like family help. Settling into Memphis. Or wrangling with Mom and Dad."

At that I managed a shaky laugh. "I may need that."

"Come back in. You're freezing."

Once we were inside, the back door opened and banged shut, and the smell of barbecued ribs wafted from the kitchen. We were Memphians. What else would we eat? But we were Jews, and at home, for our own cultural reasons, we ate beef ribs. Nothing could diminish my pleasure in the meal. The ribs. The slaw. The biscuits. I'd never been the kind of New Yorker who picked at her food, and now I found I had an appetite for the taste of home.

As I ate, Nana said, "Mike, your father's yahrzeit is coming up in a few weeks."

"I know, Mama."

"Do you need a candle? I can pick one up at the Temple gift shop. A nice one."

"No, Mama, I'm all right." My father had never been religious—he'd been raised Reform at Temple Israel, and he'd spent his life crafting a dual identity for Josh and me —but I was surprised that he'd be diffident about remembering his own father, whom he'd not only loved but revered when he was alive.

"Because it's no trouble."

My father, a clothing retailer who spent his days in diplomacy, tamped down his discomfort. He smiled at his mother and said, "Of course it isn't."

My mother had learned to deflect her mother-in-law's determination. She smiled too. "Don't hock him, Lillian."

Nana laughed. "You learned that expression from me."

"After thirty years, what do you expect?"

In the lightened mood, I asked my father, "I was wondering what happened to Grandpa's record collection. Didn't he have all those singles from Stax?"

Nana said, "Oh, they're gone. Your father wanted to throw them out, but I wouldn't hear of it. I sold them, and I was surprised how much I got for them."

"They're all gone?" I asked, disappointed.

In surprise, my father said, "Why would you want vinyl? Don't you stream all your music these days?"

"Sure, to listen to. But I wanted something of Grandpa's as a memento." Grandpa Mo had left me something more significant than his record collection. He'd left both of us, Josh and me, a bequest of $50,000. We'd each used it the same way, to make a down payment on a house.

Josh said, "Dad, don't we still own the building downtown?"

"You still own that? I thought you'd sold it," I said.

"I should sell it."

The building had housed the clothing store that my great-grandfather established and that my grandfather had built up. We had a moment of Memphis notoriety when my grandfather decided to serve Black customers in the early 1960s. My father had parlayed Raskin's into his current business, a chain of pricey women's boutiques in Memphis's ritzy suburbs. Coming from a family in the rag trade had made all of us snappy dressers.

Josh asked, "Any progress on renting it?"

"No luck yet."

My mother said, "I'm beginning to think the building is cursed. Nothing lasts longer than a year there."

My father said, "It's just retail. The last tenants had a tough go. I didn't think they'd be there long."

Nana said, "The last time I stopped in there, I swear I could feel Mo's ghost. Maybe he won't let it go."

I reached for my father's hand. "I've been in a lot of places that have a ghost," I said.

He rose and kissed my hair as he had when I was a little girl. He smiled. "Don't worry, we won't sell it anytime soon."

I WAS IDLE, frittering away my days in the house in Germantown, and my mother worried about me. She offered to take me shopping, an activity that had always entertained me when I was a teenager but had little appeal at the moment. She didn't care for antiques, but she suggested excursions to antique shops, which interested me even less. She kept trying. She said, "There's a vintage market in Cordova this weekend. Do you want to go?"

"No antiques, please."

"No, it's mostly newer stuff. Crafts, too. What your father would call tchotchkes. It's fun. It's indoors, in this weather."

My father said, "It's lively, Nat. Crowded. It should remind you of New York."

I'd never minded the crowd in New York. Every day in Manhattan, the streets were more crowded than Memphis. "All right," I said.

It was fun. I wasn't looking for anything, and I followed my mother's lead when I didn't let the crowd pull me along. I suspended my Sotheby's snobbery. When my mother stopped to admire some hand-thrown pottery, saying, "Isn't this nice, Nat?" I replied, "Yes."

We were looking at hand-loomed scarves when a woman said to me, "Nat? Nat Raskin, is that you?"

I stared at her, trying hard to place her. I said, "I'm sorry, but if I used to know you, it's been too long."

"I look a lot different. Jude Phelps."

We'd been in high school together, and she was right, she'd changed too much for recognition. Judy Phelps had been a bouncy blonde. This woman was gaunt and pale—stress, I hoped, not sickness—and her close-cropped hair was black streaked with dark blue.

"Now I'm really embarrassed," I said.

"Don't be. Seeing you is like seeing a ghost. You swore you'd never come back to Memphis."

Looking at her, I said, "Obviously a lot can change in fifteen years."

"Are you really back? Not just visiting?"

"Really back."

"What are you doing?"

"Recovering from a divorce."

She snorted. "Oh, man. Been through the changes?"

I nodded. "You, too?"

"You see how I changed."

"What are you up to?"

"I was an interior designer until I got tired of it. I still find stuff for designers, but I'm mostly an antique dealer now."

"What's your area?"

She smiled, and I could see the suburban belle's charm

flicker on her face. "Mid-century modern. Modern Memphis." She dug out a card from her shoulder bag.

I took it. "I worked at Sotheby's in New York," I said. "Early American. I don't know what I'm going to do with it in modern Memphis."

"You'd be surprised," she said.

I looked at her card.

She asked, "Would you like to get together for coffee?"

A FEW DAYS LATER, we met in Midtown. Jude's words had been resonating with me. I still wasn't all right. I didn't miss a single human being I'd known in New York. I missed the feel of porcelain, crystal, and mahogany in my hands.

Over coffee, I asked her how she made a living as an antique dealer.

"I have some cases in a mall and another in a vintage shop," she said. "And if I find something good enough, it goes to auction. Not always in Memphis. I'll take it to Nashville or New Orleans, or send it to New York."

"Hand to mouth."

"Sometimes yes, sometimes no. I have a bit of a cushion. I took my ex to the cleaners. Believe me, he deserved it." She pushed her hair behind her ears, and her earrings glittered.

I couldn't help it. I didn't know much about jewelry, but I recognized Edwardian design when I saw it, and I doubted that the bits that caught the light were glass. "I like your earrings," I said.

"Family heirloom," she said, fingering them. "From my grandmother."

"Are you a collector?"

She nodded. "And a dealer, too. I'm a gemologist, so I know my way around estate jewelry."

"That and mid-century modern."

"Why not? I've always liked sparkly things. And I learned a lot from selling the stuff my ex gave me."

I said, "So you got what you deserved, too."

She laughed. "I did."

I asked her, "Have you thought about running your own shop?"

"I've thought about it. I've decided against it. I can't take the risk. I wish I could find a better place to showcase the bigger things. My merch doesn't do well in the malls, and being a case dealer limits me to smaller stuff. I keep eyeing the shops in town and wondering which one would be a good fit."

"And you haven't found one."

"Not yet." She sipped her coffee from the tall paper cup, as dainty a gesture as a debutante taking tea.

I liked her. I empathized with her, fleeing a bad marriage and surviving its breakup. And after we talked, I thought again about the building on South Main.

I called her a few days later. "Can you meet me on South Main? I have something to show you."

We met on the sidewalk outside the building. She looked puzzled. I said, "This building is going to be vacant at the end of the month."

"How do you know?"

"My family owns it."

"Would they rent it to you?"

"They might."

"And what would you do with it?"

"It might be right for an antique shop," I said. "I wanted you to take a look. I'd like your opinion."

"What's gone wrong with the current business?"

"I don't know. We'll ask."

The shop, a gift shop aimed at tourists, wasn't well-stocked. They were clearly winding down. The owner, a tired-looking woman in her sixties, greeted us and invited us to look around.

Jude didn't bother to look at the merchandise. She looked at the space. "The front windows are great," she said. "A lot of light, and room for displays." She wound around the shelves and tables that were depleted of merchandise. "A lot of room for floor groupings, too. And for cases. Six cases? Ten?"

The owner didn't pretend that she couldn't hear us. "Are you thinking of renting the place?"

I said, "Maybe."

"How's business been?" Jude asked.

"Not what we hoped," she said. "We thought it would be fun to run a shop after my husband retired. It's too much for us. That's why we're closing it up."

Jude said, "It's a lot of work."

"What kind of business are you in? What would you put in here?"

Jude let me answer. "An antique shop."

"I'm sure you'd do all right here."

"You never know," Jude said.

On the sidewalk, she said, "It's a great space. It could

work. It depends on the numbers."

"I can talk to my father about the rent. But I don't know anything about the operating expenses for an antique shop."

"Me neither, beyond making my case rent. But I know someone who does. He deals in music memorabilia, and he used to be a partner in a shop that just shut down."

"Why?"

"The owner began to have health problems, and he couldn't keep the place going. Gideon would have taken it over, but he couldn't afford it. I know how much he misses having a shop to run. He doesn't like being a case dealer, either." She looked up. "He's a good friend of mine, and I'm sure he'd be glad to talk to you."

WHEN I WALKED into the Cozy Corner, the smell of barbecue, smoke and pork, wrapped me like a blanket. We didn't eat pork at home, but as Dad told me, "We can eat whatever we like in restaurants." Barbecue was the smell of Memphis, and I'd missed it. Otis Redding was on the jukebox, singing "A Change Is Gonna Come," the version I'd always liked better than Aretha's. The place was so small that I didn't have to search for Jude and her companion. I sat, and Jude introduced me.

He was a little older than me, fortyish, with the kind of Southern bad-boy looks that no amount of wear would spoil. Sandy hair, with a curl that fell over his forehead. Bright blue eyes, the crow's-feet pronounced at the corners. A crooked smile. Teeth too white to be natural.

Tennessee born and bred, although the accent was hard to place. His hand was warm, the fingers rough and calloused, the handshake confident.

I asked him how he got into dealing in music memorabilia.

"I was a country musician for a long time," he said. "Worked in Nashville as a session musician. Played the guitar. Never did break out, much as I wanted to. So I finally hung it up and moved here and kind of fell into working in Jim's shop."

"Do you still play?"

"Of course I still play. Just don't expect it to amount to anything, that's all."

He'd already learned a hard lesson about dashed expectations. "I'm sorry about the shop. The one that closed."

"Well, Jim was mighty sick. Didn't have long. Didn't last long after he closed it down."

"Even sorrier."

He nodded. "So you're thinking about going into the antique business."

"I'm thinking about opening a shop. I've been in the antique business for a long time. Didn't Jude tell you? I was a specialist at Sotheby's in New York."

"That don't hurt. But it ain't the same as running a small business."

"I'm aware of that."

"Just making sure. I've met people who think it's going to be fun to run a little antique shop. Then they find out what it's really like. Long hours. Customers who ain't always nice. Toting. No one ever thinks about all the toting. And dust and dirt."

I said, "What do you think we did at Sotheby's? Waved our painted fingernails over the pieces to learn about them through ESP? I've done my fair share of toting. I've handled stuff that had centuries of dust and dirt on it. And as for difficult customers, who do you think consigns at Sotheby's? Or buys at Sotheby's? Crazy rich people, and I dealt them day in and day out. I don't have any illusions about having fun playing with cute old things. I know better than that."

"That's a start," he said.

"Why didn't you take over the business when your partner left? Why aren't you running your own shop?"

"Couldn't afford it," he said. "I'd be glad to rent some floor space and a few cases. But it's too much to take on all the overhead. I'd rather let someone else do that."

Then he smiled, and I saw full-on charm. That startled me. New Yorkers didn't bother with that kind of charm. I was half a Raskin, and I'd been furious at him for impugning my business sense. But I was also half a Beardsley, a Southern girl who'd had a big crush on Dwight Yoakam in junior high school. This man was softening me up, and I should have been mad about that, too. But I wasn't. "Well, I can understand that," I said.

"I think we understand each other," he said.

THAT EVENING, after diner, I asked my father, "Are you still looking to rent the old clothing store?"

"Of course I am. You have a lead on a tenant?"

"Would you rent it to me?"

"It depends on what you're planning to do with it."

"I'm thinking about an antique shop."

"You're serious about this? It isn't just a rebound thing?"

"It is a rebound thing, but it's serious, too."

He said, "Well, it's risky, but no riskier than a gift shop or a bookstore or a café. Have you put together a business plan?"

"I can."

"Three-year plan. I can give you estimates for rent and other expenses."

I knew who had better estimates than my father's, and I had his number.

I DIDN'T MIND GOING BACK to the Cozy Corner to meet Gideon again, this time without Jude. He was leaning back in his chair and chewing a toothpick, like a caricature of a country boy. When he saw me, he removed the toothpick so he could grin at me. "Nice to see you again," he said.

Two could play at that game. I sat and fluttered my eyelashes a little. I exaggerated my accent. "Oh, Mr. Fairchild, the pleasure is all mine," I said.

He laughed. "The cotillion's long over."

"So is the hoedown. I came here to talk business with you. I have a lead on some retail space for an antique shop. I need to get a better idea about overhead before I talk about a lease."

"Is this the property your daddy owns?"

"Jude told you that?"

"Will he give you a break on the rent?"

I said, "He wants to see a business plan first. And I can't put one together unless I know what it costs to run an antique business. I hoped you'd be able to fill me in."

"You're serious."

"Yes. You want to talk business or not?"

"Yes, ma'am, I do."

I said, "Put the toothpick back in your mouth. You'll need it for your hayseed act. Or is it an act? Where in Tennessee are you from?"

"Nashville."

"Before Nashville."

"I was born again in a Nashville recording studio," he said.

"How do I know I can trust you enough to go into business with you?"

He grinned. "You don't," he said.

2

HOUSEWARMING

MY FATHER BROUGHT THE LEASE FOR THE RASKIN BUILDING to the dinner table, and both my parents watched as I signed it. I put the pen down and said, "Now I know I'll be staying here."

They both beamed at me.

"Mama, Daddy, I can't tell you how much I appreciate the way you've welcomed me back. Now it's really time for me to move."

"There's no rush," my mother said. "You can stay here as long as you need to."

"Thanks. But I think I've recovered enough to want my own place."

My father put his hand over my mother's. "There are some nice rentals in Germantown. Townhouses, too, if you want to buy."

I smiled. "No, I'd like to have a house, not an apartment. I want to live in the city."

My mother said, "It's one thing to work in town. But to live there—"

"Most neighborhoods in Memphis aren't safe, and we'd worry about you," my father added.

I laughed. "I used to live in Manhattan. I think I can handle Memphis."

My mother said, "If you really want to look, I know a good real estate agent."

"I've looked for a house before. I can manage."

"My mothering days aren't over yet. Let me give you his name."

"Mama, would it make you feel better if I called him?"

"Yes."

A FEW DAYS LATER, Simon Beaufort picked me up in Germantown. His salesmanship was muted by a soft patrician Delta accent. After talking on the phone, he said, "Let me show you some houses in Evergreen."

As he drove, he told me that the neighborhood was a historic district, full of houses built in the 1920s. "Nice old houses. Lovely old trees, too." The first house wasn't right. It had red shutters, a cottagey detail I disliked, and it was too small, even for one person. The second house had been modernized beyond recognition, a bungalow forced into an open plan. I said, "I know that historic designation is for exteriors only, but what some people do to their interiors is criminal."

He said, "I have another house to show you."

The house was a one-story bungalow with a sloping roof and a porch flanked by stone pillars. Living in Manhattan, I'd forgotten that every Southern house worth its salt had a porch. A sign on the lawn advertised the Evergreen Historic District. I asked, "Does that come with the house?"

"The owner was very active in the Historic District Association."

Inside, the house smelled of beeswax furniture polish. The walls had been freshly painted a creamy white, but in the idiom of the neighborhood, everything else had been preserved. The original boards of the pine floors gleamed. The undisturbed red oak of the woodwork glowed. The furniture in the living room and the dining room belonged to the decade the house was built, and it had been as carefully maintained as the interior.

Simon took me on the tour. The kitchen had new appliances, but it retained its original galley shape. No open plan here. The bathroom was tiny by Germantown's standards, but everything fit, and the subway tile on the walls shone. Even the hex tile beneath my feet sparkled.

As we walked into the backyard, Simon told me about the furnace and the water heater and the air-conditioning system, all recently updated, but I was no longer listening. I followed him back into the house, and in the living room, without thinking, sat in the Morris chair that had pride of place. I sank comfortably into it.

He sat, too, and told me what the seller was asking.

I said, "Two hundred nineteen thousand for eighteen hundred square feet, a front yard and a backyard, and a garage?"

He said softly, "We can ask them to come down, if you want to."

"Do you have any idea what I sold my condo in Manhattan for?"

"That's a very different market, I hear."

"Add a zero."

At that he laughed. "We can ask them to raise the price, if it makes you feel better."

In the embrace of the Morris chair, I felt the presence of the owner who had cherished and preserved this house. "Ask them if they'll sell the furniture."

"You look like you're home," he said.

"I am."

Outside, at the neighboring house, two women sat on their porch, despite the chill in the air. One of them called, "Simon? Back again to show Miss Augusta's house?"

He waved. "Yes, and my client has come all the way from New York to see it."

"Really?" she asked, rising. She wore her braids pulled back, and they emphasized her cheekbones. In her sweat-shirt and leggings, she had the lithe, muscular look of a runner.

Her companion said, "Val, don't busybody her." Hers was a patrician accent, like Simon's, and her tone was one of longtime affection. She was tanned and sturdy, and if her mama had ever fussed over her looks, she'd stopped caring a long time ago.

I said, "It's all right. I'm going to be your neighbor, if all goes well. I'm going to put in an offer on the house."

She said, "I'm Emmy, this is Val, and I hope you get the house."

Val asked, "Are you from New York?"

"I lived there for years, but I grew up in Memphis."

"Where in Memphis?" asked Val.

"Germantown."

Emmy said, "This is about as far from Germantown as you can get."

"I know. That's why I like it."

Val laughed. "Welcome to the neighborhood."

ON THE DAY I moved in, Val waved to me and came bounding down the sidewalk. As I pulled a box from my trunk, she asked, "Do you need any help?"

"Thanks, but I'm fine. I bought the furniture in the living room and dining room, and I'm having the bed delivered later today. This is just the stuff my mother found in the attic and insisted she didn't need."

Val laughed. "Your mama in Germantown? What does she think of your living in the city?"

"She's still nervous."

"Is she planning to visit anytime soon?"

"She's stopping by to bring me more stuff from the attic. Tomorrow afternoon."

"What time?"

"Twoish."

Val gave me a grin that was more than neighborly. It was complicit. "We'll be home tomorrow," she said. "We may drop by."

My mother came over on schedule. As she opened her trunk, she said, "I found a few more odds and ends I thought you might be able to use."

I laughed and helped her carry the boxes into the house. As soon as she'd sat down, accepting my offer of coffee, the doorbell rang. Val and Emmy stood on the porch. Emmy held a foil-covered plate in her hands. "Cookies," she said. "Not vegan. I hope that's all right."

Val said, "I told her you don't bring vegan cookies for a housewarming gift."

"Come on in," I said. "You can meet my mother."

Val grinned at me, and I grinned back.

They stepped inside. "Mama, these are my neighbors, Emmy and Val. I'm sorry, I don't know your last names."

Val held out her hand. "Valerie Jackson, ma'am." My mother shook it.

Emmy laughed. "When was the last time anyone called you Valerie?"

Val said, "My mama, when I told her my shift was on Sunday and I couldn't get to church. You're one to talk, Emmeline."

Now Emmy laughed too. "Miz Raskin, I'm Emmy Fuller," she said.

I saw my mother stifle a look of surprise. Not at the relationship. My mother was too progressive for that. But at the polite address, which proved that my new neighbors had both been properly brought up by their respective Southern mamas.

"It's a pleasure to meet both of you," my mother said.

"Val, Emmy, there's coffee, if you want any."

"No, we can't stay long," Val said.

"Just for a moment," Emmy added, and they sat down.

My mother asked, "How long have you lived in the neighborhood?"

Val said, "We moved in when our son was just a baby. He's five now."

"Is he in school yet?"

Val said, "Yes, he's in kindergarten over at Vollentine. He's happy there, and we've been happy with the school, too."

"What do you do for a living, Ms. Jackson?"

Emmy said, "Val rescues people for a living. She's an EMT."

My mother's eyebrows rose, just a hair. She took in Val's broad shoulders.

Val reached out to rest her hand on Emmy's knee. "You save lives too, sugar," she said, her voice full of affection. To my mother and me, she said, "Trees. Emmy's an arborist."

"And now we're busybodies for the whole block," Emmy said. "We just got elected block captains. Eyes and ears."

Val said, "We got used to looking in on Miss Augusta, the woman who used to live here," she explained. "We'd stop by a few times a week to make sure she was all right."

"Where did she move to?" my mother asked, as I hadn't.

Emmy said, "She broke her hip, and the house was too much for her. She's in assisted living now, and she's doing well there. We visit her every few weeks. We told her all about Nat. She's just overjoyed that Nat bought her furniture along with the house."

"It belongs to the house," I said. "Especially that big chair."

Emmy said, "That was always Miss Augusta's chair. Little tiny woman, and she loved that chair."

That explained the way I sensed her presence in it. "Could I come with you sometime? Meet her?"

Emmy said, "She'd be thrilled to meet you."

My mother asked, "Is this a quiet neighborhood?"

Val knew exactly what she meant. "Yes, ma'am, it is. The biggest commotion we ever had was when the ambulance came for Miss Augusta after she fell."

My mother asked, "Really? Nothing worse than that?" I knew that tone. Out on the street, in New York or in Memphis, it meant, *You're fooling with me.*

Emmy said, "Well, we did have some vandalism on Halloween last year. The squirrels wrecked our pumpkins." She started to laugh. "Ate them into a mush!"

Val said, "People will stop by to meet you, but once it gets a little warmer, we'll have a barbecue, and you can meet everyone properly."

"I'd like that," I said.

"Don't wait until you've finished the cookies to stop by again. Come over, and you can meet our son, and our cat, who will love you up by trying to trip you."

"I'd like that, too."

Emmy said, "It was lovely to meet you, Mrs. Raskin. Nat, we really do have to go. We have to retrieve Leo before he moves into the house down the block. They just got a puppy."

After they left, my mother said, "They laid it on a little thick, I think. I can't believe there's never been a burglary in this neighborhood." She permitted herself a small smile. "But if anything goes wrong on this block, Miss Valerie Jackson is the one to handle it."

I wanted to laugh. *Don't worry, suburban mama, we'll take good care of your baby in the big bad city.*

NANA CALLED and insisted on coming to see me. "Don't worry, I can drive in from Germantown. And I can't wait to see your new house."

"What did my mother tell you?"

She said, "You'd think no one ever lived in a city before. For years you lived in a city that was bigger and more dangerous than Memphis."

"Don't tell me she worried the whole time I was in New York."

"Don't start," Nana said.

When I opened the door to her, she held a foil-covered plate in her hands, just as Emmy had. She said, "It's lovely. The neighborhood, the block, the house. One of your neighbors waved to me as I walked up."

"The tall one or the short one?"

"A tall Black woman."

"That's Val. And Emmy, and their little boy, Leo, and their tuxedo cat."

"Neighborly?"

"Very."

She said, "Let me put this in the kitchen for you."

I peeked, although the smell of cinnamon and yeast gave it away. "Babka!"

She smiled. "For you, what else?"

"There's coffee. Shall we have some?"

"Oh, I shouldn't," she said.

"You look fine, Nana."

"No, I meant I shouldn't eat up the babka I made for you."

"That's what it's for, isn't it? To enjoy?"

She said, "The only time I was thin was just after your grandfather died. I was too miserable to eat." A shadow passed over her face.

She still missed him.

I took the plate. "I'll give you the tour, then we'll have coffee and babka."

The morning sun slanted into the living room, warming the reddish-brown finish on the furniture and turning the yellow pine floors to gold. She nodded and smiled as I showed her the neat little kitchen, the guest room, and my bedroom, where the bedding was so new it still smelled of sizing.

She sniffed and said, "Now that's the smell of new dry goods."

I laughed. "That must be why I like it."

At the dining room table, coffee and cake before us, she said, "I can tell you'll be very comfortable here."

"You didn't say happy.'"

"That no one knows." She reached for my hand. "I was so sad to hear about your divorce, *ziskeyt*. So sorry. I thought he was a decent man."

"So did I, until he wasn't." I raised my hand to my eyes. "After the miscarriages…"

She had been one of the few people who hadn't said

anything stupid in trying to console me about my miscarriages. She'd known what to say.

I rubbed my forehead and took my hand away. "Nothing was right after the miscarriages." I took a deep breath. "We should have talked about IVF or adoption. I couldn't, and he didn't."

She didn't press me.

"I keep thinking it was my fault. If I hadn't been so depressed. If I hadn't pulled into myself so much. If I'd had something in me to give to him."

She tightened her grasp on my hand. "If he'd shown you how much he loved you and cared about you."

I shook my head. "You and Grandpa. Almost sixty years together. A marriage that only death could end."

Her hand tightened on mine again, a pressure that was almost painful. "We had our ups and downs," she said.

"I don't know if I'll ever find someone to love me like that."

She released my hand. She looked as tired and sad as she'd looked during the week of shiva. "That no one knows, either."

3

OPENING DAY

ON THE SUNDAY BEFORE THE SHOP OPENED, I WENT BACK
to Germantown to eat bagels and lox with my parents. I
sat at the breakfast bar with my father. My mother had
refused my help in the kitchen, and I heard water running
and flatware rattling as she loaded the dishwasher.

Since I'd signed the lease, which spared me rent but
put me on the hook for taxes and utilities, my father had
been hands-off about my effort to get the shop ready to
open. He didn't offer advice, and he didn't stop by to
check on my progress. I'd been surprised. Now I asked
him, "You haven't asked me how I'm coming along with
the shop. I thought you'd want to know."

He sighed. "When it's a family business, you step back.
I learned the hard way when I started the boutiques."

I'd been too young to pay attention to the business
then, and I'd never had reason to ask later. "Did you have
trouble with your father?"

"He had a tough time letting go. And even though he
didn't run my new business for me, he stayed interested.

Too interested. We had a few arguments about it. So yes, I did." He gave me a rueful expression. "I don't want to have that kind of trouble with you."

I felt a rush of gratitude, and it made me candid. "Do you think I'm doing the right thing? Do you think it will work?"

"It's a good idea, and your financials are sound. Whether it will work—well, that's up to the customers, and they're a fickle bunch. It won't help if I hang over your shoulder and give you advice you don't need."

"Thank you," I said, and I had to blink because my eyes were wet.

"Can I stop by before you open?" He smiled. "Would that be all right?"

"Sure," I said. "Is it normal to feel terrified?"

"Absolutely," he said, and he put his arm around my shoulders to hug me close.

THE DAY before the shop opened, as Jude, Gideon, and I were putting the finishing touches on the place, my father knocked on the door. He held a parcel under his arm. I brought him inside to meet Jude and Gideon.

He said to Jude, "It's nice to see you again," even though he couldn't have remembered her from Germantown High. He shook Gideon's hand. "The man with the plan," he said. "You've run an antique shop before."

Gideon was surprisingly deferential. "I have, sir."

My father laughed. "Call me Mike," he said, and he looked around.

The sun slanted through the big glass windows, and the air had a floral scent. My mother and grandmother had tapped their friends to consign the silver, porcelain, and brown furniture I knew so well, and Jude had emptied her storage unit to add her mid-century furniture and lighting. Gideon trusted our security system enough to bring in his guitars.

"Nat, it's beautiful. It doesn't look like the same space. I like the groupings. People can see how they'd use these things in their own homes."

Jude had made everything fit together, the Staffordshire figurines and the Victorian lamps sitting easily on the Scandinavian teak tables. *Old South and New*. The tagline on our business cards and our website.

"That's Jude's doing. She has the eye for design."

"And those guitars make a great display. Never mind playing them. They're like pieces of sculpture." He looked at Gideon. "Yours?"

Gideon grinned. "Eye candy, even if you don't play. The collectors and the musicians will go crazy for them."

My father stopped before each case. "The cases are just right. Enough stuff to interest the eye, but not so much to overwhelm it. And it suits the price point. It says the merchandise is good but affordable. Very nice." He looked around again and smiled at Jude and Gideon, then said to me, "Your grandfather would be pleased to see this. He'd be proud of you."

"I swear he's here," I said. "The friendliest ghost. I can just hear him reminding me, 'Nat, *ziskeyt*, buy low and sell high. And don't discount the new merchandise! Give it thirty days. Better yet, sixty!'"

"I brought you something, and it's even more appropriate than I realized." He set his parcel on the counter, and I unwrapped it as Jude and Gideon watched.

It was a photo of a man in his twenties, slender and debonair, in a well-cut suit and a fedora hat. He leaned against a counter. A familiar counter. The one where my father and I now stood. "Is that Grandpa?"

"It is indeed. Taken in 1946, just after the war. In the shop."

"Well turned out."

"As always."

I held it up for Jude and Gideon. "Our patron saint, if Jewish retailers can have them."

My father laughed, and in the way his eyes crinkled, I saw the Raskin family resemblance that ran from my grandfather to my father to myself. "Why not?"

"I HAVEN'T BEEN SO nervous since my bat mitzvah," I said to Jude, who stood behind the counter.

Gideon said, "I've already disarmed the security system. Go ahead, unlock the door."

I wiped my hands on my pants legs. I unlocked the door and turned our sign to "open."

Outside, a man and a woman peered through the window, and I opened the door to invite them in.

"Are you open?" the man asked.

I grinned. "Yes, we are. Come on in."

Once inside, the man said, "Your shop wasn't in the tour guide on the Memphis website."

I felt a little dizzy. "We just opened today. You're the first in the door."

"Lucky for us!" the woman said.

Gideon asked them, "Where are you from?"

"Cincinnati," the woman said.

"Have you come to see Graceland?"

The man laughed. "No, Beale Street."

"Is there anything you collect?"

"Whatever we like!"

Jude had worn her heirloom earrings today, telling me they brought her luck. She fingered them as she smiled at our first customers. "Please, look around."

They lingered. Pointed at a few things. Picked up others. They made the rounds of the shop, and when they were done, the man approached the counter and pointed. "There's something I want to see in this case."

"That's mine," Gideon said. He took the key from the drawer. "What can I show you?"

"The photograph of the jug band," the man said.

Gideon opened the case and pulled it out. "The Beale Street Jug Band," he said. "They played on the street in the 1930s. Dewey Corley."

"You ever hear any recordings?"

"Not the band. Dewey Corley recorded solo late in his life. The Memphis Jug Band and the Cannon Jug Band made some records, and I've heard them. They're great."

As he held the photograph, the man asked his wife, "What do you think?"

"What better souvenir?"

It was only a ten-dollar sale, but it was our first, and as Gideon rang it up, Jude wrapped it, a tag team who knew what they were doing. I was still having trouble with the card reader. I thanked them for stopping by. "Tell your friends back in Cincinnati about us," I said.

The security system was set to jangle when the door opened, like an old-fashioned bell. Our second customer was a friend of Jude's, an interior designer, tall and willowy like Jude herself, dressed in a style that my mother and I called "Tory Burch splendor."

Jude introduced all of us.

"I had to stop in on your first day." She looked around. "It's lovely."

"Thank you."

"Your doing?"

"Some of it," Jude said. "Are you looking for stuff for clients?"

"Always."

"Please, look around."

"I already see some things I like. Do you mind if I take some pictures?"

"Go ahead."

After a leisurely round through the shop, she said, "I have my eye on a few things. If the clients like it."

"Let me know," Jude said. "Designer's discount."

She laughed. "I'm not done yet. I still want to look for sparklies for myself." She pointed to the costume jewelry in the nearest case. "Is that yours?"

"Give me the key," Jude said, and I handed it to her.

She bought a nice pair of 1950s rhinestone earrings for $50.

The next time the bell jangled, a short, grizzled, pony-tailed man walked into the shop. He looked around, sighted Gideon, and stepped up to the counter, letting his elbows rest on the glass. I'd cleaned the glass this morning, and now I could see smudges on it. "So this is where you ended up, you rascal. Is this your place?"

Gideon said, "It belongs to Miss Minerva over here."

I laughed and blushed as I extended my hand. "I'm usually known as Nat Raskin."

He said, "I'm a musician when I'm not at my day job. That's how I met this layabout." He said to Gideon, "So have you found Robert Johnson's guitar yet?"

I said, "Robert Johnson's guitar? That must be worth a few dollars."

Gideon laughed. "He's pulling my leg. No one's going to find it. It doesn't exist."

The part-time musician asked, "Are you still playing around town?"

"Pickups," Gideon said. "When I feel like it."

He looked around the shop but didn't bring anything to the counter. He waved as he left. "Keep the faith, brother," he said to Gideon.

After he left, Gideon snorted. "He never bought a damn thing at the old shop, either. Just wanted to hang out and shoot the breeze." He looked at me and smothered a smile. "Robert Johnson's guitar," he said.

I let myself get the slightest bit indignant. "I know silver. How much do you know about silver?"

We had a few more people stray in, and when they left, Jude called them "looky-loos," meaning people who didn't buy.

I asked, "Is this normal? Sixty dollars in sales?"

Jude and Gideon looked at each other and laughed.

Around two in the afternoon, two women walked in, one middle-aged, the other young enough to be her daughter. The older woman came up to the counter and smiled at me as though we'd met before. I'd gotten used to being embarrassed at not remembering someone who had seen me every week in Temple or whose kid had been a friend of mine in junior high school. She solved the mystery for me. "Your mother told us all about this place."

"How do you know my mother?"

"We volunteer together."

"It's our first day open," I said.

"I know. I made a note in my calendar."

Looking around, the daughter said, "Your shop is just darling." She was my age, dressed in white trousers and a Tory Burch tunic. Her handbag, a designer number, had set her back a few dollars. She wore diamond studs in her ears, just the right size for daytime. Those had set someone back a few dollars, too. She was clearly a woman of leisure, free to shop on a Thursday afternoon.

They strolled through the shop, touching things, picking them up, exclaiming and laughing. I wondered if they'd had a little liquid for lunch. At Sotheby's, the champagne had flowed at every auction. We'd never minded getting our customers likkered up, not a bit.

The daughter found a modern lamp, big and striking, with a red glass base and a drum shade. It was too big to heft. She touched the glass and said, "Wouldn't this be perfect for the den?"

Her mother said, "Oh, it would. It would look great with your new sectional."

She looked at the tag.

"Oh, don't worry about it," her mother said. "It's gorgeous."

I'd seen this happen in many a department store. Women egging each other on.

"It's so you!"

The daughter laughed. "It is," she said. "I want it, and I'm going to get it."

Jude said, "Let me take it to the counter for you." She knew a tipsy customer when she saw one.

"We aren't done yet," the daughter said. "We want to look around some more."

Jude set the lamp on the counter, and I checked the price. $275. Her mother hadn't batted an eyelash. Maybe they'd want to dicker when they settled the bill.

They kept roaming. "What do you think of this picture for Olivia's room?" the mother asked. It was a sentimental print of kittens in a basket, priced at $25, but we'd take it. It joined the lamp on the counter.

The mother stood before Jude's case, examining the estate jewelry. She said to the daughter, "I need something for that gala this spring. To go with the new dress."

Jude slipped onto the floor, key in hand. The woman said, "Those diamond earrings," and pointed. I'd come to learn that people always pointed, as though you needed special instructions to find your own merchandise in the case.

Jude opened the case and handed the mother the earrings. She put them on by feel, not needing to look in a mirror. "What do you think?" she asked her daughter.

"I'm not sure."

Jude asked, "What's the dress like?"

The mother explained.

Jude pulled out a pair of earrings, diamond-and-sapphire drops. "Give these a try."

The woman put them on, and Jude pointed her to the nearby mirror. The mother checked her reflection. As she turned her head, the diamonds sparkled in the afternoon sun.

"Those are gorgeous," the daughter said.

"Will they work with the dress?"

"Yes," the daughter said. "You have to get them. If you don't, I will!"

The diamond-and-sapphire earrings found their way to the counter. $450.

The daughter leaned over the front case, where I'd arranged my silver. She pointed. "What is that?"

Gideon asked, "The tongs?"

"What's that on the ends? Is it feet?"

He smiled at her. "Chicken feet."

She laughed. "You're kidding!"

"The Victorians thought it was the height of bad manners to touch a piece of food, so they had silverware for everything. They liked to use the design to tell you what it was for. Those were for fried chicken."

What did he know about silver? Plenty.

More laughter. "Can you see me using this at our next picnic?"

Gideon laid the tongs on the counter. I'd seen him smile like that before. He'd smiled at me when he was flirting with me. Now he was flirting with the daughter, a Cordova matron in training if I'd ever seen one, and she liked it.

The mother said, "Silver's such a nuisance. You have to polish it."

The daughter picked up the tongs and began to handle them as though she didn't want to let them go. I'd seen people do that at auction previews. *This is mine.*

Gideon leaned over the counter, pretending he needed to come close see better. She looked up, a gleam in her eyes.

He said, "If you seal silver in a plastic bag, you keep the air out, and it tarnishes less. But the best way to keep it bright is to use it."

She held the tongs as though she couldn't bear to be parted from them. "How old are they?"

"Nat?" Gideon asked. "Your expert opinion?"

"Go ahead," I said. "You're doing so well." *You're egging her on, in your own special way.*

"Either side of 1900," he said. "It's American silver. Gorham. They made the same pattern for a long time."

Still holding the tongs, she said, "Chicken feet! I have to have these."

Her mother said, "Well, you're the one who'll be polishing them."

She looked up and smiled at Gideon, in love with the chicken feet and with him as well, just a little. "I'll take them." $195.

When they left, I turned to Gideon, "Where did you learn about silver?"

"Years of doing estate sales. You pick it up."

"I'd better brush up on Robert Johnson. You didn't mind selling my stuff instead of yours?"

Jude laughed. "Can't you tell? He likes selling, and he doesn't care whose merch it is."

I said, "I think he likes flirting."

"Whatever works," Gideon said.

I leaned against the counter. "We've just paid our monthly expenses, and we'll be all right, even if we don't do a lick of business again."

Gideon said, "Sometimes it's like that."

Jude laughed. "And sometimes it's not."

NOT EVERY DAY was a thousand-dollar day, but we did better than I'd expected. Gideon's old customers found him and bought from us. Jude's designers did too. And my mother never stopped telling her friends—nagging her friends—to stop by, and once they enjoyed themselves there, they told their friends too. Since South Main was a vibrant shopping district with a lot of foot traffic, we had plenty of random visitors off the street. I was surprised by how many people knew us through our website. Jude knew a website designer who made it for us in exchange for some furniture for his place.

But there was a question we heard over and over.

"Minerva's Place," I said into the phone. "How can I help you?"

I hadn't tired of saying that every time the phone rang. I delighted in telling the caller, "We're open Thursday through Sunday, ten to five. We're on South Main. There's a parking lot behind the shop."

"Do you have any Elvis stuff?" said the voice over the phone.

As a Memphian, I owed a debt to Elvis and Graceland, which brought the tourists to town, and many of them came to South Main to find us. I've never cared for Elvis. I don't mind Johnny Cash, but I'm an Otis Redding fan. But I learned to be polite to the people who loved the King.

"Elvis? As a matter of fact, we do. Is there anything in particular you're interested in?"

Gideon, who was rearranging the bottom shelf of his case, had been eavesdropping. He straightened up and mouthed to me, "Tell him about the playbill."

I listened, as I had since we opened, to someone who collected Elvis commemoratives. "We don't, but one of our dealers specializes in music memorabilia, and he has some unusual paper items. And a lot of other stuff, too. Come by to see us!"

When I hung up, Gideon said, "I can guess what he was asking about."

"Someday, I'm going to lose my religion and tell an Elvis collector the best thing he can do with his commemorative plate is take it out and shoot skeet with it."

Gideon straightened up and laughed. "Why, Miss Minerva, I believe you're getting the hang of running an antique shop!"

Gideon had been the first to ask me, "Who was Minerva?"

"Minerva is my middle name," I told him. "After my great-grandmother."

"Your Jewish great-grandmother was named Minerva Raskin?"

I shouldn't be surprised. Nashville, where he had lived for a long time, was full of music producers from New York record companies. Jews. "On my mother's side. Their name was Beardsley."

Now, when he bantered with me, he called me "Miss Minerva."

After I signed the lease, I'd offered him a spot as a case dealer. He'd rented three of my ten cases and taken space as a floor dealer, too. After Jude signed an agreement as a floor dealer for her furniture and rented three more cases for her smalls, I was close to covering my monthly expenses.

The four empty cases nagged at me, and I pestered both Jude and Gideon to spread the word that we had room for dealers with interesting stuff. Jude told me, "I know someone who might be interested in renting a case."

The more time I spent with Jude, the more I liked her. Under the wounded Southern goth was a brisk business-woman with a designer's eye for arrangement and a consummate seller's ear for what people didn't realize they wanted.

"What's his area?"

"African American. Not the racist stuff, thank goodness. And Memphis history. And all kinds of other things that catch his eye, which is a good one."

Thomas Waverley was the most dapper-looking antique dealer I'd seen in Memphis. To meet me, he wore a three-piece suit, and the face above his bow tie was light brown in complexion and serene in expression.

He extended a beautifully groomed hand and told me,

in an accent that had been educated far from Memphis, that he was pleased to make my acquaintance. "Just one thing," he said. "Don't call me Tom. It's Thomas."

Tom. Uncle Tom. These racial moments were like splinters that had never worked their way out. I hadn't felt them in New York, but now, back in Memphis, I felt them more often than I cared to. "My middle name is Minerva, and as long as you never call me Memphis Minnie, we should be all right."

At that he laughed. "You have my word. May I look around?"

"Please do."

When his inspection was finished, he said, "Very nice." He was assessing us, too.

"That's what we're aiming for," I said, my reflexive answer for customers.

"How much are you charging for a case?"

"Fifty dollars a month."

"I like the pair against the far wall. Good traffic flow. I can pay you for three months in advance." He took out his checkbook. "Would that be all right?"

"That would be spectacular," I said.

We shook hands again.

After he left, I asked Jude, "Am I right in assuming he's gay, too?"

She nodded.

"And there's a lot going on beneath that elegant surface."

Her voice was a little sharp. "It's a business relationship, Nat. Not more than that. How much do you need to know for fifty dollars a month in case rent?"

THAT SUNDAY MORNING, the first person through the door was a Black man who looked to be in his seventies, slender and dapper, as though he'd just come from church. He wore a fedora at a jaunty angle, and he had the coolest two-tone oxford shoes I'd ever seen. I envied them and yearned for a pair myself.

He came up to the counter and said to me, "I used to come in here when this was Raskin's Clothing, back in the day."

"Really?"

"I saw the piece in the *Appeal* about your shop. Another Raskin in the building. Had to stop by to see what you've done with it." He looked around with appreciation.

"Morris Raskin was my grandfather. I'm Natalie Raskin."

He smiled. "I bought all my suits here when I was singing in the blues clubs on Beale Street," he said. "Mr. Raskin was always courteous to me. And whatever he sold me didn't break the bank."

"My grandfather was very stylish himself," I said. "Did you see the photo?"

He looked at it and laughed. "I remember him looking like that. He made sure I was stylish, too. I brought all my fellow musicians here. Your grandfather dressed many a bluesman on Beale Street."

"I didn't know that."

He said, "I spent a lot of time in the record shop, too, when it was open."

"Record shop?"

"He sold all kinds of music, but he always had the latest from Sun and Stax. If you recorded a disc and pressed a few, he'd take them and try to sell them for you. He liked the music, and he liked us. He was tight with all the musicians, the session men and the men who played in the clubs on Beale Street. We all hung out there."

"I never heard a word about this. Not from him or from my father."

"He paid a price for it, back in the day."

"Really?"

"The Klan didn't like it. Not the music and not the musicians. At Stax and Sun, white men and Black men played together in the studio. The Klan organized a boycott. There were demonstrations on the sidewalk outside the shop—the clothing store and the record store. They told Mr. Raskin to quit. Broke his windows more than once. I heard someone hurled a brick with a message wrapped around it. Called him a n—lover and told him to quit or else. Signed it KKK."

"That I've heard about. It's awful. But thank you for telling me."

I introduced Gideon, who had been eavesdropping with interest. I said, "Gideon is a musician, too."

"What do you play?" the elderly bluesman asked.

"Guitar. Mostly country, but I jam with bluesmen too."

"On Beale Street?"

"Sometimes," Gideon said. "I didn't catch your name."

"Joe Jordan. Known as Little Joe in my singing days."

Gideon's face broke into a smile. "I never heard you perform live. But I've heard your recordings. That's the purest Delta sound I've ever heard. Guitar ringing like a bell."

Joe Jordan let a small smile play over his face. "Always a pleasure to meet a fan," he said. He looked around. "This is a nice place you have here. Your grandfather would be proud of you, Miss Raskin."

He swore he wasn't a collector, but he found a photograph of Beale Street as he remembered it in the early 1960s. Gideon had marked it $10, but he said, "I got it for nothing at an estate sale. I'd let you have it for two dollars."

"Thank you kindly," Joe Jordan said, tucking the photograph into his jacket pocket.

After he left, I said to Gideon, "I didn't know you played the blues."

"Now you do."

I glanced at the photo of my grandfather and said, "I never knew he ran a record shop. I never knew he liked and encouraged the musicians. Do you think he met Otis Redding?"

"Maybe," Gideon said.

"I can't imagine why my father's never talked about it."

***

DESPITE OUR POSTED HOURS, we often found ourselves staying open later than that on Friday and Saturday nights, our best days for walk-in business. That Friday, because it was already dark when we left, Gideon waited for me as I locked the door. "Let me walk you to your car."

I lingered for a moment, waiting for the alarm system

to stop beeping, a sign that the door was secure. I said, "It's all right. You really don't have to escort me."

"I don't get the impulse to be a Southern gentleman very often. Let me do it."

"Southern gentleman, my eye. Showing me up in my own area of expertise."

"Miss Minerva, I'm happy to sell your silver."

"You like charming the customers. Not just the ladies. You charmed that Bubba who came in looking for a vintage whiskey jug."

"Well, I know something about old whiskey jugs."

"The ones that moonshine comes in? And where in Tennessee did you say you were from?"

He didn't say. He wouldn't. Jude and I were blabber-mouths in the shop. We talked about what we did—or didn't do much of—in our lives outside the shop, but Gideon never said a word about his personal life. I didn't know where he lived in Memphis. I didn't know whether he had a wife or a girlfriend. I didn't know how he spent his free time, except for the estate sales and auctions he told us he attended. I'd never worked with anyone who held himself so close.

As we turned to cut through to the alley, I heard an unearthly call from the backyard. We didn't have much of a yard, but we had a live oak tree in the corner, which was probably as old as the building itself and needed a good pruning. "Did you hear that?"

He smiled at me. "I sure did."

"What is it?"

"You're such a city kid," he said. "Don't you know the

call of a great horned owl?" He listened as the bird called again. "It's a girl owl. The boys have a deeper call."

"In town?"

"They find a lot to eat in town. Restaurant dumpsters attract mice and rats."

"Do you think we'll be able to see it?"

"Let's go look."

We went into the backyard, and we both saw her perched on a branch. She was as big as a cat. I had never seen an owl so close up, and I was awestruck by the way she looked right at us, her tufts pricked up, her yellow eyes aglow.

I turned to Gideon. "The owl," I said. "She's sacred to Minerva."

He moved nearer. I could smell the clean scent of his shirt. "Ain't Minerva's owl a little bitty thing?"

I'd seen the Roman mosaics that showed her bitty owl on her arm, like a hunting falcon, or on her shoulder, like a pet. "How would you know that?"

He smiled, the crooked smile that belonged on an album cover. "There are a lot of things I know," he said.

4

ROBERT JOHNSON'S GUITAR

Since Joe Jordan's visit to the shop, I'd been bothered by his story about Raskin's Records. I called my father during the day, which I rarely did, because I wanted to talk to him privately. "Nat!" he said. "Is everything all right?"

"Sure," I said. "Just fine. Why would you worry?"

"I never hear from you like this."

"Oh, it's just that someone came into the shop, and it's top of mind."

"Business?"

"Not really. Family history. I need your memory."

"I'll do my best. What do you want to know?"

"The record shop," I said. "Raskin's Records. I never heard you mention it."

"How did you find out?" He sounded guarded and a little upset.

"One of Grandpa's old customers walked in. A blues guitarist named Joe Jordan. He told me he used to hang out there."

My father said, "It wasn't a serious business. A hobby, really. Something my father played around with because he wasn't sure he wanted to be in the rag trade." He took in a breath. "He had some trouble with his father about that, I think."

I was more puzzled than ever. "It sounded like the Klan took it pretty seriously. According to Joe, they harassed Mo about the record shop, not the clothing store."

My father said, "What I remember—and I remember this pretty well—is that the Klan didn't like anything the Raskin family did."

"I was surprised you never mentioned it, that's all."

"We've always been in the clothing business. Not the record business."

"Dad, is there something bothering you about this?"

"No, Nat," he said. "It's all ancient history. Nothing to worry about."

He was lying, and that disturbed me.

He said, "I've got to go. We'll see you soon? Friday night? Or Sunday brunch?"

"Yes," I said. "I'll call Mama."

He wanted me to believe that the record business had been a hobby. *Eyn kleynigkeyt,* as my grandmother would put it. A mere trifle.

But it wasn't. What was my father not telling me? And why?

51

"WISH ME LUCK, NAT," Gideon said as he shrugged into his leather jacket.

"Where are you off to?"

"Got a guitar to look at."

"Something good?"

"A 1964 Fender Stratocaster. The last year Mr. Fender made the guitars himself. And in one of their best finishes. Candy-apple red."

"Value?"

"Five thousand."

"Not shabby."

"No. But this may be something better. It may be Bobby Swann's red Strat."

"Bobby Swann? Who's that?"

"Session musician for Stax. Legendary guitarist. Backed up all the greats. Played on all the hits. Musicians know him, even if most people don't."

"Is there really a guitar? This isn't like Robert Johnson's guitar?" Robert Johnson's guitar had become a running joke between us. I hadn't known it was a myth. Gideon still teased me about my ignorance.

"No, this one really existed. We just don't know where it went. If this is Swann's guitar, it's worth more than five thousand. It's worth fifty thousand, maybe more."

"Worth the trouble to find out."

"That's why I'm looking. I'll be looking for documentation, too."

"Provenance," I said. My expertise when I worked for Sotheby's.

"I may need your help with that."

"You mean it?"

"I've seen you in action. I know you're good for it."

"Able to admit I might know a few things myself?"

He laughed. "I'll let you know," he said as he left.

As we closed the shop on Saturday evening, Jude watched me tally the daily sales. We'd been busy all day, and I was happy with the total. "You did all right today," I said. "Paid your rent in one fell swoop." One of my grandmother's friends had come in and bought a thousand dollars' worth of garnet jewelry.

"We should celebrate," she said.

I shook my head. "I should get home."

"Why? Since you don't even have the excuse of a cat to feed? I'd like to go out for a drink. Join me."

Cat! I smarted a little at her spinster jibe. "All right. But not a pickup joint, please. Someplace where we can eat, too."

She nodded, and after we closed, we walked down South Main to Earnestine and Hazel's. E&H had been a soul food restaurant when I was growing up, but it had become a bar while I was gone. Like the Cozy Corner, the music was soul. At the smell of French fries, I was suddenly ravenous. I ordered a burger with my beer, and both tasted wonderful. "Hungrier than I thought," I said.

"You want another beer?"

"I do." I took a swig and set the glass down. "Jude, do you think Gideon's happy being a dealer in the shop?"

"I'm sure he is. Why would you doubt it?"

"He razzes me a lot."

She laughed. "No, he teases you. That's different. He likes you, and he thinks highly of you."

"What is this, junior high? We're grown up, and we're in business together."

"He just holds his cards close, that's all."

"Some of them aren't worth holding close. Where does he live? What does he do in his free time? Sometimes I think he really works for the CIA."

She said, "Don't push him. If he trusts you, he'll tell you."

"Does he trust you?"

She said, "We go back a few years. We've done auctions and estate sales together. We've been in shops together. He met me right after I got divorced, and he helped me out. But there are things I still don't know about him, and that I don't ask him about."

I shook my head. "I tell my friends all kinds of stuff, and they do the same for me."

She laughed. "Your blabby New York friends? He's different."

"Where in Tennessee is he from?"

"He won't say, and I don't ask him. I still don't know."

GIDEON CAME in the next day a little red-eyed. "Late night?" I asked.

He rubbed his eyes. "Played a few sets in a bar."

"You need some ibuprofen?"

"No, Miss Minerva, I'm all right, I managed to dose myself at home."

I reached into my purse and rattled the bottle. "There's more, if you need it."

"I'll let you know." He took a swig of coffee from the cup he carried.

"So what happened with the guitar? I can't wait to hear."

He brightened. "It's a beauty. A '64, from Fender's hand, and it's in perfect condition."

"You didn't buy it on the spot?"

"The seller didn't have a receipt handy."

"That's strange, if he was serious about selling."

"He's a musician who bought it from another musician. They were probably both drunk at the time. It's not like buying from Sotheby's. Or even like buying from my old shop."

"Didn't he want to insure it?"

"No, he hadn't bothered with that either."

"Do you think it's hot?"

He shook his head. "I told him to dig out whatever proof of sale he's got. He's digging. He said he'd call me when he finds it. His wife just had a baby. No one is sleeping in that house. He looked cross-eyed tired."

"Did he know anything about the connection with Bobby Swann?"

"No. He said he'd never heard anything about it."

My Sotheby's training stirred and woke. "Maybe we can work from the other end. Is Swann still around?"

"From what I know, he died in 1984. Sad story. Drugs and drink."

"Family?"

"I don't know. But that's something an old bluesman might know."

"Joe Jordan," I said. "He was there, and he seems to remember everything. Where does he live? Should we call first, or just go there?"

"Let me ask around."

JOE JORDAN LIVED in Orange Mound, the historic Black neighborhood not ten minutes' drive from my own historic neighborhood in Midtown. Evergreen, a neighborhood full of lovingly maintained bungalows and Tudors, had an active preservation association. Orange Mound, which was full of pride, had no money to back it up.

Gideon insisted on giving me careful directions, as though Orange Mound, five minutes' drive from Evergreen, was a foreign country. He wasn't far off. I'd never set foot in that part of Memphis.

We met in the street outside Joe's house, which had no front yard, just a carpark. His house was half the size of my bungalow, built by someone who had no use for frills or ornaments. Or no money. Like all the houses on the block, it looked the worse for wear. The woodwork was weathered and cracked, and the paint was peeling.

Joe was more casually dressed at home than at the shop—no sport coat, no tie—but he still looked dapper. He was glad to see us. "Gideon, Miss Natalie, come on in. You want anything? Tea? Cola?"

"Don't go to any trouble," I said.

But he was already in the kitchen. The house was so small that anyone in the kitchen could easily see into the rest, which was divided into a tiny dining room crowded with a dinette set and a living room dominated by a beat-up sectional sofa and a large-screen TV. An electric guitar, worn with use, stood in the corner of the living room.

I asked, "Is that a Fender?"

He returned with two glasses of iced tea. Smiling, he said, "Stratocaster. Starburst. Bought it in 1957, and I'm still playing it."

"It's beautiful."

"You've been schooling her?" he asked Gideon.

Gideon and I laughed at the same time. I said, "About guitars, yes."

Gideon said, "Nat's right, your guitar is a beauty."

Joe said, "You want to play it?"

"Your guitar? You'd let me play it, just like that?"

"Since you're a guitar man."

I sipped the tea and put it down. It was very sweet.

Gideon said, "It would be an honor to play your guitar."

Joe reached for the instrument and carefully handed it to Gideon. Gideon took it with equal care. He curled his fingers around the frets and rested his hand on the strings. "Is there anything you want to hear?"

"You choose," Joe said, smiling.

I didn't know the song, but from the first bars, Joe recognized it. "'Bringing it Back Home to Me.' That's sweet. That's the way BB used to play it."

Gideon paused and smiled. "I know." He took up the riff again and began to sing. Joe nodded and joined him in harmony, his reedy, slightly cracked tenor twining around Gideon's bluesy baritone, a lovely, easy harmony.

I was captivated and entertained, just as they wanted me to be. An audience of one was big enough.

After Gideon played the last notes, Joe looked pleased. "You know what you're doing."

"I was a session man in Nashville for a long time."

"Country?"

"Whatever they needed to back the song. If they wanted you to play bossa nova or Beethoven, you'd do it."

"What happened? Why you give it up?"

"Wanted to be out front. That didn't happen. You ever do session work?"

"No, I'm just a downhome Delta bluesman," he said.

At that Gideon laughed.

Joe cleared his throat. "Bobby Swann," he said. "You want to know about Bobby Swann."

"Whatever you remember," I said.

"I remember all of it," he said. "You folks ready for a story?"

I nodded, and Joe rested his hands on his knees, a griot's posture.

"Bobby Swann," Joe said, summoning the man and his memories of him. "I met him just after he came to Memphis. He came up in the Delta, like I did. Cotton country. His father was a sharecropper, and he didn't want that for himself. He had more ambition than that. Wasn't sure where he'd go or how he'd get there. Just had to get out." He nodded at Gideon.

"He'd just got married when I met him. Virgie Lee. Met her in church. He was still a churchgoing man back then, but he had a dilemma. He grew up in the Baptist Church. Now, it's a funny thing. Singing is just fine with God if you're a Baptist. So is playing the piano while you sing. But the guitar ain't all right. It ain't sanctified. It's the devil's instrument for playing the devil's music. Bobby had a God-given talent for the guitar, but he couldn't honor God with it.

"He was working to get by. If I remember right, he was a garbageman, working with those men who went on strike. The men the Reverend King came to help. It was a bad job, but it was with the city, and it was steady money. He hated it. He was itching to play in the bars and clubs."

Gideon smiled at that.

"He knew all about the blues clubs, the ones Virgie Lee didn't approve of, even though he didn't play there. Even she couldn't stop him from going to Raskin's Records, where all us musicians hung out, and he met the men who played in the clubs and did session work for Stax. Blues and jazz men both. He went over to Stax—for a few bucks, they let anyone cut a demo—and the head man at Stax, Jim Stewart, heard him play and asked him if he'd like to do session work. They found him a better guitar, and he started to sit in on some sessions. Virgie Lee wasn't happy, and she was even less happy when he began to make more money, like the other session men did, by playing in the clubs at night. She'd drag him to church on Sunday mornings, and he'd go there, his eyes heavy and bloodshot, still wanting to please her." Joe sighed.

"Back in those days, they offered the musicians a cut of the royalties. If the record took off, you made more than just your pay for the time in the studio. Bobby played on a few records that hit, and he made some money. In fact, he made enough money so he could quit playing at night. He was a Stax man from then on. Didn't work anywhere else."

"What did his wife think about that?" I asked.

Joe said, "Well, things weren't going too well before then, but when he quit his city job to work for Stax full-time, she was mighty unhappy. They had a kid by then, a daughter. Virgie Lee thought Bobby owed the family a steady living, and music wasn't it. But he'd found a way for himself, and he wasn't going back." Joe looked at Gideon again.

"He changed after he began to play for Stax. It made him confident in a way that was dangerous for a Black man in Memphis in the mid-1960s. That really worried Virgie Lee. He was spending his time playing music inspired by the devil, in her mind, and he was acting in ways that could get him in trouble."

We both waited for more. "1968" echoed in my mind, the year of the Reverend King's assassination and the urban fury, born of grief and despair, just after it. But Joe shook his head and sighed.

Then he looked at me. "He wanted a better guitar. He knew Mo pretty well by then, and they had a friendly, kidding relationship. Mo stocked records from Stax, and he knew how well Bobby played. Told Bobby he was impressed by his versatility and his musicianship." Joe chuckled. "A fancy way of saying he could play bossa nova or Beethoven, and it came easy to him. Bobby was always moaning about not having a decent guitar. And one day— I remember it well, because I was in the record shop myself—Mo asked him, 'How would you like a new instrument?'

"Bobby laughed. He said, 'I would love me a brand-new Fender Stratocaster. Candy-apple red. Why? Are you Santa Claus?'

"And Mo laughed too. He said, 'A Jewish Santa Claus. Sure, why not? I could lend you the money.'

"Bobby said, 'Strat is a pile of money.'

"Mo told him, 'You could pay me back over time. No interest. I'm not that kind of a guy.' And that's how Bobby Swann got himself that red Fender Strat."

Gideon and I were both quiet for a moment. I asked, "Is Virgie Lee still around?"

Joe said, "She is. Lives in Whitehaven."

"Would she talk to us?"

Joe said, "Let me ask around, find out."

I asked, "Is she still mad?"

Joe laughed. "No shit," he said. "But if you ask her right, she might want to tell you all about it." He looked at me. "Might feel better letting it out to you."

5

AMAZING GRACE

AS I WAS BUSY LOOKING FOR A CHECK TO GIVE THOMAS Waverley, who waited at the counter, Gideon came from the back room, holding his phone in one hand and rubbing his ear with the other. Jude asked him, "What's wrong with you?"

"I just got an earful."

I looked up. "From who?"

He said, "I called Virgie Lee Swann."

"What did she say?"

"First of all, she wanted to know who the devil I was. Then she wanted to know who the devil had given me her name, and when she heard it was Joe Jordan, she called him a miserable sinner. Then she wanted to know why the devil I was calling, and when I explained, she said, 'I don't want to think about that man. I don't want to talk about that man. I don't want to talk to you. Don't call me again.' And it must give her a lot of satisfaction to have a landline, because she slammed down the phone so hard my ear is still ringing."

"Did you say Swann?" Thomas asked.

"Yes, Virgie Lee Swann. Bobby Swann's first wife. Ex-wife. You ever hear of him?"

"Of course," Thomas said. "Guitarist, right? Played for Stax in its heyday?"

"That's the one."

"You're looking for something, aren't you?"

"Maybe," Gideon said. "Doing some research. Nat is helping me out."

"Provenance," I said.

"Find anything yet?" Thomas asked.

Gideon said, "Just that Virgie Lee Swann has an attitude about her ex-husband, even though it's been forty years since she divorced him."

Thomas permitted himself a small smile.

I didn't know Thomas well—he hadn't encouraged it—but I felt enough at ease to talk to him with the same teasing tone I used with Jude and Gideon. I asked him, "You wouldn't happen to know Virgie Lee Swann, would you?"

He raised his eyebrows, just a little. "You don't really think we all know each other, do you?"

I flushed. "This is a small town," I said. "Tightly knit. My grandmother knows everyone who lives in Cordova, and my parents know everyone in the Jewish community. That's what I thought of. That's why I asked."

He tucked his check into the inner pocket of his suitcoat. "I'm afraid I'll have to disappoint you," he said. "I don't."

Jude asked, "What about the guy who gave you her name in the first place?"

I said, "Joe Jordan? Now we know she hates him, too."

Thomas said, "I know Joe Jordan. Not well, but he lives in my neighborhood. He really does know everyone Black in Memphis. If I were you, I'd ask him again." He turned to go.

Jude, who had learned to say "bless your heart" at her mother's knee, putting the barb in the honey, said sweetly, "Why, thank you, Mr. Waverley."

Unlike Jude, I was out of practice at being a Southerner. After he left, I said to no one in particular, "Man, he's touchy."

Jude looked at me and laughed. "Look who's talking."

I OFFERED to call Joe Jordan. On the phone, he called me "Miss Natalie," inquired politely after my well-being, and told me he hoped the shop was flourishing. I invited him to stop by the shop the next time he was in Midtown. He promised that he would.

He asked, "You get a chance to talk to Virgie Lee yet?"

"Well, we tried to. Gideon called her, and she blistered his ear off. Told him in no uncertain terms she didn't want to talk about Bobby Swann to anyone."

He chuckled. "So she still has an attitude about Bobby."

"You knew?"

"Thought she might have let it go a little. It's been forty years."

"Evidently not."

He said, "Her daughter might talk to you."

Daughter? "Do you know her?"

"I know her name. Brenda. She was just a little bitty thing when I knew her father. I don't know if she'd know me. But she might be easier to talk to than Virgie Lee."

"I hope so."

"She got married. Doesn't go by Swann anymore. Her name is Sawyer now."

"Why didn't you mention her before?"

"Well, she was only a little girl when her mama and daddy got divorced. I don't know how much she can help you. But I guess it's worth a try."

He didn't have a phone number for her, but I looked for her online, where I found her on the website of Baptist Memorial Hospital. She'd done well there. She was a manager in the medical records department. She'd been photographed as she received an award for her activity as a United Way committee volunteer. She wore a practical navy-blue pantsuit, and her hair was carefully pressed. Despite the occasion, her expression was profoundly serious. She held herself close, even at a celebration.

I called Baptist Memorial, and without the kind of obstruction or demur I'd get in New York, a receptionist with a pleasant voice connected me with Brenda Sawyer's voicemail. Like her appearance, Brenda's voice was careful and restrained. In my message, I put on my best professional demeanor, emphasizing my interest in her father's guitar rather than in his life and my hope that she would talk to me.

To my surprise, she called back several hours later, her voice guarded. "I don't quite understand why an antique dealer would want to talk to me."

"I'm researching the history of the guitar that belonged to your father," I said.

"I'm not sure what I can tell you."

"I'd be grateful for anything you might be able to tell me."

"What are you going to do with the information?"

I knew what was bothering her. "I can assure you that whatever I find will stay confidential, unless you tell me otherwise."

"That's all to the good, but why are you interested in the first place?"

"It may have turned up," I said.

"In Memphis? Someone in Memphis owns it?"

"That has to stay confidential, too."

"You aren't planning to talk to the newspaper?"

"I used to work at Sotheby's in New York, and believe me, if I'd told the press about something like this, they would have fired me on the spot."

"Sotheby's," she said.

"You can look me up online."

There was a silence. Clearly she already had.

I said, "I just have a few questions about the guitar. And if there's something you don't want to talk about, let me know. I'll respect that."

Another pause. "All right," she said. "I'll talk to you."

BRENDA LIVED IN WHITEHAVEN, just east of Orange Mound. Despite its name, it was a Black neighborhood, and I'd never been there, any more than I'd visited Orange

Mound before I talked to Joe Jordan. Like Orange Mound, the houses in Whitehaven were small and run-down. The residents parked beater cars on the streets and in the front yards. As I approached Brenda's block, the neighborhood changed to slightly bigger houses, built more substantially from brick and better maintained. The cars improved, too. Brenda's house was a stripped-down version of a house in any white suburb. The minuscule front lawn was immaculate, and there were beds of flowers by the house, along with low-growing shrubs that would be fragrant when they budded in a few weeks.

As I got out of the car, I could feel eyes on me. In this neighborhood, as in Orange Mound, I was anomalous, a white visitor in a brand-new car. I thought of my own neighborhood, where the neighbors also watched for people who didn't belong.

I met Gideon on the sidewalk. At the door, Gideon said, "You ring the bell."

I said, "When I called, she did agree to see me, even if she didn't sound keen on it."

"Does she know about me?"

"I told her you'd be coming."

"I'll step back, just in case she feels uneasy seeing me."

I said, "I bet you can charm your way out of it."

Brenda answered the door and invited us in. She was taller than I expected, and in person, her straightened hair looked stylish. Even on the weekend, at home, she was carefully and soberly dressed, in navy-blue trousers and a blouse to match, enhanced with a scarf in a subdued print.

The house had an old-fashioned smell of good house-keeping, beeswax and pine-scented cleanser. The living room furniture, a sectional sofa, two end tables, and two wing chairs, had been good quality when it was new and had been carefully maintained. There was no television in this room. They must keep it in the den. On the walls hung photographs of Memphis, cityscapes and landscapes, all in black and white. I recognized a good eye and an expert's hand and wondered who the artist was.

The man on the sectional rose as we came in, and Brenda introduced him as her husband, Edwin. Like his wife, he was casually dressed but well put together. I shook his hand and introduced Gideon to them both.

Edwin said, "I looked up your shop online. I told Brenda we should stop by."

Brenda said, "He likes to watch *Antiques Roadshow*. Never misses an episode."

"Are you a collector?" I asked.

"I get a kick out of seeing something that's worth a lot."

"I like your photographs," I said. "If you don't mind my asking, who is the artist?"

Edwin said, "I am. I took them."

"They're beautiful."

"It's my hobby. Been doing it for years."

"Have you ever shown them anywhere?"

"No, they're just for my enjoyment."

I'd meant to praise and encourage. But Edwin Sawyer clearly felt defensive about getting attention from a white antique dealer whose motives he didn't trust.

Gideon did his best. "You'll have to excuse both of us. We're antique dealers, and we can't help ourselves looking at stuff."

And judging it, I thought. Both of the Sawyers were cautious and self-protective, and they had good reason for it. I reminded myself to be careful.

Brenda and Edwin sat side by side on the sofa, and Gideon and I perched in the wing chairs that flanked it. The chair was much too big for me, and I leaned forward, trying to get comfortable in it.

Edwin said, "I understand you're interested in a guitar that belonged to Brenda's dad."

I said, "Yes, that's right. We're doing some research. Trying to figure out what happened to it. Who might have owned it after he did."

"Provenance," he said.

"*Antiques Roadshow*," I said, smiling.

Brenda tightened her hands in her lap. "Like I told you over the phone, there's not a lot I can tell you. I was a little girl when my parents divorced."

"Anything you can remember will be helpful." I asked, "Do you know when he bought it?"

I'd made a lucky remark. She unbent enough to smile a little. "Well," she said, "I remember my fourth birthday. I remember him playing me 'Happy Birthday' on his new guitar. I remember how pretty I thought it was. Bright red and shiny."

But she didn't lose herself in the memory. She smoothed her expression and forced her voice to remain level. There was more to tell, a lot more, but I didn't dare pressure her.

Gideon said, "I hate to ask a lady to reveal her age, but do you recall what year that was?"

Edwin said, "Provenance, sugar."

"Oh, I'm not vain about my age. My birthday was in August. August 1964."

Gideon nodded.

She said, "I know he took the guitar to work. I was so proud that he didn't work for the city or in a factory like my friends' dads. He worked at Stax. That was exciting when I was a little girl."

"I can imagine," I said.

She didn't reply in response to my sympathy. Clearly, she didn't trust it, either. "I was only eight when my parents got divorced. But I know he took the guitar with him when he left."

"That must have been hard for you."

Her voice remained level. "My mother was very unhappy with him after the divorce, and I didn't see him much afterward. I have no idea what happened to the guitar. You'd have to ask his second wife about it." She anticipated my question. "Her name was Micki. Michelle. I think she remarried a few years ago. I don't know what her name is now."

Edwin reached for his wife's hand and held it tightly. He asked both of us, "What is the guitar worth?"

Gideon said, "A 1964 Fender Stratocaster in good condition, just on its own merits, is worth several thousand dollars. It could do as well as five thousand at auction."

Still holding Brenda's hand, Edwin said, "But the same guitar, owned by someone famous—owned by a celebrity —that would be worth a lot more."

"It could be," Gideon admitted.

"How much more?" Edwin asked.

"It's hard to say." Gideon knew, all too well, what happened when someone got fixated on a number.

"Your best guess." Edwin wasn't going to let it go.

Deadpan, Gideon said, "I'd guess it might go for somewhere between twenty-five to fifty thousand at auction."

"Fifty thousand?" Brenda asked. She turned to Edwin. "If I wanted it back, that's way out of my reach."

Did she want it back? My reflex as an antique dealer was to offer hope. "We're dealing with a lot of ifs," I said. "If it's really his guitar. If we can get a clear provenance. If the current owner wants to sell. If it does well at auction. A lot of ifs."

Edwin let go of Brenda's hand. "You have a lead on that guitar, don't you?" he asked Gideon.

Gideon said, "A lot of ifs."

Edwin shook his head.

Brenda sighed. To me, she said, "I wish there was more I could tell you."

"This has been helpful."

Brenda said, "My mother knows a lot more than I do."

I said, "I know it's not easy for her to talk about your father. But we'd be very grateful if she'd talk to us. Just about the guitar. It doesn't have to be personal."

Brenda said, "She's never gotten over the divorce."

Edwin said, "You should tell her how much it's worth."

Brenda snorted.

"She might still be mad, but she might be interested."

Brenda looked at me. "I'll give it a try. And I'll let you know."

Outside, on the sidewalk, I said to Gideon, "There's a lot she's not telling us."

"I can tell."

"I've seen this before. It complicates things."

"I know. If she wants it back—"

"A lot of ifs," I reminded him.

BRENDA CALLED me a few days later. "I talked to my mother," she said.

"I appreciate it."

"I told her how much it might be worth. That did get her attention."

I was glad she used the words *might be*. I wondered if her mother had heard them. "What did she say?"

"She'll see you. God knows what she'll say to you."

"Any words of advice for us?"

Brenda snorted again. "Are you a praying woman?"

I thought of every selfish appeal I'd ever made to the Almighty. At work, *Let it hit reserve.* And at home, after each of my hospital visits, *Why did this happen to me?* "Sometimes."

"Pray before you go. And tell that dealer friend of yours to pray, too."

LIKE BRENDA, Virgie Lee lived in Whitehaven. Poverty marked her block. On one neighboring lot, a battered car sat on the front lawn, and another was strewn with trash. Virgie Lee's house was neater than her neighbors', but it was older and smaller than her daughter's. Brenda and

Edwin strived mightily to live in the middle class, but Virgie Lee couldn't afford to.

The woman who answered the door was short and stocky. Her face was lightly lined, but her hair was completely gray, processed into an old-fashioned style as durable as a helmet. She was probably in her sixties, but she looked a decade older. Her clothes were an old woman's, a beige cardigan in a pointelle pattern and polyester pants to match. Her shoes were sturdy, dowdy lace-ups, shoes to spare sore feet. Her appearance spoke to a lack of money but also a lack of vanity.

I introduced myself and Gideon and reminded her that I'd called at Brenda's urging. "Mrs. Swann, is this still a good time for you?"

She nodded slightly. "Yes, it is. Come in."

The interior of the house was tidy and well-kept. The walls were beige, but the paint had been refreshed. The furniture was too old for careful maintenance to freshen it, but in this house, a new large-screen TV had pride of place. Against the far wall stood an etagere full of framed photographs, children and grandchildren. On the wall opposite the TV was a carefully framed poster of Van Gogh's *Sunflowers*. As we sat, I saw the sculpture of praying hands on the etagere, which alerted both the snob and the Jew in me, and I reminded myself, *You aren't evaluating anything here. Shut up and listen.*

Once we were settled with glasses of sweet tea—as when we'd visited Joe, it was very sweet—she spoke to Gideon first. "Young man, are you a churchgoer?"

I'd told Gideon what Brenda said about prayer, and he'd shrugged it off. Now he replied with cheer as well as courtesy. "My granddaddy was a preacher," he said. "And his daddy was a traveling playing preacher."

"A musician?"

"Yes, ma'am. Saved many a soul with that guitar of his."

"A preacher who played the guitar?"

"I'm named for him. Gideon Fairchild."

She blinked in surprise. "What's your favorite hymn?"

Without missing a beat, he said, "'Amazing Grace.'"

Our housekeeper, Mavis, had loomed large in my early childhood and my brother's. When we came home from school, it was often Mavis who fed us and who inquired after our doings and our well-being. My mother wasn't surprised that many of my earliest notions of religion came from Mavis. My father, who liked Mavis and didn't mind trusting us to her care, was less pleased to discover how much I knew about Jesus before I was old enough to attend Temple Israel's Sunday school.

Still, I'd never seen a Christian morality play this obvious. I was only a little surprised to hear it from Virgie Lee, but I was astonished to hear it from Gideon.

Unless he was fooling with her, and with me.

She asked me, "And you, young lady? Where do you go to church?"

I was ready. "I've got it all covered. St. Mary's on the Christian holidays, and Temple Israel on the Jewish ones."

Her eyes glittered. "Raskin, you said your name was?"

"Yes, ma'am."

"Any relation to that Morris Raskin?"

"He was my grandfather."

"He's passed on?"

"Yes, four years ago."

I didn't see sympathy in her face. She looked back at Gideon and nodded. This was another audition, and for the moment, he'd done all right. She was clearly on the fence about me.

Gideon threw me a glance and took the lead. "Ma'am, is there anything you want to ask us before we ask you about the guitar?"

"Brenda told me you were antique dealers." Her voice was full of doubt that antique dealers were honest in their dealings.

"Yes, ma'am, we are. We help out people who have something and want to know more about it. I know someone who has a guitar that resembles the one your ex-husband used to own. We're looking into the guitar's history so we can tell him what he's got and what it's worth."

Aw shucks, Mr. Fairchild, I thought.

"Brenda said it's worth more if it was his guitar."

Carefully, respectfully, Gideon said, "It may be."

"Preacher's grandson," she said, looking at him. "You being straight with me?"

"Doing my best."

"Who has that guitar now?"

Gideon said, "People trust us to keep that kind of thing in confidence. We do that for everyone. That's why I can't say, ma'am."

She shook her head. "The Lord knows I don't want to see that thing again. I was just curious."

Gideon asked, "Ma'am, when did Mr. Swann buy that guitar? The red Fender Stratocaster?"

She hesitated. "Well, before I get to that, there's something else I need to tell you." She threw a glance at me, but she was talking to the preacher's grandson. "Because there was trouble, and it didn't start when he bought that red guitar. It started a long time before that."

She took a swallow of her tea and set it down on the coaster. "Robert Swann," she said, her tone suddenly gentle, as though she were going to deliver an elegy. "He was the sweetest man when I met him. Sweet smile. Sweet nature. He even smelled sweet." She sighed. "We met in church. And when we got married in church, everyone turned out to wish us well."

She shook her head. "I knew he played the guitar, but I didn't know how much he wanted to go down to Beale Street until after we got married. I begged him not to, because I knew the devil lurked there. But he wanted to play that guitar something awful, and once, he went to a club to play. Oh, was I mad! We had a terrible fight, and I thought about leaving him."

Evidently, she hadn't.

"We made up, and I got pregnant. I had a bad time, didn't feel well. He stayed close by to take care of me, and I thought, *Once the baby comes, he'll give up that guitar.* But after our daughter was born, and I recovered, he got the urge for Beale Street again. It called to him. But he resisted. I thought we'd be all right.

"Then I found out he'd been hanging around Raskin's Records, where all the bluesmen spent their idle time. When I asked him why, he got mad at me, like he'd never done before. 'Just listening to music, Virgie. How can you deny me that?' He was right. Even though I didn't like it, I couldn't." She gave me a reproving look.

"He came home one Saturday afternoon all excited. 'I went to cut a record at Stax,' he said. 'The head man, Jim Stewart, he liked my playing so much he asked me to play backup on another record they were making. Told me I could be a session man if I wanted to.' I told him, 'Quit your job to play the guitar? That's the last thing I'd want.'

"A few weeks later, he came home with a lot of money. He'd never gambled, and I hoped he hadn't started. I asked him, 'Where did you get that?' He laughed. 'That song I played on for Stax was a hit,' he said. 'This is my share. Look, Virgie, more than I make in two weeks with the city.'

"I didn't like it, not one bit, but he quit his job, and he went to work for Stax."

She sighed again and looked down at her hands, which were graceful and long-fingered and ropy with veins. She looked up. "He said he needed a good guitar. He told me how much it would cost, and I was just horrified. Hundreds of dollars. But he was lusting after a good guitar, the way he'd once lusted after Beale Street. It didn't matter what I said. He wasn't going to change his mind about getting his hands on one."

She looked at me. "That Mr. Raskin always liked him. He helped many of the musicians who hung around his shop. Lent them money to cut a record or to go on the road. Robert told me that Mo Raskin thought he had a real gift. He said, 'He'll lend me the money for a decent guitar.' I said, 'What's a decent guitar? How much money?' He said, 'Fender Stratocaster, and don't worry about the money, because he'll let me pay it back as I can, and he won't charge me interest.' I said, 'It's bad enough to be in debt. It's worse to be in debt to a Jew. I don't care what he says about the interest.'"

As politely as I could, I asked, "Why would you say that?"

"We'd been in debt to the grocer, that Mr. Stein, and the furniture store owner, that Mr. Weiss. They were grasping men. Wanted their money. I didn't like it, and I didn't like them."

I remained polite, even though I was upset. "It sounds like my grandfather was trying to do Bobby Swann a favor."

"That didn't matter to me," she said.

I struggled to tell myself that her attitude was anti-Raskinism and not anti-Semitism. It didn't help. This was another racial splinter, and it hurt.

She spoke to Gideon again. "We had that terrible year in Memphis, 1968, when the Reverend Martin Luther King was shot and the whole city went up in flames. Raskin's Records, too. Otis Redding died that year, and everyone thought it would be the end of Stax. But it wasn't. The new co-owner, Al Bell, thought a lot of Robert and kept him on as a session man. Stax flourished, and it became Robert's new home. His new family. We barely recognized him. All the Stax musicians dressed like pimps in those days. Wild hair. Wild clothes. They all wanted to be like Isaac Hayes, who was a big star at Stax in those years. He was a crazy man. Bald as an egg, and he performed half-naked. Dressed himself up in chains instead of clothes. Talk about the devil's doing! He wasn't my Robert anymore. He was Bobby Swann, and I didn't know him."

She swallowed the tea like it was bourbon. "And then he met her. The woman who ruined our lives. Backup singer for Stax. Just as bad as the musicians. Afro out to here"—she showed us—"and in pants, but everything else low-cut and tight. I took one look at her and thought, *Homewrecker.*"

More tea. I wished she was drinking bourbon. It might ease her bitterness.

Her gaze moved from Gideon to me. "When he left us for good, all he took was that guitar. That bright red candy-apple devil's plaything. I can still see him picking it up to put it in the case, giving us both a last look before he walked out the door."

It was time to go. We thanked her and left. Outside, on the sidewalk, I asked him, "All that stuff about the preachers in your family. Were you just trying to make her feel better, or was that true?"

"That was true."

"How do I know? I never do, with you."

"That's enough religion for one day," he said. "Maybe for a year. Can I take you out for a beer?"

I shook my head. "I can't believe that you and I and Virgie all lived in Tennessee at the same time. Hearing her talk, it's like I was in Germantown and you two were on Mars." I looked at him. "You are from Tennessee, aren't you? Where did you grow up?"

"Mars," he said, grinning at me.

"Someday I'm going to find out what you're sitting on. Where in Tennessee you're from," I said.

"Maybe," the preacher's son said to me, his eyes bright. "And maybe not."

6

MY MICHELLE

By the time I got home, it was dark enough that I turned on every lamp in the living room, wondering as usual why it had been built without overhead lighting. The low light suited my mood. I poured myself a glass of wine, fired up Otis Redding on the iPod, and perched in the Morris chair, the big mission armchair that Miss Augusta had liked so much.

The word *homewrecker* had stayed with me. The woman my ex-husband had fallen in love with had ruined my marriage and torn apart my home, but I'd never thought of her that way. In the half dark, I took out my phone, and as I rarely did, searched for my ex-husband's name.

I found the wedding announcement from the *New York Times*. Her parents, who must have been loaded, had paid for a Sunday spread and a photo. The man I'd once loved held his new wife's hand and gazed at her with goofy adoration. She wore a strapless satin dress that didn't hide her baby bump. I stared at her image. Alyssa Gordon, nominally Jewish, six years younger than myself. Taller and thinner, too. She stared back at the man she'd taken from me with a knowing smile on her face.

THE NEXT MORNING, I woke up with a headache, and I took it into the shop.

Gideon teased me, "You have a late night?"

"Otis Redding and I had a great time," I said.

"You need anything? Water? Ibuprofen?"

It was kind of him to offer. "I'm all right for the moment, thanks."

"Is it anything you want to mention?"

I shook my head. "Let's go find the homewrecker."

Gideon said, "Homewrecker? That's harsh."

I saw Alyssa's smile again, but I said, "Virgie Lee got to me."

"I grew up with people like that. Hate the sin and no sympathy for the sinner, either."

"Hell must be full."

"Good company, though," he said.

"I'm not so sure about that." My head throbbed. "I can go dig up the past on Michelle. Homewrecker or not."

"You need any help?"

"To read microfilm at the library? It would bore you stupid. Let me do it."

I'D DONE research in the reading rooms of grand libraries built in the nineteenth century, and I'd sat in county courthouses where the archive boxes were filthy with dust and spiderwebs. It was strange to walk into the Memphis Public Library, built while I was gone. I shared this welcoming contemporary space with toddlers listening to story hour and job seekers at computer terminals, polishing their resumes.

The library of my childhood had been staffed by white librarians, and to my surprise and my satisfaction, the librarian in the history department was a young Black woman who smiled when I walked in. "Can I help you?" she asked. I heard the faintest echo of her original accent through her education.

"I hope so." I told her about my quarry. "She was married to a Stax musician named Bobby Swann. Her first name was Michelle. He died in the 1980s, and she's since remarried. I don't know when, and I don't know to whom."

"Let's check the index to the *Appeal*."

"I didn't see that online."

"We're a little old-fashioned in the history department. It's not online. And the back issues are still on microfilm."

"I've read microfilm before." I mimed rubbing my eyes.

She laughed. "I hope we can spare your eyesight."

She quickly found me the wedding announcement from 1989. "Michelle Swann and James Montgomery wed." She pulled the microfilm reel for me.

I sat at the microfilm reader, listening to it whir. And there they were. Michelle Swann, widow of musician Robert Swann, was joined in marriage with James Montgomery, owner of Montgomery Real Estate Development. In the *Appeal*, as in the *New York Times*, money bought a lot of newsprint and a photograph. The groom, handsome and sober in his business suit, stood decorously next to the bride. Michelle was tall—nearly as tall as her husband—and she appeared lean and lithe, even in a dress that was a cloud of satin and lace. Her smile dazzled inside her veil. I felt a twinge of sympathy for Virgie Lee, who might have been pretty as a young woman but who had never been drop-dead gorgeous like Michelle.

Now that I knew how to find both Montgomerys, I went back to the index. These days, money and success made James Montgomery newsworthy. Michelle Montgomery, like Michelle Obama, basked in the reflected glory of her husband. She was also notable in her own right as a philanthropist in Memphis. She had done her duty for United Way and the library, and recently she'd started raising money to encourage the museum to acquire some works by Black artists.

I wondered where they lived. The newspaper pieces didn't give that information away. Evidently, they were rich enough to protect their privacy, like my grandmother Beardsley.

What had Michelle's life been before she became a Montgomery? I went back to the *Appeal*'s index to look at the 1960s and 1970s, and discovered there was no mention of anyone named Swann in the *Appeal* in those years. Bobby Swann had been law-abiding as a younger man and later invisible as a studio musician. There was no mention of Bobby's divorce from Virgie Lee or his subsequent marriage to Michelle. I sighed, shook my head, and closed the index.

I went back to the librarian. "I'm curious about this woman's first husband. The Stax musician. I can't find him in the *Appeal*."

She said, "The *Appeal* sometimes covered the hit singers, but everything else is iffy. You want to look at the *Tri-State Defender*. It's the local African American community newspaper."

I knew the Jewish community paper well, and I'd grown up reading the Germantown community paper too. I'd never seen the *Defender*, let alone read it, and I thought again about the Black and white worlds of Memphis, so close together and so far apart. "Please tell me there's an index."

She checked online for me. "Yes, there is," she said.

I worked backward to check the *Defender* for any mention of the Swanns, either Bobby or Michelle, but I couldn't find them. The *Defender* was full of strivers and preferred to profile the achievements of ministers and educators. Singers at Stax, especially if they had hit records, were mentioned, but session musicians were not.

I wondered if Michelle had worn satin and lace when she married Bobby Swann. Curious, I checked the index for any mention of her. Nothing. In those days, she had been invisible to the *Defender*, too.

I returned the index to the shelf.

"Any luck?" the librarian asked me.

"I think I've had all the luck I'm going to have today."

She smiled. "Don't get discouraged. Keep looking. You never know."

BACK AT THE SHOP, I said to Gideon, "Let me buy you a beer and show you what I found about Michelle Swann."

"My treat. I found something, too."

"I thought you hated research."

He said, "Does it count as research if you hear about it in a blues bar?"

I laughed. "I've never done any research in a blues bar."

We didn't go to E&H, because I insisted we needed enough light for him to see my photocopies. "She's come up in the world." I showed him the wedding announcement.

"Left the music business behind, from the look of it."

"Here's how she spends her time now." I showed him the article in the *Appeal* about her role in raising money for the museum for a Black art collection. "Good causes. Like my mother's friends. Do you know where she lives now?"

"You'll never guess."

"I won't, because you're dying to surprise me."

"Cordova."

"The land of rich white people? You can't be serious."

"Did you know that Isaac Hayes bought a house in Cordova in the 1970s?"

"Now that was chutzpah," I said.

"Maybe they were neighbors back in the day."

I said, "I know someone who knows a lot of people in Cordova. My mama, who grew up there, went to high school there, and came out as a deb in the country club there."

"I thought you were Jewish."

"That's on my father's side. On my mother's side, I'm descended from the Beardsleys, who settled Shelby County in the 1820s and grew cotton for decades. They were slaveowners, I'm sorry to say."

"And all those people know each other."

"Yes, they do, just like everyone in Orange Mound knows each other. Let me ask her if she knows anyone who can smooth our way to Michelle Swann Montgomery, now of Cordova."

I INVITED myself for brunch at my parents', which wasn't difficult. Over bagels and lox, my mother squeezed my hand and said, "It's so good to see you." My father asked me about the shop.

"It's doing great," I said.

"More coffee?" my mother asked, pouring me some before I could reply.

"Mama, can I ask you for a favor?"

My mother laughed. "How big a favor?"

"Not too big. You still talk to some people in Cordova, don't you?"

"A few of my high school friends, sure. Why?"

"I'm helping Gideon research a guitar. Dad, you met him, he's the dealer who's an expert on vintage instruments. We think the guitar may have belonged to a musician whose widow lives in Cordova now."

My father asked, "Who was the musician?"

"He was a session man for Stax. He isn't well-known. Bobby Swann."

Both my parents shook their heads. My mother asked, "Does she still go by Swann?"

"No, she's remarried, to James Montgomery, the developer. They live in Cordova, which is why I'm asking. You don't just drop in. It's like dealing with any rich collector or art patron. I wondered if you knew anyone who knows her."

"She's married to James Montgomery? I didn't realize they lived in Cordova."

My father said, "Did you know Isaac Hayes lives out in Cordova, too?"

"Yes, I just found out. That must have surprised some people."

"Oh, it did," my mother said.

"Is he still there?"

"As far as I know," my father said.

I said, "She's done a lot of charitable work. United Way, the library, the museum."

My mother said, "Let me ask around. I might know someone who's sat on a committee with her."

MY MOTHER FOUND an acquaintance of Michelle Montgomery's, and she got Michelle's telephone number, too. When I finally connected with Michelle, she was gracious. She was intrigued that anyone cared enough about Bobby Swann's history to interview her, and she invited both Gideon and me to visit her at home.

On the day of the interview, I drove northward to Cordova. My mother's mother lived in Cordova, and when I was a child, we always spent Christmas with her. Her house, built in the 1960s, predated the McMansion bloat of the past twenty years. Since then, vast houses had popped up all over Cordova like mushrooms.

Curious about Isaac Hayes, I'd gone back to the public library to look him up too. His purchase of the house had been newsworthy enough for the *Appeal*, which had treated him like a local magnate, not a Black man trespassing where he wasn't wanted. I wondered if he'd really been welcome in Cordova. He still lived in the house.

I didn't go out of my way to drive past.

Michelle's place had a discreet numbered sign and a long, curving path meant to imitate the approach to a plantation. The house was white and fronted by tall pillars, a Memphis developer's fantasy of Tara Plantation. Seeing it, I thought with longing of the old Beardsley house in rural Shelby County, where I spent my childhood summers, a planter's house. The real thing.

It took some chutzpah to live in a house like Michelle's if you were Black, no matter how much money you had.

Michelle herself answered the door to meet Gideon and me. She was still gorgeous, tall, lithe and muscular like the woman who had been unrelentingly in the public eye since her husband became president. She welcomed us inside.

"You must be Nat," she said, holding out her hand. "I hope you don't mind that I looked you up. I'm impressed. Columbia degree and all those years at Sotheby's." Her fingers were warm and dry.

"No, I don't mind."

"And I got a good report from Susan Ainsley. She told me you have family in Cordova."

"My grandmother, Eleanor Beardsley, lives nearby."

She laughed. "I won't hold that against you." She turned to Gideon. "I looked you up, too, but you're a man of mystery."

"I lived in Nashville for a long time," he said, as though that explained his low profile online.

"Were you a musician?"

"Session man for Warner, for many years."

"But you gave it up?"

"Got tired of being in back."

With a flash of recognition, she said, "And you couldn't jump out front."

"Turned out it wasn't worth it."

"Ain't that the truth," she said, and beneath the Cordova matron she'd become, I saw a flash of the girl she'd been.

From the foyer, next to the big staircase, I spotted the painting, which was big and bright enough to see across a football field. "Is that a Kehinde Wiley?" I asked her.

She broke into a smile.

"I haven't seen his work since I left New York. Do you mind if I take a closer look?"

"Not at all."

It was one of his iconic pieces, a rapper posed to look like a Gainsborough. I looked, and I admired. "That's a beautiful piece," I said. I turned. "And is that a Romare Bearden?"

She said, "Bearden is my husband's taste. Wiley is mine."

I couldn't help myself. "I hope you have it properly insured."

She laughed. "Us? We're insured to the eyeballs."

She sat us in the living room, a big space with a fifteen-foot ceiling and a cathedral window that someone had to get on a ladder to clean. She had set out coffee. Like my grandmother, she had a nineteenth-century silver set. Gorham, late Victorian, if I was right. But she poured the coffee into sturdy ceramic mugs. "You don't mind being informal?" she asked me.

"Not at all." I'd been ready to put her at ease, and instead, she was charming and disarming me. I knew it was dangerous to be captivated by a rich collector. But I couldn't help liking it. I liked her. "Are you from Memphis?" I asked her.

"I am. My parents both came from Mississippi—Sunflower County—but I grew up near Beale Street. Not so far from Stax." She sighed. "They left Mississippi to better themselves, but in Memphis, my father had a job in a warehouse, and my mother was as a maid. They worked themselves to the bone. When they were in their thirties, they looked decades older. I swore I'd never live like that."

"When did you start singing?" Gideon asked.

"Youth choir at church. I was ten. I graduated to the adult choir when I was sixteen. But I always had my eye on Stax." She looked at Gideon. "When I graduated from high school, I went over there. They offered me session work. Being in back. I didn't mind. I thought I'd have my chance."

Gideon looked back at her. He wasn't smiling; he hadn't been charmed by her, as I was.

"I did, but not the one I expected." Looking at me, she said, "After you called, I looked through some of my old stuff, and I found a few photos to show you."

As with her art, she'd assembled a gallery for us.

She pulled out a photo and laid it on the coffee table for us to look at. This was Michelle herself, her full Afro adding to her height. She wore a low-cut blouse, knotted to show off a taut midriff, and low-slung bell-bottomed jeans. She chuckled when she saw the expression on my face. "Soul child, running wild," she said. "That was in 1970."

Gideon said, "You would have given Pam Grier a run for her money."

"You aren't the first person to say that."

At a loss, I asked, "Who was Pam Grier?"

Gideon said, "Actress in blaxpoitation movies in the 1970s. *Coffy. Foxy Brown.*"

I shook my head. "Before my time."

"Hot buttered soul," Gideon said, looking at me. "Isaac Hayes."

She smiled, a rueful smile. "Ike and Bobby were tight back then."

I thought of Virgie Lee's contempt for Isaac Hayes. "What was he like? Isaac Hayes?"

She laughed. "Oh, man. He was wild, too. Black and proud and crazy. He used to perform half-naked, wearing chains from the waist up. We never knew whether he was making an ironic statement about slavery or letting the world know about his private kink. Some of both, I think now."

"Do you know him? Still see him?"

"Not for a long time. He hit a rough patch after he left *South Park*. And he's reclusive now. I hear he's not well."

"I'm sorry to hear that," I said, meaning it.

"You came here for Bobby, not Ike Hayes. I have something else to show you." She slid the photograph across the coffee table.

He was tall and broad-shouldered, and he wore a white suit that suggested Elvis without copying him. He held the gorgeous red guitar at crotch level, the sexuality obvious.

"That was Bobby when I first met him," she said. "When he walked into the studio, he looked just like that. I took one look at him, and he took one look at me, and it was like we'd both been hit by lightning. We were crazy about each other. Virgie Lee? She might as well have been on Mars."

I shot Gideon a look, but he stayed deadpan.

"But that's how he looked in those days. Black and proud and fine. And that's how I remember him."

I said, "I see why you fell for him."

"Like being hit by lightning." She looked at me. "Did that ever happen to you?"

Why was it easy to confide in her? "Yes, in high school."

"High school romance? What happened to him?"

I didn't care that Gideon was listening. "Long gone. I grew out of it."

She said, "When I met Bobby, he was still married to

Virgie Lee. Oh, I knew what she thought of me. Have you talked to her?"

We both nodded.

"Did she call me a Jezebel?"

I said, "Close enough."

Michelle looked at me. "When a marriage goes wrong, it takes two. She never saw that."

Did she know I was divorced? I'd never thought my divorce was my fault.

Gideon gestured toward the photo. "When was that taken?"

"This one? It was a publicity still from Wattstax. 1972."

"Wattstax?" I asked.

She smiled at me. "Before your time. Stax held a benefit in LA to commemorate the fifth-year anniversary of the riots in Watts. It was something! Like Woodstock, but Black and urban. Everyone from Stax played in the concert. Bobby was onstage for hours." She looked away, lost in the memory of the people they had been, Black and beautiful. "When we got back from LA, we were on cloud nine, the two of us, and when he proposed that we get married, I didn't have to think about it. I said yes. And when our son, Jeffrey, came along, Bobby was crazy about him too. Just adored him."

She smiled, but her face was tinged with sadness. "After we got married, I stopped singing at Stax because Bobby was doing so well. Stax was flying high in those days, and all the musicians were part of it. Stax was making a pile of money, and so was he. By then he was flying high in every way. They all were. It wasn't just the money. It was the drugs. They liked cocaine. They all said it made them play better."

Gideon said curtly, "It doesn't."

She looked at him, the sadness more pronounced. "Session man. So you know."

"Too well," Gideon said.

She laid her hand on the photo, reclaiming it. "Bobby said that cocaine gave him wings, and he wanted to fly as high as he could."

Gideon asked, "And what happened when he came down?"

"I bet you can guess."

Gideon said, "I don't like to guess. I'd rather know."

"All right. This isn't easy to talk about, but it's never been a secret. When he wasn't doing cocaine, he was low. Really low. I always hoped I could love him out of it. But of course I couldn't." She looked down at the photo of Bobby in one of his highest moments. "I worried about him, and I nagged him about going to the doctor. He'd tell me that no doctor could cure him of the pain of being a Black man. He was bipolar, for God's sake. He was sick. Black or white, they can treat it. But he didn't want treatment."

She looked at Gideon. "And then Stax went bankrupt."

"What happened then?" Gideon asked, his voice flat. I wondered why.

"He tried to keep making a living as a musician. He'd play the clubs in Memphis. Atlantic hired him for some session work at Muscle Shoals and New York. It wasn't enough. Not just the money. It wasn't Stax. Stax had been his home and his family for ten years. And then it was gone. It was over. Except for the cocaine."

She looked at Gideon, a steady gaze, and he met her eyes. Until he looked away.

"When he died, there was no money. No insurance. I didn't know what to do. Mo Raskin had always felt responsible for Bobby. He'd helped him out from the beginning, and he was still trying to help when Bobby died. I went to see Mo to ask for his advice. He told me the guitar was worth something. A fair amount, he said. He told me he'd take me to Diamond Pawn and get me what it was worth." She met my eyes, and I nodded.

"And he did. He got Ike Levy at Diamond Pawn to put five thousand dollars into my hand. We needed that money, my son Jeffrey and I."

Gideon asked, "When did you sell it?"

"Two weeks after he died. That was on June 8, 1984."

I made my voice gentle. "Did you keep the receipt?"

"I can't remember, and even if I did, I cleaned out everything when I moved. I threw boxes and boxes of junk away. I'm sure I don't still have it."

WE LEFT the house to stand in the pleasantly cool air in the driveway. Gideon looked pale and drawn. I said, "Icarus."

His thoughts were elsewhere, and he looked at me in surprise.

"You knew about Minerva. I thought you'd know that story, too."

He blinked. "I do. Wax wings. Hubris. Soared too close to the sun and came crashing down to earth."

He kept surprising me. With Virgie, he'd been the scion of a long line of Baptist preachers. With me, he knew his Greek mythology. I wanted to reach for his hand, and I knew how wrong that was. Our friendship, tethered by the shop, wasn't strong enough for it. I said, "Why do you think she told us all that?"

"She liked you." He looked at something behind my head, then met my eyes.

All the men I'd loved had been brown-eyed, and it was strange to look deeply into eyes that were blue.

He asked, "Have you ever tried cocaine?"

"I tried it once at a party. I didn't care for it." I let the unspoken words hang in the air. He hadn't just tried cocaine. He'd lived in its haze in Nashville, just as Bobby had at Stax. And I couldn't ask him about it outright, because he wouldn't tell me.

He said, "Well, now we know where the guitar went after he died. Do you think Diamond Pawn has records that far back?"

"I don't know. I can talk to Ben Levy, who took over the business from his father. If they have the records, he'll let me know." I wanted to distract Gideon, and I said, "I went out with his son in high school. Adam Levy. The high school romance. We were crazy about each other."

It worked. He was distracted by hearing about my love life. "The one you grew out of." So he'd been listening while Michelle and I made girl talk.

I said, "He thought we should be together forever. I didn't."

WHEN GIDEON OFFERED to accompany me to Diamond Pawn, I told him, "It's just to get a receipt. You don't have to."

"No, it's all right. Ben knows me. I've bought from him, and I've done valuations, too."

I made a face.

He said, "Does he have a daughter who's single? I can ask her out. Just so we both have a personal relationship with the Levy family."

"I'll never hear the end of that," I said. "And I don't even know if you've been married or not."

He shook his head.

Several days later, Gideon and I walked into Diamond Pawn together. I'd never set foot in a pawn shop, either in Manhattan or in Memphis, and I was surprised by how well-lit and well-organized Diamond Pawn was. The customers, who were predominantly Black, didn't look any different from people who shopped at Walmart. Most of the employees were Black, including a broad-shouldered, thick-necked man in a security guard's uniform that was reminiscent of a cop's. His eyes roamed the place, alert for trouble, but when he saw Gideon he held out his hand for a high five. "Gid, my man, are you here to buy today?"

"No, we're here to see Ben."

"He expect you?"

"We have an appointment," I said.

"And who's this pretty lady?"

Old-fashioned Southern sexism. I told myself I'd heard

worse in New York. "I'm Nat Raskin. I own an antique shop on South Main. Gideon rents dealer space from me."

"Ben's in back," the guard said, smiling.

I'd been worried about seeing Ben Levy. I'd never known what Adam told him about our breakup, which had been ugly and painful, even if it was years in the past. But Ben Levy rose as we walked in and greeted me with warmth, reaching out to take my hand.

As a teenager, I'd thought of him as Adam's dad, and I hadn't seen how handsome he was. Now I did. He had a canny, weary look, as though he'd been on the lookout for deception for so long that he was tired of it. I thought, *At Sotheby's, we always cloaked it in connoisseurship. But we were professional skeptics, too.*

Ben said, "At Temple, I hear all about your shop from your family." The Levys had always been big shots at Temple Israel. They'd donated handsomely to the building fund, and they paid extra for seats in the front row on the High Holy Days.

"It's doing well. I'm really pleased with how well."

"You like being back in Memphis?" Did he know that I'd sworn never to return?

"Yes, pleased and surprised by that, too."

"You don't miss New York?"

"Just a little," I said, and for a moment I missed it fiercely. *I'm here now*, I reminded myself.

He turned to Gideon. "It's good to see you, too. I take it you're not in the market for a guitar today."

Gideon grinned. "I might be. What have you got?"

"Take a look out front. If you're interested, we can do a deal." He motioned to both of us to sit. "You're tracking down the provenance on a guitar. Bobby Swann's guitar, you tell me."

Gideon said, "We know it's Bobby Swann's guitar. We just talked to his widow." He added, "Michelle Montgomery, now."

"Didn't Swann play for Stax back in the day?"

"He did. Michelle told us his guitar ended up at Diamond Pawn."

"When?"

"Just after he died. 1984."

He laughed. "Ancient history."

I asked, "Do you have records that go back that far?"

"We have records that go back to the 1920s when the shop opened."

"So you'd remember the transaction," I said.

"Nat, I'm your dad's age, not Methuselah's."

"June of 1984. Weren't you working in the shop by then?"

"I was, but I don't remember the transaction."

"I think your father handled it."

"That's why. He didn't get me involved."

"Michelle Swann brought it in. She was a knockout. Do you remember her?"

He shook his head.

I pressed him. "Do you remember the guitar? Fender Stratocaster, candy-apple red finish?"

"Nat, we've had so many guitars through here over the years. A fair number of Strats. I don't."

I began to feel bothered. I doubted that he'd forget the sight of Michelle Swann, striking all by herself, if she'd pulled out Bobby's stunning guitar from its case. I said, "My grandfather came in with her."

"And I'm sure he went right in back to huddle with my father, his old buddy. Nat, do you know how many objects run through this place? Valuable objects? I can barely remember what came in last month, let alone what came in almost twenty-five years ago."

I thought of my father telling me that the record shop was a hobby and not a real business. "But you have the records from 1984, you said. The receipts. That's all we'd need for provenance."

"You didn't ask the widow for the receipt?"

"We did. She didn't save it."

He said, "Nothing was computerized back then. It's all paper. You'd have to dig for it in the paper files."

I leaned forward. "I don't mind. I used to do that all the time for Sotheby's."

"When in 1984? Do you know?"

"June. Shortly after he died, early in June. If we could look at a month or two after that, that would be great."

"I'll dig the boxes out."

"What about the record of a sale? Would you have that, too?"

"We would, but I couldn't for the life of me tell you when that was."

"I know. Could you take a look at the computerized records first? See what comes up?"

Ben looked at Gideon, who said, "What can I say, Ben? She's good at this. She used to work for Sotheby's."

He said, "Sure, I can do that right now." He turned to

the monitor on his desk and began to tap on the keys. He frowned. "No, nothing shows up."

"When did you computerize?" I asked, still the Sotheby's-trained sleuth.

"In 1989."

"So it might have sold sometime between mid-1984 and 1989."

He looked at both of us. "That's a lot of records. A lot of files."

Without consulting Gideon, I said, "I don't mind. If I could sit and look—"

He began to look at me with a quizzical expression. "You really want to do this?"

"It's what I did for a living for fifteen years. I haven't forgotten how to do it. I've handled records a lot worse than yours. Papers with centuries of dust and dirt on them. Boxes full of mouse droppings. Twentieth-century files a few decades old? Stored in a climate-controlled office? Piece of cake."

Gideon said, "Speak for yourself."

"Didn't you once tell me that the antique business involved a mess of dirt?"

"We'll pull them, and we'll set up some time for you to take a look," Ben said.

"Thank you," I said.

Ben said, "Nat, while you're here, there's something I'd like to show you, if you don't mind."

Gideon said, "I know that tone, Ben. You need a valuation?"

"It's not a guitar."

I'd walked into that one, being so insistent with him, just short of rude. I modulated my tone. "Sure, what is it?"

"It's an oil painting. It's been sitting here for a while. We're not savvy about oil paintings, not like you are, Nat. Would you mind taking a look?"

"It's just a valuation, right? Not an appraisal for insurance?"

"No, I bought it outright, and I plan to sell it. I just want to know what it's worth."

I took a deep breath. "A quick look and a little online search? I do that all the time in the shop. I don't charge for that."

He rose. "It's back in the warehouse. I'll show you."

"Is the warehouse climate-controlled too?"

"Of course we air condition the warehouse. Otherwise, the employees would keel over in the heat in the summer."

The warehouse, like the shop, was well-lit and well-organized. The muscular Black men who worked there wore bright yellow polo shirts with "Diamond Pawn" embroidered on the pocket. Mr. Levy found the picture and set it on a nearby table, pushing aside a cardboard box to make room. I bent over to look, Gideon at my elbow. He crowded me a little, but I didn't mind.

It was in an ornate gilded frame, a pleasant landscape showing an island in the ocean. I checked for a signature. I could make out the date—1883—but the artist's name was too hard to read. "Do you have a magnifying glass?" I asked.

"I have a loupe," he said, pulling it from his pocket. "I

started with diamonds, and diamonds are still good to us. I always carry a loupe."

The first name looked like "Robert" but the last name could be "Eamon." Or "Eaton." Or "Easton."

Gideon leaned in closer.

"Can you read that?" I asked him.

"No."

"I hate artists who sign with a squiggle. The first lesson in art school should be about branding your pictures with a legible signature."

Ben said, "Don't we wish."

I turned the picture around and was rewarded with a scrawl in pencil: "St. Helena Island, South Carolina." But not the artist's name.

"Let me try a quick online search." I checked Live Auctioneers and Worthpoint and smiled.

"You found something?" Gideon asked.

"We got lucky. Robert Eamon, 1840 to 1918. Born in Charleston, South Carolina. Studied art in Paris just after the Civil War. Returned to the US to live in Charleston. Painted South Carolina landscapes. One of his pictures didn't sell at Toomey in Chicago a few years ago, but there's a price realized at Brunk in Asheville last year. Estimate of eight to twelve thousand, sold for seven plus commission."

Ben said, "It is worth something."

"Local interest in the South. I'd send it to Brunk without a reserve. If it sells, you can probably get about five thousand for it."

"I paid less than that."

I laughed. "Buy cheap, sell high. The Raskin motto, too."

He halted and looked at me, nostalgia infusing his face. "I remember when my boy Adam took you to the prom," he said.

He remembered that just fine. "Not recently."

"It seems like yesterday." He asked, "Do you ever talk to Adam?"

What did he know? "No." Jarred into politeness, I asked, "How is he?"

"He went to law school, and he decided to specialize in entertainment law. He's in Nashville, working for Warner Music. He seems to like it." He was looking at me with a rueful expression. "He's married. Nashville girl. Jewish, but quite a princess. It's his job to make a living and hers to spend it."

"Do they have any children?"

"No, not yet, even though his mother and I keep hoping."

I said, "Gideon used to live in Nashville. He worked for Warner, too, as a musician."

Ben said, "I didn't know that. Did you ever run into my son in Nashville? Adam Levy?"

Gideon's face and voice were deadpan. "No, I didn't."

7

————

THE MIRROR IMAGE

A week later, Michelle Montgomery walked into the shop. Jude was on duty with me, but there was something forbidding in Michelle's expression, and I didn't introduce them. I said pleasantly to Michelle, "It's nice to see you. Please look around."

"I will."

Jude's eyes followed her as she meandered through the shop.

"Don't do that," I said.

"No, no. She looks like a jewelry buyer, that's all. Well-off suburban matron. Hope springs eternal."

I wasn't going to out her as a collector of contemporary Black art. "Let her look," I said.

Michelle came to the counter. "Nat, there's something in the case in back I want to see."

"Which case?"

"There's a lot of Black history stuff in it."

Thomas Waverley's case. Thomas never hung around to sell. For that, he relied on us. Jude handed me the key.

"Sure," I said, and she followed me into the corner, a spot where Jude couldn't overhear us. "What can I show you?"

She said, "Nothing, really. I came to talk to you."

"You could have called me."

"It didn't feel right. I had to think about it for a long time. I decided to ask you in person."

The depth of emotion meant it was either very good or very bad.

"It's even harder than talking to you about Bobby. There were happy memories along with the bad ones. But this—there's nothing but pain."

I said, "We have a good lead on the ownership of the guitar. You don't have to share anything more, especially if it's hard for you."

"It's about my son Jeffrey," she said.

Softly, like Gideon, I said, "It's all right to leave some things alone."

She raised her eyes to mine. "I know. I can't."

I waited. I'd learned a long time ago that my silence encouraged someone else to open up. I let her talk.

"Jeffrey is just like his father."

"He's a musician?"

"And a cocaine addict."

The son was also an Icarus, flying too close to the sun with wings held together with wax. "I'm so sorry," I said. "But I don't know how I can help."

"Will you talk to him? And take your friend with you. He'll understand."

She'd correctly figured Gideon for a man who'd had his own trouble with drugs.

"I'll ask him. I can't promise anything on his behalf."

She laid her fingers on my arm. She had the long, lustrous, beautifully shaped nails of a woman who didn't work with her hands. "He'll say yes if you ask him."

"Maybe."

"No, he will. Because he cares about you."

"We're business partners. That's how we're friends."

"No, I can see it's more than that." She tightened her grasp. "Please, go talk to Jeffrey, both of you."

———

GIDEON WAS dubious about visiting Jeffrey Swann. "We already know where the guitar went. What more can he tell us?"

I hadn't told him about Michelle's plea. "When you're researching provenance, you never ignore a source of information. We don't know what he might be able to tell us."

Gideon said, "I have better things to do with my time."

I felt a flash of irritation, because he'd also refused to accompany me to Diamond Pawn to work through the receipts. He'd become edgy since we'd interviewed Michelle. The story of Bobby's downward spiral had really gotten to him. It wasn't kind of me to subject him to Jeffrey Swann, who took after his father in both musicality and self-destruction.

———

JEFFREY LIVED downtown in an old two-story building that had once been a commercial space and had since become apartments. Now, like the area, like the block, it was run-down.

Gideon put his hands in his pockets and hunched his shoulders. "If he lives here, he's broke."

"Or frugal."

"No, broke."

I was learning what his irritation meant. He'd lived in a place like this when he was broke. He didn't like remembering it. I said, "It's just research." I tapped him on the arm. "History."

"Maybe, and maybe not."

I said, "Look, you don't have to talk to him. I can probably manage to ask him a few questions all by myself. But you can speak to him, musician to musician, in a way I can't."

Now I'd tapped on his ego. His professional pride. He unhunched his shoulders. "Okay."

The man who opened the apartment door to us wore a white shirt too big for him, and he was barefoot. But he was heartbreakingly beautiful, his face a lovely combination of his mother's and his father's. "Come on in," he said.

His place was small, and the furniture was sparse, a stark contrast to the opulent comfort of his mother's house in Cordova. Unlike hers, the walls were bare. A lot of melamine, like a student's place. Michelle hadn't bought her son's furniture.

Maybe she had, and he'd sold it.

The room was chilly. I wondered if he ran hot or if he was economizing on his utility bill.

The best thing in the place was the guitar propped in the corner, as Joe Jordan's had been. Jeffrey's instrument was new, and its starburst finish gleamed in the low gray light.

I saw Gideon's eyes travel to it and linger there.

Jeffrey said, "I don't have much to offer you. There's some cola in the fridge, and I have tap water." Like his mother, he didn't have the usual Black accent of Memphis, with its heavy Delta overlay. The Delta and the South had been stripped from his speech.

He gestured for us to sit on the sofa, and he brought over a dining chair for himself. "My mother told me about you," he said. His voice was soft and melodic. I wondered if he sang, too. "That you're both antique dealers. I looked up your shop online. It's really nice."

"Thank you," I said, my reflex.

"She also told me that you're researching my father's guitar."

"Yes, that's right," I said.

A faint smile played over his face. He looked just like his mother, melancholy with memory. "His life, too."

Gideon had laid his hands on his pants legs, the tendons prominent as though he were making a physical effort.

"We don't mean to make this difficult," I said, my voice soft.

"I can always tell you to stop. Or go away." But he was smiling. He'd inherited charm from both sides of the family.

"We will."

Reassured, he settled back onto the sofa. "I don't know how much I can help you," he said. "I know my father owned that guitar, because I saw it around the house. I heard him play it. But I don't know what good that does you."

I thought of Brenda. "Whatever you remember," I said.

He smiled. "Oh, I remember that guitar," he said. "I thought it was the prettiest thing I'd ever seen. I remember how much I wanted to learn to play it. My father knew my hands were too small, and he bought me a beginner's guitar. I remember him covering my hands with his own to teach me how to finger a chord." His face was sweet. Was that the expression Virgie Lee had seen in his father? "I remember how proud he was when I learned how to play C major."

Gideon explained, "That's the easiest chord you can learn. The first."

He looked at Gideon, musician to musician. "How old were you when you learned to play?"

Surprised, he said, "Honestly? I started so young I don't remember."

"Who taught you?"

Musician to musician. Gideon unbent a little. "My family was full of guitar players. My grandpa. My uncles. My mama was a singer. She sang in church. She was a soprano. Lovely, lovely voice."

That was more than he'd ever told me about his mother.

"What was the first song you played?"

He hesitated. Was it reluctance to share it, or pain for the memory? "'Amazing Grace.'"

"Accompanying your mother?"

"Yes." He was tense again.

"I never played for my mother. I wish I had. She won't sing anymore."

"Why not?" I asked.

"It hurts too much to remember."

"She told us she sold the guitar," I said.

"I understood why she had to. But it broke my heart. It was bad enough that he was gone. But I wished we could have kept the guitar to remember him by."

"Did you ever think about trying to buy it back?"

"I lost track of it. And then other things got in the way."

I didn't ask what they were.

He rubbed his nose. "I thought I'd never see it again." He looked at me, then at Gideon. "Has it shown up?"

"We don't know," I said.

Gideon talked over me, his voice brusque. "If it surfaces, it will probably go to auction, with a big price tag."

"Thousands of dollars?" he asked.

"Tens of thousands."

He sighed. "I'd love to hold it in my hands again. Play it for him. Remember him at his best." His eyes lingered on me, then moved to Gideon. He hesitated, not for us, I thought, but for himself. "I was twelve when he died. Old enough to know how troubled he was. I knew he did cocaine, and I know he died from an overdose. My mother didn't tell me. She didn't have to."

I felt Michelle's presence in the room like her perfume. *Talk to him…* I didn't know what to say.

He looked at Gideon. "You're a guitar man, aren't you? Used to do session work, like my dad did?"

"I was a session musician in Nashville for a long time," Gideon said.

"But not anymore. Why did you quit?"

Stiffly, Gideon said, "I needed a change of scene."

Very softly, Jeffrey asked, "Does it snow in the studio in Nashville, like it does in New York and LA?"

Gideon went very still. "I reckon you know."

"Oh, I do," he said. He gestured toward the pristine, gleaming instrument propped in the corner. "Can I play for you?"

I knew the expression on Gideon's face, as Jeffrey did not: *This ain't none of your business.* But he said, "It's a lovely instrument. PRS-24?"

"Yes, it is."

"Beautiful sound," Gideon said, his voice flat, as though he'd come here to appraise it.

"Do you want to hear it?" Jeffrey asked.

Before Gideon could reply—or refuse—Jeffrey rose and retrieved the guitar and the amp. He plugged in the amp, and he held his guitar on his lap as gently as a father would cradle a baby. He looked up and smiled, his father's sweet, sweet smile. "This is for both of us, session men," he said.

He played "Hurt," a song of addiction and despair, about a man who had hurt—and lost—everyone who loved him, a man so badly hurt he'd never recover. I'd heard Johnny Cash's version, which Gideon undoubtedly knew.

Jeffrey smiled as he sang, the smile he'd inherited from his father, the smile that had beguiled Virgie Lee and had struck Michelle like lightning. I watched as Gideon listened to the song, going stiff and silent. I looked from one damaged man to another.

Jeffrey Swann, who had been hurt, also knew how to hurt.

When he finished, he asked, "My mother put you up to this, didn't she?"

Gideon stared at me. "Did she?"

Jeffrey had played us as deftly as he'd played his guitar, a talent he'd inherited from his mother. I was so upset with them both, Jeffrey and Michelle, that I couldn't give Gideon an answer.

Gideon rose.

Mortified, I said, "Jeffrey, you've been very helpful." As I stood, I said, "Thank you."

Gideon moved toward the door, unable to say anything polite.

I shook Jeffrey's hand. "If you think of anything else, you can call me." I gave him my card. "It's all right, we'll see ourselves out."

ON THE SIDEWALK I caught up with Gideon. He turned to me. "What the hell, Nat?" I'd never seen him so angry. "Did you know he was a cocaine addict? Did Michelle tell you that? Why didn't you tell me?"

I was afraid, and it came out as anger to match his. "Because I didn't think it was important. We came here to do some research, not to stage an intervention!"

"Did Michelle talk to you about that, too?"

"I reminded her we were doing research. And that's all we were going to do."

"So that's why you dragged me along. One musician to another. Is that what you thought?"

I was beginning to get an inkling of why he was so angry. "This isn't about Jeffrey. Or that I withheld something from you. What are you really mad about?"

He faced me. "I reckon that's none of your damn business," he said.

"Really? As your partner in business and your friend?"

He was close enough that I could smell the leather of his jacket and the scent of the cologne he wore. I reached for his arm to lay my hand on it.

He shook me off. "Don't you dare come on to me."

Shocked, I said, "I wasn't."

"Don't kid yourself."

Now I was thoroughly angry, too. "What's wrong with you?"

He said, "I don't want to talk about this anymore." He backed away. "Leave it alone. And leave me alone." He turned to go, and I stood unmoving on the sidewalk and watched as he walked away.

8

THE GUN UNDER THE COUNTER

After our visit to Jeffrey Swann, Gideon kept his duty hours at the shop, but he no longer hung around when he wasn't scheduled. He was so brusque with me that Jude noticed. "I asked him if something was going on with the two of you. He said, 'Back off, Jude.' So I have." She shook her head. "Now I know for sure."

With Gideon, it wasn't a personal connection to mend but a business relationship. I'd had relationship problems before in my professional life. It might be painful, but I would handle it accordingly.

On one of Gideon's duty days, I asked him, "Hey, can we talk?"

He folded his arms.

"Privately?" I threw Jude a look. She nodded.

He said, "You're taking me out behind the woodshed?"

I shook my head. "Let's go in back."

We sat at the table in back. He folded his arms again. "Go ahead," he said.

Deep breath. *I can do this.* "Things have been awkward

between us since we talked to Jeffrey Swann," I said. "I'm worried that it's affecting our relationship. Our business relationship."

He inclined his head and didn't reply.

"I know you were mad. I'm sorry it went like that. But we still have to work together."

"Business?" he said curtly, sounding like he had when Jeffrey got to him. "I'm here to do business."

"Sure," I said. "So am I. But it's a lot easier to do business when we're both pleasant with each other."

He looked like an unhappy, overgrown kid. *You're not the boss of me.*

Another deep breath, I thought. "I wanted to tell you how much I appreciate having you as a dealer in the shop. Not just for the merch you bring in, but for everything you do in working with the customers and selling all of our stuff." I stopped there.

He looked up. He nodded. "Okay," he said.

"I'm not your boss. I know that. Look, I like having you in the shop. I just like it better when we act friendly in a professional way."

He laid his hands on the edge of the table, and I saw how the tendons tightened. "Don't push me," he said.

I looked at him, and he looked away. "I won't," I said.

"Is that it?"

I nodded.

He rose and left.

I remained at the table, more upset than before. Under my polite, professional veneer, I was hurt. Not as badly as he was, but hurt nonetheless.

After Gideon left that afternoon, Jude said, "You talked to him?"

I nodded.

"And it didn't do any good."

"He told me to back off, too."

She said, "Would you tell me what happened between the two of you?"

"Just my side of it. You have time for a drink at E&H?"

At E&H, I played with my beer bottle, peeling the label instead of drinking.

Jude asked, "What was it? How bad was it?"

"We went to talk to Bobby Swann's son, Jeffrey. He's a guitarist. Pretty good, as far as I could tell, since he played for us. He's also a drug addict. The more he talked, the more upset Gideon got. Really upset." I shook my head, remembering. "When we left, I felt awful for him, and I wanted to make a friendly gesture. I put my hand on his arm, and he thought I was coming on to him. And that only made it worse."

"Were you?"

I said, "He was upset. He's a friend. I didn't mean to make a mess of it."

Jude sighed.

I said, "I'd guess he had some trouble with drugs in Nashville. You don't have to tell on him."

Jude said, "Oh, I will. You're absolutely right. I bet Jeffrey Swann held the mirror up for him, and he didn't like what he saw."

"How bad was it?"

"He said it got to the point where he'd be lucky to end up in the emergency room. And if he didn't, he'd end up in the graveyard. That's when he stopped using and he left Nashville."

I shivered.

She shook her head. "He still drinks too much. He doesn't do cocaine anymore."

"Why wouldn't he tell me?"

"He doesn't like to remember, and he doesn't like anyone to know."

"Does he really believe I'd think less of him for having had a problem?"

She said, "Isn't it obvious? He's ashamed."

I shook my head. When I met Jeffrey, I'd thought, *I've never met a cocaine addict before*. "Can I fix this?" At Jude's expression, I said, "No, not him. I'm not touching that. I mean the situation. I'd hate to see him leave the shop."

"Oh, he won't," Jude said. "He really likes being in the shop. He'd have my hide if I said he loves it, even though he does. And he really likes you. He says you have good business sense and you're reasonable and fair. He's not going anywhere."

"What should I do?"

"What did he say he wanted?"

"To give him room."

"Then do that. He'll hide out and sulk for a while yet, but he'll be all right."

"Jude, were you and Gideon ever—"

She said, "Thank the Lord, no. We did a lot of estate sales together. That's how we got to be friends. And he was really kind to me when I got divorced. Helped me out. But getting involved with him that way? I'd just as soon pour Tabasco sauce in my eye."

I began to laugh. "I'm sorry. That's terrible. But it's funny, too."

A FEW DAYS LATER, shortly after I opened the shop, I answered the phone. An unfamiliar voice said, "Ms. Raskin? We haven't met, but my name is Todd Whittaker, and I'm a lawyer with Whittaker, White, and Whittaker."

I wondered how he'd gotten my name. "Is this about an estate? Or an appraisal?"

"It is about an antique that I believe has some value."

"Do you need a valuation?"

"We might. My client is also interested in the history of its ownership."

"I'm a licensed appraiser. I can provide both of those things. Is this for insurance purposes?"

"It would have to stand up in court. Can you provide something like that?"

I began to have an uncomfortable feeling. "Yes, I could. Is your client filing a suit?"

"We all hope it won't come to that," he said.

A very uncomfortable feeling. "What is the object? What can you tell me about it?"

"It's a musical instrument."

I bet it's not a Stradivarius.

He continued, "A vintage guitar, which used to belong to a musician well-known in Memphis."

I said, "Is this about Bobby Swann's Fender Stratocaster?"

"As a matter of fact, it is."

Discomfort began to turn to anger. "Are you aware that I'm already looking into the provenance?"

"I've heard that you know something about it."

"Can you tell me who you're working for?"

"No, I'm afraid I can't."

"Mr. Whittaker, is this really about an appraisal? Or is it a warning?"

He said, "We'd prefer not to go to court."

I was suddenly very angry. No one wanted or needed an appraisal here. Todd Whittaker was letting me know that someone in the Swann family had approached him about a lawsuit. "Then we're in agreement, Mr. Whittaker."

He thanked me for my time and hung up.

He'd been pussyfootin' me, as my Shelby County relatives liked to say. I had a pretty good idea who his client was. Were there grounds for a suit? I'd been spared this kind of fight at Sotheby's. I was aware of lawsuits to recover stolen or looted art, but this was different.

I called my brother. "Josh, do you have a moment?"

"What have you got?"

"I just got a call from a lawyer at Whittaker, White, and Whittaker. Do you know them?"

"Only by reputation."

I was pretty sure of the answer, but I asked anyway. "Are they estate lawyers?"

"No, they specialize in civil litigation. Why were they calling you? Don't tell me someone is suing you."

"I doubt it. It has to do with something I'm researching. I have a couple of questions about estate law. You can bill me if you need to."

"Nat, would I do that? You can owe me lunch. Somewhere nice. What's the question?"

I told him about the fractured Swann family and the sale of the guitar after Bobby Swann's death. "Would either of his children have a claim on the guitar now, as part of his estate?"

"Did he have a will?"

"I doubt it. He was a musician, and I hear that he died stone broke."

"So there was nothing to go to probate."

"I don't think so. The guitar was the only thing of value that he owned, and his widow was desperate for money."

"When did this happen?"

"He died in 1984."

"Well, technically speaking, unless there's a will that specifies otherwise, the probate court will divide an estate between the surviving spouse and the surviving children. But there was no will, and no one thought to go to probate court. There was no estate to settle. And even if there had been, Tennessee won't hold on to a probate case for more than ten years. This happened twenty-five years ago. The probate court wouldn't bother with it."

"Could one of the children sue to get it back?"

"Who owns it now?"

"I don't know for sure. That's what I'm researching."

"Well, there's something called tortious denial of inheritance. You have to prove that the heir was damaged by being denied part of the estate. But that's a hard row to hoe if there was never a will."

"But a member of the family could file a suit."

"Look, you can sue anyone for any reason. But most lawyers would tell someone in that situation not to bother. It would be a waste of a lawyer's time and a waste of their money. That's what I'd tell a client like that if they came to me."

"If this is who I suspect, it's someone who's gone to a lawyer because they're angry and upset."

"I see that all the time. I let them get the anger out, and then I let them know there's no standing for a suit. Why can't this person just buy it back from the current owner? Once you find out who it is?"

"Well, when it surfaces, it's likely to be worth tens of thousands of dollars, because Bobby Swann was a well-known guitarist with Stax. A celebrity of sorts. This person doesn't have the money."

He sighed. "What about negotiating a deal with the current owner? Or getting a deal from whoever is handling the sale?"

"It will probably go to auction, and both the auction house and the owner will want top dollar for it. I don't see either of those parties feeling generous because the guitarist's family wants it for sentimental reasons."

"Well, that's not a legal problem, Nat. It's a personal problem, and it would be a waste of time, energy, and money to handle it legally. I'm surprised this lawyer didn't tell his client that."

"You don't think there are grounds for a suit."

"No. I doubt it will go anywhere."

"I think I know why he called me." I didn't watch what I said. "Someone in the family wants me to know they've gone to a lawyer. They want me to know they're angry and upset."

"It's annoying, but it's just smoke. I wouldn't worry about it."

"Are you talking as my brother or as a lawyer?"

"As a lawyer. I mean it."

I DIDN'T SHARE Josh's confidence. I was uneasy knowing that someone in the Swann family was angry enough to badger a lawyer about a suit. I'd fibbed to Todd Whittaker about having a client for a formal appraisal, but I saw the value of making the inquiry official. I needed a signed contract from Gideon. Better still, from the owner of the guitar, whose identity I didn't know, since Gideon was protecting him, too.

But I wasn't ready to say any of that to Gideon, not yet.

Everyone we'd talked to had referred to my grandfather and his shop. As Gideon nursed his sense of injury, I thought I'd make a detour and research Mo Raskin and Raskin's Records.

I went back to the public library. En route to the index for the microfilmed records of the *Appeal*, I passed the city directories. On a whim, I pulled out the volume for 1968, and I found all the Raskin listings, home, clothing store, and record shop. I tried 1970. The record shop was gone. Intrigued, I worked backward this time and found the record shop's first listing in 1954.

Raskin's Records had been in business for fifteen

years. That was a long time for a hobby that wasn't really a business.

I put the earliest city directory away and pulled out the index to the *Appeal*.

Raskin's had advertised weekly in the *Appeal* for decades, but I didn't care about the ads. I wanted to find articles that mentioned my grandfather. And there he was, Morris Raskin, in 1965, 1967, and 1968.

And as Joe Jordan had told me, the site of protest hadn't been the clothing store but the record shop.

It started in 1965, when white protesters clogged the sidewalk outside the shop. My grandfather was quoted as saying that he believed in serving every customer who walked into the shop, a code for "Negroes welcome," and that anyone who disagreed with him was free to shop elsewhere. He told the *Appeal* that he'd called the police to clear the sidewalk outside his front door.

In 1967, Raskin's Records was in the news again, for hiring a Black man as a salesclerk, and a few months later, for receiving a brick through the window. I thought of the plate glass window of the clothing store, which now held our display, and felt queasy at the thought of the glass shattering. My grandfather reported that the brick had come with a message: N— lover. He said, "We'll fix the window, and we'll keep welcoming all our customers."

That was the legacy the Raskin family—and the aging musicians of Beale Street—remembered and cherished. I was proud of my grandpa.

And here was another article, also from 1968, but well after things had calmed down in Memphis. September of 1968.

. . .

Buddy Griffen of Memphis was shot yesterday when he entered Raskin's Records on South Main Street, brandishing a pistol. Owner Morris Raskin told police that he warned Griffen to put down the pistol, and when he refused, Raskin shot the man in the arm, wounding him. The wounded man was taken to Baptist Memorial Hospital.

Detective John Ivey, who was summoned to the scene, said that armed robbery had been a problem for the merchants on South Main for several years now and had gotten worse since the unrest after Dr. King's death.

Who was the man Morris Raskin shot? And why did my grandfather shoot him? I checked the index for Buddy Griffen, but he didn't appear. Not newsworthy, except for getting shot. I needed to find him.

I had better luck with Detective Ivey. He'd been a member of the first class in the Memphis police academy to accept Black men back in 1952, and he'd been promoted to the rank of detective at the end of 1967, one of four detectives identified as "colored" in the article in the *Appeal*. Just in time for the worst unrest in Memphis in decades. Cynicism washed through me. I could see why the Memphis Police Department had hired and promoted Black officers to arrest Black lawbreakers.

Was Detective Ivey still alive? Still living in Memphis? I could find out.

First I wanted to learn more about the man my grandfather shot.

I CALLED JOE JORDAN. He sounded breathy and tired.

"All you all right, Mr. Jordan?" I asked.

"Just a bad cold, sugar. But even a cold takes it out of you when you're my age."

"I won't bother you, then. You rest up and get better." I felt guilty as I remembered that he'd never married and didn't have children in Memphis. "Is there anyone to take care of you?"

"Oh, the neighbor ladies have been in here fussing over me. Bringing me soup, feeding me aspirin, putting blankets over me. They drive me crazy. If they left me alone for a few hours, I'll get better all by myself."

"I can call you in a week or two, once you've recovered."

"No, don't hang up, I'm bored from being sick. You have a question for me?"

"I do. You have to promise me you're not too tired—"

"Don't you fuss over me, too. If I'm tired, I'll tell you. What do you want to know?"

I tried to sound as matter-of-fact as I could. "Did you ever run across a man named Buddy Griffen on Beale Street?"

He snorted, and it turned into a sneeze. "Excuse me. Now there's a name I haven't heard for years. Yes, I did."

"Who was he?"

"Called himself an agent. Talent agent, booking agent. He booked girl singers on Beale Street and in West Memphis. Only managed one at a time. They were his girlfriends, too."

"Not so good for business."

"He was no good at business, and no good in other ways, too. He'd find some poor girl who wanted to sing—he liked them country, young, and not too smart—and he'd promise her a singing career. And once he'd made a little money booking her, she'd get her hopes up, and she'd stick to him like glue. And then he'd get tired of her and start knocking her around. None of those girls ever made it as singers."

"How did he stay in business?"

"He dealt on the side. Weed, pills, cocaine. I don't recall if he ever sold anything harder. That was his real business."

"Did he know my grandfather?"

"Everyone in the music business hung out at Raskin's Records. I'm sure they knew each other."

I waited to hear more. I wanted to hear more. But Joe began to cough, and when he stopped, he said, "Miss Natalie, I am beginning to feel tired. I'm sorry."

"No, you eat some soup and lie down and take it easy. Thanks for talking to me."

"You get what you need?"

At that I laughed. "Do we ever? Take care, Mr. Jordan."

I HAD a standing invitation with my parents for dinner on Friday night, and I managed to join them once a month. After talking to Joe Jordan, I had a question for my father. I wanted to ask it, more than I wanted to eat roast chicken, even if it was tasty chicken roasted with two lemons.

Even though we'd never been religious, Friday night dinner had always been leisurely and special, the end of the workweek. When I was a kid, my father let his managers take over the boutiques on Friday night so he could go to Temple, where he smiled and charmed and drummed up business for the coming week. Everyone who went to Temple did the same thing. No one thought it was strange to gladhand in God's house.

My mother lit candles, not out of religious feeling but because she liked the way they glowed on the sideboard. Both she and my father asked me about the shop. I thanked my mother for telling her friends about us. "Thanks to you, we hardly need to advertise."

My mother laughed. "Second nature. I've been sending them to the boutiques for years now."

"And I appreciate it," my father said.

I'd been saving a funny story to tell them. I told him about my favorite customer this week. "Huge guy. Long hair, long beard, wearing overalls."

"Bubba," my father said. My mother shot him a reproving glance. She had redneck relatives, and my father knew better.

I said, "Did I get a lesson about making assumptions. He was a serious collector, and you'd never guess what he collected."

"I won't even try," my father said.

"Netsuke. Fasteners for kimonos. Gorgeous little figurines. It was quite a sight, seeing him cradle those itty-bitty fragile objects in his big palm, smiling at them like they were pets."

My father said, "You can't go by appearances. My father taught me that. We welcome everyone, and we sell to everyone." He smiled. "One of the Raskin business mottoes."

"I've been thinking about Grandpa lately."

"Has he been haunting you? More than usual?"

"What?" my mother asked.

"I swear Grandpa's ghost is still hanging around the shop. No, that's not it. I'm doing some research on a guitar that might be worth a lot. A Fender Stratocaster from the 1960s. There's a possible connection to a local musician who worked at Stax."

Both my parents looked at me in surprise. "You're researching a guitar?" my father asked.

"For Gideon. You met him, remember? He sells vintage guitars."

"Right, right," my father said.

"Grandpa's name keeps coming up. Everyone we talk to remembers him and his record shop."

My father said, "Really?"

"Dad, I saw the city directories. He was in business for fifteen years. It's hard to believe it was just a hobby for him."

My father set down his fork. Irritation crept into his voice. "Nat, I don't know why you're digging into this."

"Just curious. Like I'd be curious about any valuable object. Looking for context."

"This isn't context. It's family history." He picked up his fork again, and his hand trembled.

"I know. But I've gotten the bug to find something out, that's all."

My father's expression was unhappy, as it was when the boutiques had a bad month. "You found something."

"I did. It was really strange. It was so strange I wonder if the *Appeal* got it right."

"What was it?"

I told him about the shooting. "Was it true? Do you remember it?"

It was a good thing my father didn't play poker, because he couldn't bluff to save his life. He said, "Dad never talked about it."

"So you don't know anything?"

"I wasn't there. I never asked."

My father had been fifteen—he'd talked about being bar mitzvah in 1966 at civil-rights-conscious Temple Israel—and he was certainly old enough to hang out, and even help out, in the shop. "Nothing? You really didn't know?"

He shook his head, an obvious lie. "Leave it alone, Nat. It's nothing to remember, much less to commemorate."

"I just wondered," I said.

"Stop wondering."

"Dad, what is this about?"

"Please, Nat, just drop it," he said, and I heard an edge —and a warning—that I'd never heard in his voice before.

"Dad?" I looked at my mother. "Mama?"

My mother laid her hand on my arm, her own warning. "Please, Nat, leave it alone."

I'D NEVER SEEN my parents upset like that. But the incident mattered, and I was more determined than ever to find out why.

I went looking for Detective Ivey.

He'd had a long career in the Memphis Police Department, and even though he was now retired, he showed up in the *Appeal* and the *Tri-State Defender*, the local Black paper, as the father of kids who graduated proudly from college and married well. The latest family announcement, the engagement of a daughter, put him in Whitehaven. I wondered if he and Virgie Lee were near neighbors.

I sent him a message through his Facebook page, and he called me at the shop. Jude was on duty with me, and I excused myself to stand in the yard, where it was now pleasant instead of winter cool. I thanked him for getting in touch with me.

He had a deep, gravelly voice, which must have carried well when he was on the street. "What exactly is this about?" he asked. "You're not a reporter, are you?"

"No, I'm not. This is personal. I'm looking into some family history. It goes back to the days when you were a detective on South Main, and I wondered if I could tap your recollections."

At that he laughed, a sound like rocks tumbling. "The old days," he said. "The bad old days."

"The 1960s."

He said, "I always told my men to interview people in person. We got better answers. Why don't you come to see me?"

"I'd be glad to."

Now I knew the way to Whitehaven, and I knew the neighborhood. It was a few blocks from Virgie Lee and Brenda, a middle-class area. The detective's block was tidy and well-maintained. I wondered if his presence continued to deter crime in his immediate vicinity.

The woman who answered the door was in her seventies, but she was slender and spry, with a lightly lined face. "You must be Miss Raskin," she said.

"Please, call me Nat."

"Come on in. John is looking forward to seeing you. There aren't too many people who remember those days."

I was momentarily sobered, thinking of all of those who were no longer here to remember them.

I was now used to rooms crowded with furniture and etageres full of photographs of children and grandchildren. On the wall opposite the sectional—it looked well-used, as though several generations had bounced and piled onto it over the years—was a diptych of photographs, the Reverend Martin Luther King and President Barack Obama.

Mrs. Ivey offered me coffee, which I gratefully accepted, because I could forgo the sugar.

Detective Ivey sat in his recliner as though it were a throne. Even seated, I could see how massive a man he was. I'd found his photograph in the *Appeal* from the late 1960s. It was clear he'd been large and in charge back then, and he hadn't changed.

He was a sepia brown, light enough to show the freckles on his nose, and his skin was pitted and rough. He gave me a shrewd, appraising gaze. "The 1960s," he said. "In 1968?" He gestured toward the image of Dr. King.

"Among other things," I said.

He said, "To make sense of what happened that year, you have to start a few years back." He sat up, and the chair folded up with him. He leaned forward, his knees apart, and rested his hands on his still-bulky thighs. Like Joe Jordan, he had a story to tell, and he would tell it at his own pace.

"I graduated from the academy in 1952. That was the first year the department admitted Black men. We were an experiment, and we knew it. Of course they sent us out to the Black neighborhoods. Downtown, Midtown, and Orange Mound. Black police officers for the Black community, and it wasn't because the department was so forward-thinking. The white patrolmen didn't like the Black neighborhoods. They were glad to give them up to us."

I sighed.

"You didn't have to be much of a race man to see that Black poverty and Black crime went hand in hand with racism. If you think it's still bad in Memphis, you should have seen it in the 1950s. We Black policemen knew what we'd been hired to do, but we all had relations and neighbors who were suffering under the burden of Jim Crow. We walked a fine line, policing the Black community."

I thought of Mo Raskin opening his record shop in 1954, when Jim Crow was alive and well on South Main.

"It didn't get easier in the 1960s. You had young men, just kids, coming up into an economy that wouldn't hire them. They'd get a record, and that made it worse. Too many kids poor and angry and unemployed. Guns and drugs, a real mess on the streets. You know the reason I got promoted to be a detective?"

I had my theory, but I let him talk.

"Nineteen sixty-seven was the worst year in memory for armed robbery on Beale and South Main. It wasn't enough to have Black officers on patrol. The police department wanted Black detectives in robbery and homicide. That's how we got promoted, four of us. The department had a real problem with white officers roughing up Black men. They figured it would be better all around if Black detectives roughed up the Black men they arrested."

I shook my head.

"It was like the Wild West that year. Armed robbery after armed robbery. Every merchant on Beale and South Main kept a gun under the counter. I talked to store-keepers who'd been robbed three, four, five times."

I asked, "Were the Jewish merchants hit any harder than the others?"

"No, but there were a lot of Jewish merchants down-town and in Midtown. Kind of a sore point all around, Black people and Jewish storekeepers."

I'd heard all about that from my father well before I heard it from Virgie Lee Swann. "Do you remember Raskin's Records on South Main?"

"I remember Raskin's Clothing Store and the record shop right next to it. They had some trouble with the Klan, as I recall. Demonstrations and intimidation, too."

"I read about the Klan attacks on the record shop."

He nodded. "Mo Raskin had a reputation as a friend to

the Black community, and that got under the Klan's skin. But the real problem for the Raskins was armed robbery. Mo and his dad both kept a gun under the counter."

"I read about an altercation in Raskin's Records in 1968. You were on the scene. The *Appeal* quoted you."

He said, "Let me recall; 1968, that was one long altercation, between the strike, Dr. King's visit and then his assassination, and the way the city blew up after he was assassinated. When was it?"

"August of 1968."

He frowned.

I said, "Does the name Buddy Griffen ring a bell?"

"I remember him as a lowlife and a part-time drug dealer. He had a sheet as long as my arm. August of 1968, you say?"

He remembers, I thought. *He's being cagey, like they've all been.* "Mo Raskin shot him."

He concentrated. "Nothing ever came of it," he said. "We didn't arrest anybody. Buddy wasn't badly hurt, even though he went to the hospital. He agreed not to press charges. I heard that Mo Raskin paid his hospital bill."

"That doesn't sound like armed robbery."

"Well, it was settled as far as the department was concerned. We still had a bellyful of trouble in Memphis. We weren't going to run after two guys who settled something between themselves."

"Something personal? Detective, what did you think it was?"

"I didn't turn back to think about it. I was too busy doing my job, keeping the city from blowing up again."

As I left, I realized he wasn't the only Black person

who'd been evasive with me. The connection between Mo Raskin and me shut these people up. It wasn't as bad as it had been in the 1960s, but it was the grandchild of Jim Crow, and Black people were still censoring themselves around white people. What were they keeping from me? What had made Buddy Griffen mad enough to wave a pistol at Mo Raskin, and Mo Raskin agitated enough to shoot him?

Why had they cut a deal afterwards? What was between the two of them?

Who would know?

9

LITTLE LADY

Just after we opened, the electronic bell jangled, and a customer came in, hesitating just inside the door. Jude had run down the street for coffee, and I was alone in the shop.

He was a burly man who wore a cowboy hat over his graying hair. Under his unbuttoned jacket, his belly strained at his shirt buttons, and below it he wore a belt with an oversized buckle. His face was weather-beaten, a white man who'd been out in the sun a lot.

I reminded myself not to make assumptions, but he looked so much like an Elvis collector that I had my hackles up. Jude didn't care about Elvis, one way or another, and as a musician, Gideon had an ambivalent relationship with the King. But for my money, I'd be glad never to see another Elvis fan.

"Nice shop you've got here," he said, in the accent that Nashville singers affected.

I'd never felt uneasy being alone in the shop in broad

daylight before. I wished Jude would haul herself back from getting coffee. "Thank you," I said politely.

His gaze traveled to the back wall, where Gideon displayed his guitars, but he didn't comment on them.

Something was bothering me. He wasn't just taking it in as most customers did. "Can I help you?" I asked.

He came up to the counter and rested his hands on the glass countertop. His fingers were short and thick, and on his right hand, he wore a heavy class ring. "I hope so, little lady."

The one thing I'd hated since I came back to Memphis was the way Southern men of a certain age called every woman "little lady." I drew myself up to my full height. "Is there something in particular you're interested in?"

He leaned over the counter. He smelled of Old Spice and cigarettes. "I'm a guitar collector," he said, gesturing toward Gideon's display.

"Well, you've come to the right place." Where the hell was Jude?

"And a guitar dealer, too, for the right kind of guitar."

I wished Gideon wasn't still mad at me. I wished he was here. He'd know if this guy was on the level, and if he was, he could talk guitars until they were both blue in the face. I nodded.

He leaned closer, and I couldn't help myself. I backed away. He said, "I hear that you have a lead on a guitar that used to belong to Bobby Swann."

I was so surprised that I said, "Where did you hear that?"

He shook his head and smiled at me. His teeth were

surprisingly white for a smoker. "I'm afraid I can't say," he said.

"You have a client," I said.

"Have to keep that under my hat." He touched the brim.

I said, "Well, your client must be an optimist, because no one knows where Bobby Swann's guitar is."

"I hear different."

Had he? Or was he bluffing? I said, "You know, I'm not the person you need to talk to. The guitars"—I gestured toward them—"those aren't mine. They belong to another dealer, Gideon Fairchild. He's not here right now, but if you leave your contact information, I can have him get in touch with you."

"No, I'd rather not do that."

Why? I thought. But I remained polite. "Well, he's always here on Friday and Saturday. You could talk to him then."

"Stop by?"

"Sure, or call if it's not convenient for you."

"It's a shame he ain't here today."

For my own reasons, I thought, *Yes, it is.* "You'd be certain of catching him on a Friday or a Saturday," I said. "We're open from ten to five both days." I handed him a shop card. "That's our number, and our email address, too."

He tucked the card into his shirt pocket. "Oh, I already got that," he said. "I went to your website."

I reminded myself that our website existed so people could find us and decide to visit us. Why did he sound like he'd stalked us?

The door opened, and Jude came in, a cup of coffee in her hand. "New help at the coffeeshop," she said. "Took forever to get a latte." She looked at the man at the counter.

He gave Jude a once-over. I thought, *If you call her little lady, she'll belt you.* He said, "I was just leaving," as he turned to go.

He hesitated at the door and gave the shop another survey. My scalp prickled, and I was glad that our cameras recorded the face of everyone who came and went.

After he left, Jude asked, "Who the hell was that?"

"He wouldn't say."

"What did he want?"

"He wants Bobby Swann's guitar."

Jude set down her coffee. "Isn't that Gideon's department?"

"That's what I told him," I said. "I don't know why, but he gave me the creeps."

"He is a creep. He ogled me."

"Did you see the way he looked around the shop?"

"I did, and I didn't like that either."

"Should I tell Gideon about him?"

"Of course you should."

"I still feel funny about talking to Gideon."

"He should know about this guy. In case he comes back."

I must have looked dubious, because Jude said, "It's just business."

I said, "A professional courtesy, you mean."

"Right."

THE NEXT DAY, when Gideon came in for his shift, I asked, "Can I talk to you about something?"

"We going behind the woodshed again?"

Cut that out. "No, it's about a customer. Came in looking for a guitar. For Bobby Swann's guitar, as a matter of fact."

"Who was it?"

"He wouldn't leave his name. Maybe you'd know him."

"What did he look like?"

"He looked like half the guys who go to gawk at Graceland. He's on video. I downloaded it."

"Why? What'd he do?"

"Take a look."

I showed him the video on my phone screen, and he said, "No, I've never seen him before. Don't have a clue who he is." He looked from the screen to me. "He looks like he came to case the joint."

Jude said, "That's what I thought, too."

Gideon said, "Our security's tight as a drum. But I don't like the way he looked at the guitar display, either."

Gideon was there all day Friday and all day Saturday, but the man didn't return.

When I opened the shop on Sunday, Gideon was on the sidewalk, waving at me. As I unlocked the door, I said, "You aren't on duty today."

"I felt like coming in."

"To keep an eye on your guitar display?"

"Among other things," he said.

That afternoon, just before we closed, the man in the

cowboy hat walked into the shop. When he saw me, he touched his fingers to the brim of his cowboy hat in greeting.

I felt cold and angry, but I said, "Gideon, this is the customer I was telling you about. The one who stopped by to ask about Bobby Swann's guitar."

He said to Gideon, "So you're the guitar dealer."

Gideon was brusque. "Yes, I am."

The man smiled. He said, "The little lady wasn't very cooperative with me. I'm hoping things will go better with you."

I could feel Gideon's annoyance, and it let me express my own. "I gave you Gideon's name and number. I told you how to contact him. I don't know what more I could have done for you. And stop calling me 'little lady.'"

"What do you want?" Gideon asked.

The man reached inside his jacket, and Gideon tensed, but all he did was pull out his wallet and flip it open. "I'm an investigator," he said, showing us his license so quickly that neither of us could read his name.

"Who hired you?" I asked. "Was it the law firm?"

"I can't say."

"I think I know," I said.

He looked at Gideon. "I'd like to ask you a few questions about Bobby Swann's guitar."

"What do you want to know?"

"It would be mighty helpful to know who owns it now."

"I have a client, too. I can't say, either. I can't help you," Gideon said, his anger controlled but clear in his voice.

He leaned against the counter. "Just a little information," he said.

Gideon said, "Look, if you have legitimate business with us, I'd be glad to help you. But I don't want to see you back here, harassing Nat—who is not a little lady, by the way—or bothering me. I'd like you to leave."

The man shook his head as though he regretted our attitude. "All right, I get it," he said to Gideon, not speaking to me.

Once he was gone, Gideon locked the door after him and turned the sign to "closed." Back at the counter, he demanded, "What the hell was that about? What law firm?"

Ashamed and abashed, I told him about Todd Whittaker's call.

"Why didn't you tell me?"

"You haven't been talking to me much lately."

"Talk to me now. Who hired him?"

"He wouldn't say, but I'd bet it was a member of the Swann family. Virgie Lee doesn't want it. Michelle can afford to buy it if she wants to. Jeffrey might want it, and we know he's manipulative as can be, but I don't think he's vindictive enough to sue for it."

"Your money's on Brenda."

"I don't know. But that's my hunch."

"I thought you didn't work on a hunch."

"I don't."

"You want to call her?"

"No, not yet. I might call the lawyer, but I won't hold my breath for the truth."

"They have any claim?"

"Not according to my brother, Josh, who's an estate attorney. But they can certainly pester us if they want to."

He shook his head. "Sue for it! Well, at least they can't sue us. We don't own it."

"Actually, there's something I should show you. I was hoping for a better moment than this, but you might as well know."

"What is it?"

I pulled the folder from my handbag. "I went over to Diamond Pawn, and I found something interesting." I laid a receipt on the sales counter.

Gideon bent to examine it. "We already know they bought it from Michelle. Old-school, though. Writing it out by hand."

"Ike Levy, I'd bet. Look at the date. And the amount."

"A lot more than it was worth at the time."

I pulled the second receipt from the folder. "Now look at this."

"Who they sold it to."

"Look at the date on this one. And the amount."

"Same day. Same amount. They paid too much for it, but they got the money back the same day." He bent to look at it more closely. "Same lousy handwriting, too."

I pointed. "That's who Ike Levy sold it to."

He didn't say it, but his face took on an "I'll be damned" expression. "Morris Raskin."

"My grandfather."

Gideon said, "So it was a backroom deal, like Ben Levy thought."

"My grandfather would have been happy to give Michelle Swann the money outright. But I'm sure she didn't want to take charity from him. It was a ruse to spare her feelings." I felt proud of my grandfather. "A subterfuge for his charitable impulse."

Gideon said, "Do you think he had feelings for Michelle? More than charity?"

"You were there when she talked about him. I don't think so. It sounds like she appreciated the way he helped Bobby. It didn't seem romantic to me." I raised my eyes to his. They were blue and a little bloodshot. "I think it was friendship disguised as business."

He met my eyes, and I saw the first real smile in weeks. "So Mo Raskin owned the guitar for a while. Have you asked your family about it? Found out what they know?"

"My father is awfully touchy about his father's involvement in the music business. I haven't wanted to poke the wasps' nest again."

"Might be worth an inquiry."

I thought, *The will. Check the will. Ask Josh.* "It might."

"Don't sit on it."

I said, "I've missed hearing you rag on me."

"I've missed doing it. Walk you to your car?"

"Is that an apology?"

He smiled. "Don't press your luck," he said, but it was a familiar tone. A tease.

In the yard, I heard the owl's call. I stopped at the foot of the overgrown live oak. "She's still here," I said.

"Don't stand right there unless you want bird crap in your hair."

"Very funny." I looked up as the bird, who flew soundlessly, alit on a lower branch. It was eerie to watch her move her head so that she could gaze right at us. At me.

She hooted softly, her call high and sweet, then flew away.

I was unreasonably glad to see her again.

THE NEXT MORNING, I called Gideon. "I've been thinking about calling Brenda."

"Don't go it alone. Let's do it together. Both of us."

"Both of us?"

"Yeah, the guitar expert and the provenance expert."

It was good to hear that teasing tone again. I was so encouraged that I replied in kind. "So you've truly forgiven me?"

"I thought that holiday was a few months off. In the fall, right?"

"How do you know that?"

He laughed.

"All right, you know a lot of things. Now I know you went to a temple, at least once, probably in Nashville. Am I right?"

"I was invited to a wedding. You want to meet at the shop?"

We went into the back room—if we were in front, someone would knock on the door and ask to come in to poke around—and we called Brenda at work. She answered, sounding distracted and tired. "Can we make this quick? I have a meeting in a few minutes."

"Sure. Let me put you on speaker. Gideon is with me."

"What is this about?"

"We've had some communication with a lawyer about

the guitar. I wondered if you might know anything about that."

She sounded irritated. "A lawyer? Who was it?"

"Todd Whittaker, of Whittaker, White, and Whittaker."

"What did he want?"

I tried to sound light. "I think he wanted a free appraisal. I told him I couldn't oblige him in that."

"I don't know anything about it," she said.

Gideon said, "We also had a visit from a private investigator. More than one visit."

"I certainly didn't hire anyone. Maybe the lawyer did."

"Maybe," Gideon said. "The investigator wanted to know who the current owner is. Wasn't too polite about it."

"Excuse me, I've got to go, my meeting's in five minutes."

I said, "The lawyer wouldn't identify his client. But we both have a feeling it's somebody in the Swann family."

"Why are you pointing the finger at me?" Her voice had become very frosty.

Gideon said, "That's the last thing we'd do. We're just wondering if you might be able to enlighten us."

The ice was now icy rage. "Do you think I'd do such a thing? Hire a lawyer or an investigator to harass either of you? Is that what you think of me?"

I looked at Gideon. *We're in trouble now.* I said, "Of course not."

But she hung up before I could finish the sentence.

Gideon looked at me across the little table. "Touchy," he said.

I nodded. "Not proof, but it says something."

"What now, provenance expert?"

"I'm thinking it's just a matter of time before the investigator finds the current owner and starts bothering him. Or worse, spreading the news around town."

"I've thought that too."

I said, "I know how strongly you feel about confidentiality. I still don't know the current owner's name."

"That's the least I can do to protect him. By keeping my mouth shut."

"If we were doing a formal appraisal, with a contract, it would help."

"Not enough, if this investigator is as dumb and unethical as he seems."

I said, "But it would give both of us some standing to claim confidentiality. Not just about the owner's identity but the provenance and the valuation, too."

"I wish we could do more," he said.

"I'll hire you as a sub, and you'll be covered, too."

He snorted.

"Can't I protect you, just a little bit? Or are you too much the Southern gentleman to allow it?"

"You like making my life hard, don't you?" That was a full-on tease.

I said, "Yes, I surely do."

He grinned. "You can keep doing it."

THE NEXT DAY, in the shop, he asked me, "Do you have enough time to put the contract together?"

"It's boilerplate. I'll just adjust it a bit."

"Contract for what?" Jude asked.

I said, "I'm appraising the guitar. It's official." I glanced at Gideon. "We're going to see the current owner as soon as I get the contract amended."

Jude said to Gideon, "So you're talking to Nat again?"

"I never stopped talking to Nat."

Jude smothered a laugh.

I said, "We're going over there first thing tomorrow. We'll be done in time to open. You don't need to worry about coverage."

"If you're late, I can hold the fort for an hour. In the interests of fostering a good business partnership between the two of you."

"Oh, hush," I said, one Southern belle to another, as she grinned at us both.

Gideon had unveiled the name of the current owner of the guitar, the musician who had a newborn baby at home, just before we called to set up the appointment to see him. Once on the phone, I hoped to explain the appraisal process and the terms of the contract, but he was too distracted to pay attention. We could hear the baby crying in the background. "I'm sorry that I can't talk," he said. "She's been fussing up a storm today. Just come over, and I hope she'll sleep for fifteen minutes."

Justin Taylor lived in a rented house not far from Evergreen but on the end that hadn't gentrified yet. The homeowners on this block struggled to keep the yards neat and the houses maintained. The man who answered the door was slight, short, and he looked so young I was surprised he was a father. But he was clearly a new parent. He had shiners of exhaustion under his eyes, prominent on his light-brown face, and with his free arm he cradled the baby, who fussed a little, quietly, her face on her father's shoulder.

Inside, the house smelled of baby powder and used diapers, and it was in the chaos that spoke of a baby's needs and the parents' exhaustion. With both arms around the baby, he said, "It's a mess, I know." He crooned, "All this mess because of you! You little dickens!" But his voice was full of affection. He kissed the wispy hair on the top of the baby's head, next to the pink headband that told us he'd had a girl.

"What's her name?" I asked.

"Jasmine."

"How old is she?"

"Just fourteen weeks." He kissed her head again. "I don't know what's wrong." Crooning again, he said, "You aren't hungry, you aren't tired, you aren't wet, and you're fussing up a storm." He sighed. "I wish I could guarantee she'd calm down. I'll do my best to look at this contract."

"We'll manage," I said, and I pulled the contract from my handbag.

He said, "Can we trade? Will you hold her for a minute?"

Before I could reply, Gideon said, "Let me."

We both looked at him in surprise, but Justin, too tired to object, eased the baby into Gideon's outstretched arms. Justin sat on one end of the sofa, contract in hand, and I joined him on the end.

Gideon didn't sit. As Justin scanned the contract, Gideon held her, rocking back and forth, speaking in a low, sweet, singsong voice. "Hush, hush, little baby." She quieted.

Either he was the most doting uncle ever, or he'd had kids of his own. Another mystery and another question.

I spoke softly, not wanting to disturb Jasmine or Gideon. "It's all standard language, except for the part about the fee. That's a flat rate. A dollar to make it binding. Don't worry, I don't need to make any money on it."

He smiled a little and nodded.

"When I'm finished, you'll get a report on the history of the guitar's ownership and a valuation that you can give to an insurance company or an auction house."

He flipped through the pages and nodded. "It looks all right." He rummaged on the coffee table and found a pen. "Where do I sign?"

"The last page," I said, keeping my voice low.

He signed and handed me the contract. Then he looked up at Gideon, who was cradling Jasmine and singing to her, very softly.

He rose and said to Gideon, "Let me take her."

"No, leave her, she's fast asleep."

Justin asked, "How did you do that? She's been fussing all day."

I said, "Charm. He can charm anyone."

"Hush," Gideon said.

I asked Justin, "Could I see the guitar?"

"You've never seen it?"

"Only pictures."

He smiled. "Be right back."

As we waited, Jasmine sighed in her sleep but didn't wake. Gideon smiled down at her.

Justin returned with the guitar in his hands. The bright red finish blazed in the low light of the cramped living room.

"It's beautiful," I whispered.

"Isn't it?" Justin said. "I'll be sad to let it go." He glanced at the baby, who stirred and finally woke, snuffling against Gideon's chest. Justin carefully laid the guitar on the sofa and held out his arms for his child. Holding her, he kissed the top of her head once more. He looked up, his face shining. "But I've got the best reason in the world to sell it," he said. "Isn't she lovely?"

I heard Stevie Wonder's voice, sunny and joyful, lifted in song to his new daughter. And I felt a familiar ache start in my midsection. Like a headache, it promised to worsen. "Yes," I said, surprised that my voice didn't betray me. "She is." I looked away from the baby and her father. I looked at the guitar, the red finish glowing.

We thanked him and left.

Outside, on the sidewalk, Gideon asked me, "You get what you need?"

I laid my hand on my stomach, which had begun to hurt in earnest. "Yes," I said.

"You feeling okay?"

"It's nothing," I lied. "Just a little cramp."

"You don't look all right."

It hurt worse than ever. "No, it's nothing." But I bent over, hoping to ease the pain.

He said, "You're well nigh doubled over. You sure?"

My eyes were watering, but I said, "I've had it before. It's not serious."

"Do you need to go to urgent care? Or the ER?"

"I need to sit down," I said.

"Come sit in my truck. You look like you're going to pass out."

He helped me up into the seat, and I fell back against it, my hand pressed to my gut. It had never hurt this much.

"What's wrong?"

I sat up. "I've been to see a doctor about it. It's nothing to worry about. It's emotional."

"Something really got to you in there."

Gideon's face was soft. He'd once loved a woman as much as he'd loved a child. I breathed deeply against the pain, and I told him the truth, the words coming out in a sob. "I wanted children when I was married. But I had two miscarriages instead."

"Oh, Nat," he said, his voice tenderer than I'd ever heard it. "That's rough. I'm really sorry."

I looked away because I couldn't keep the tears back.

He laid his hand on my arm in consolation. A friend's touch. A brother's touch. I'd have to be crazy to think he was coming on to me. He said, "It's all right. It's really sad, and it doesn't go away."

I nodded. "Give me a minute." He patted my arm and took his hand away. I rummaged in my purse and found a tissue. I wiped my face and took another deep breath. "I'm feeling better."

"Take your time."

I nodded and held the tissue to my face. I wanted to sob and bury my face on Gideon's shoulder, as baby Jasmine had. I took another deep breath and wiped my face once more.

"Don't you dare drive yourself home until you feel all right."

I leaned back against the seat and closed my eyes. As I waited, the pain subsided. I opened my eyes and asked Gideon, "How do I look? Still green?"

"Better."

I needed to put back the distance between us. I said, "I have something on my conscience, and it's been bothering me for weeks. I have a confession to make."

"I was brought up a Baptist. We don't go in for confession."

"We didn't need to talk to Jeffrey," I said. "You certainly didn't need to be there. I dragged you there because Michelle put me up to it."

He inclined his head, waited long enough to take a breath, and met my eyes. "I thought so." He put his hand on my shoulder.

"Watch it," I said.

"I seem to recall I said something to you outside Jeffrey's place that was uncalled for. And now I'm sorry for it. Because I know it wasn't true."

Maybe not.

10

THINGS THAT GO ASTRAY

I EMAILED JOSH TO REMIND HIM THAT I OWED HIM LUNCH someplace nice, and he just laughed. "I was kidding you. I don't care where we go. I'd be glad to see you." We met at a pleasant Vietnamese place not far from his office.

He looked a little tired, but he brightened when I sat down. "It's been too long since I've seen you. We can't even manage to see Mom and Dad. The kids both have soccer. Two different teams. We're in the car all day Saturday, from one match to another."

"You don't have to apologize to me."

"I feel bad. We live next door to them, and we come over for Passover and Thanksgiving like we're across the country."

I thought of my quiet house and the weekends that were dedicated to business instead of family. "Well, I've got a family question for you, if it makes you feel any better."

"Remember, we're not on the clock," he teased.

"I know. I'm buying, remember."

"Spring rolls to share?"

"Of course."

When the food came, he said, "What's the question, Nat?"

"Did you see Grandpa's will?"

"I did. I have a copy, as a matter of fact. Not at the office. It's on my home PC. It was straightforward, as I recall. He left the business and the building downtown to Dad, those cash bequests to both of us, and everything else to Nana—the house, his investments, and the rest of the cash."

"Did the will mention an electric guitar?"

"No. He didn't spell out the contents of the house, so who knows what's up in the attic. Or in the storage unit. Dad helped Nana go through her stuff after he died. He might be able to tell you." Josh shook his head. "Why would Grandpa have a guitar?"

"Did you know he owned a record shop for fifteen years? Raskin's Records, right next door to the clothing store."

"I didn't. That explains the 45s that Nana sold. I thought he was a collector. I never knew he sold records."

"Dad was really cagey when I asked him. I don't know why."

"How did you find out?"

"I'm researching a vintage guitar for one of my dealers, remember? Josh, I found out that Grandpa shot a man in the record store. It was back in 1968."

"I've never heard a whisper about this from Dad. What did he say when you asked him about it?"

"He told me to drop it. Got upset. Mama did, too."

Josh said, "That's weird."

"It is."

"So why do you think Grandpa had a guitar? Is that something else you turned up?"

"He lent a Stax musician money to buy it, and when the guy died—it was tragic—Grandpa wanted to help his widow and his kids. He bought it back."

Josh laughed. "I'd ask Nana to check the attic. Is it worth anything?"

"It might be. No guarantees."

"Ask her to look in the storage unit, too."

JUDE WAS on duty with me on a dull, wet day—Memphis winter, when the damp came off the river as mist and not as humidity. In midafternoon, it was so gloomy that I wanted to go home to sleep. I had a pleasant fantasy about curling up on my bed under an afghan next to a purring cat.

I yawned. "I wish we could close early."

"Yes, and it would be the one day someone stops by and leaves a furious review on Yelp," Jude said.

The bell jangled, and the door opened. It was Jeffrey Swann, and he didn't look well. His eyes were bloodshot, and his nose ran. "Excuse me," he said as he held a tissue to it.

"I hope you didn't get that bug that's going around," I said.

"No, allergies."

"So you decided to visit us. Look around, see if there's anything you like."

"Well, I didn't come to buy today. I brought something for you to look at."

"Do you need a valuation?"

"I was hoping to sell it to you."

I thought of his apartment, bare of decoration. "What is it?"

He reached into a paper bag and put it on the counter, pulling away the newspaper he'd wrapped it in. *Don't assume*, I reminded myself.

It was a silver sugar bowl and creamer, and it was familiar. Unless he had a set of his own—which I doubted—it was part of his mother's silver coffee set.

I picked up the creamer and pretended to look at the mark.

"What do you think?" Jeffrey asked.

"Would you mind looking around for a few minutes? I need to do a spot of research," I fibbed.

"Okay," he said, looking a bit disappointed.

When he was out of earshot, Jude whispered, "What's going on? You could value that in your sleep."

"There's a problem," I said.

"What is it?"

"I know him. A little. He's the guy Gideon and I went to interview. The guitarist's son."

Jude's voice dropped to a whisper. "The guy with the mirror."

I nodded. "I've seen that set before. I'm sure it's his mother's silver." I dropped my voice lower than hers. "I don't think she gave it to him."

"You want me to tell him? That we don't buy off the street?"

"No. I should, because we're acquainted."

"Don't you dare say yes out of politeness."

"I won't."

Jeffrey returned to the counter. "Can we do business?" he asked, rubbing his nose.

I said, "It's really dicey for us to buy anything from someone who isn't a dealer or a collector we know."

"But you know me."

"I know your mother, too."

"You don't trust me."

I ignored this. I said, "We're really careful about what we buy. We just can't take a risk. I could lose my license as an antique dealer." I let him supply the rest: *if I buy something that's hot.*

"Don't you trust me?"

"At Sotheby's we had a saying. 'In God we trust. Everyone else brings provenance.'"

"You know me, and you aren't running Sotheby's here, either."

I ignored the dig. "Hey, the police don't keep a sharp eye on us, but it only takes one person to complain to the city that we're handling stolen merchandise. We could lose our license."

"Over something like this."

"Absolutely. That's why we don't take chances."

Disappointed, irritated, he said, "If I have to, I'll take it to a pawnshop. I thought I'd get a better deal from you."

"They're even more stringent about what they take

than antique dealers are. They get police reports. They won't risk it, either."

"I can take it to be melted."

"They'll ask, too."

"No, they won't."

How did he know? Had he taken his mother's silver for melt before?

With a pang, I said, "Please don't take it for melt. It's too nice a thing."

Was that a smile? *I know how to get to you, too.*

"Jeffrey, you and your mother need to work this out. Don't put me in the middle of it."

"She's already done it." He picked up the creamer and began to crumple the newspapers around it. It made me crazy to watch him wrap it so ineptly.

"I'm sorry."

"No, you aren't," he said, upset, as he stuffed the creamer and the sugar bowl back into the paper bag he brought them in. "A few hundred dollars. That's all I came for."

"I can't help you."

The door didn't slam after him. It was pneumatic, and the hinges sighed as the electronic chime sounded, for departures as well as arrivals.

I CALLED Michelle right away but got her voicemail. I couldn't leave her a message telling her than I suspected Jeffrey of being a thief.

That evening, just as I came home and opened the

door to turn on the nearest lamp, my phone rang. At a little after five, it was as dark as night. Michelle was calling me back.

"How are you?" I asked as I locked the door from inside and moved through the room to turn on the lamp next to my big mission armchair. I was reluctant to get down to business with her.

"I've been better."

I unbuttoned my coat and slung it over the chair's arm as I sank heavily into the leather cushions. "Did you get my message?"

"I did. What's going on?"

"I have a question for you about your silver coffee set."

"Don't tell me you want to buy it."

"Have you checked the set lately?"

"No, why?"

"Humor me. Go look."

"Okay. Bear with me." I heard her open a cabinet door. Waited as she bent to look. "Shit," she said. "Excuse me. The sugar and the creamer are missing." I heard the cabinet door slam shut. "Did they show up in your shop?"

"Yes." *I am so sorry to tell you.*

Her voice rose. "Was it Jeffrey? Did he bring them to you?"

"Yes, this afternoon."

Her voice went cold. "Did you buy it?"

"Of course not." It was a relief to repeat for her what I'd told him.

"Well, that's something." She paused. "If he sold it for scrap, I'll kill him."

"I tried to talk him out of it."

"Thank you," she said, her voice still cool.

"Michelle, I really don't want to get in the middle of this—"

She sighed, a deflating sound. "I need to talk to you," she said. "Can you come out here?"

"Now?"

"No, it's not an emergency. When would it be convenient?"

ON A MONDAY MORNING, when most people were back in the office, I drove out to Cordova to see Michelle. It was still overcast and deeply gray, raining instead of misty, and so cold for Memphis that I had pulled out one of my wool coats from New York. I drove past the too-large houses set back from the road. The live oaks that grew here never lost their foliage, even though it dulled in the winter, and the trunks were streaked black with rain.

I pulled up to Michelle's house. I stood under the portico, shivering in the cold as I waited for her to answer the door.

She looked drawn and tired, a look that her careful makeup couldn't overcome. She was dressed in a sweater and jeans, not up to her usual panache. She invited me in. "Do you mind sitting in the kitchen?" she asked. "It seems warmer than the living room."

The kitchen was too big, like the overblown kitchens in the newest McMansions in Germantown. At the island, she'd set out a big plate of muffins. Next to the china mugs sat the silver coffee set on a tray.

That was swift.

Being the good guest, I said, "The muffins look wonderful. Are they from Miss Muff'n?"

She brightened a little. "No. I made them myself." At my look of surprise, she said, "I'm not that kind of Cordova rich lady, with a housekeeper and a cook. The cleaners come in once a week, but I cook, because I like to."

I said, "My grandmother, who lives in Cordova, doesn't lift a finger for herself."

"Well, I ain't like that," she said, reminding me that as much as she'd morphed into Michelle Montgomery, the girl who'd grown up poor and sang in church was still underneath.

We sat. I took a muffin, and as I buttered it, she picked up the silver coffee pot. "Can I pour you some?"

"Thank you."

"Cream? Sugar?"

I said, "I see the rest of the set is back."

"Yes, it is." Her hand lingered on the handle of her own cup. "I called Jeffrey. I confronted him, and we had quite a fight about it. But he returned it." There were dark circles under her eyes, despite her concealer. "You did the right thing when you refused to buy it."

"It really wasn't worth risking my antique dealer's license for."

"It was more than that. I appreciate it." She took a swig of her coffee and stared into the cup. "It wasn't the first time."

"So that's how he knew about taking it for melt."

"He melted the gravy ladle. I didn't care about the

ladle. It was a gift from my husband, which was nice, but I never liked it. I was furious that he took it."

"I thought he made a living doing studio work."

"He used to. He hasn't worked in a while."

"No good projects?"

"He's not dependable anymore," she said, the worst thing a studio singer could say about a musician.

"That must be hard for all of you," I said, just to say something.

She shook her head. She was far away.

I felt Bobby Swann's presence in this Cordova kitchen, the faintest touch of long, agile, cold fingers against my cheek.

Michelle forced herself back to this room, where the bright light made the gloom outside even deeper. "It's not really worse," she said. "But it's harder than usual."

"Why? What's going on?"

"My husband is tired of putting up with it. Jeffrey was seventeen when I married Jim, and Jim has always been good to him. He paid Jeffrey's tuition at the Berklee Conservatory. He supported him when he started trying to make a career as a musician. But he's running out of patience. He said to me, 'He'll never get better if you keep propping him up.'" She raised her eyes to mine. "I'm terrified that if I stop propping him up, he won't make it. And now I'm fighting with Jim, too."

She shook her head again. "I know Jeffrey needs treatment. We tried rehab, and it didn't work. He's been on medication, too. He hated it. He told me that lithium made him feel half dead. He said no one could be an artist on lithium. He doesn't want to try again. I wish he'd see a psychiatrist to see if there's something better. But he won't go."

"I'm so sorry."

She drank more coffee and set her cup down with a thud. "Why is it that every time I talk to you, I tell you things I don't dare tell my friends?"

I wished I knew her well enough to cover her hand with my own. I'd felt affection for rich clients before, some of whom were troubled by bad marriages and wayward children and money problems. But I held back with Michelle. "Because I'm a stranger, so to speak. And I'm sworn to confidence. Like a doctor or a lawyer."

She brushed her eyes with the back of her hand. "You sell yourself short," she said.

It hurt to watch this composed woman cry. I said, "I don't know how I can help, but if there's anything I can do for you, let me know."

She was the one to reach for my hand and squeeze it. "Thank you."

"It's all right."

We sat like that for a moment, and then she took her hand away. She worked hard to compose herself again. She lifted the coffeepot. "More coffee?" she asked, and I nodded.

I sipped the coffee, giving her time to recover. When I set it down, I choose the easiest connection between us, art. "Have you picked up anything good lately?"

She looked better. "I'm bidding on a Kehinde Wiley that's coming up for auction. It won't go cheap. I'm not sure how high I want to go."

"How much do you like it?"

"Not enough to make my husband think I'm crazy."

I thought of his ire about her son. "Crazy for art? That's okay."

At that she laughed. "You're right. And even Jim would agree with that."

The silence between us was easier. I thought of my grandfather, who had been so secretive about doing her a favor after Bobby died. I didn't want to bring that up, but I could ask her about something farther away. "May I ask you a question?"

"About what?"

"Not about any of this. About something that happened back in the day. In the 1960s, when you were singing for Stax."

A husky laugh. "It couldn't be worse than anything we've already talked about."

"I don't think so."

"Sure, I owe you. Go ahead."

Despite her invitation, I thought, *Be careful.* I wasn't a cop or a detective or a lawyer, obligated to dig out the truth. This was personal, and I was prying. I couldn't ask her straight-out why my grandfather shot Buddy Griffen. I went at it obliquely, as I had with Joe Jordan. "Do you remember a guy named Buddy Griffen? Small-time talent agent?"

"Oh my God," she said. "Buddy Griffen. How did his name come up?"

"It's in connection with some research I'm doing."

"Is this about the guitar?"

"It's related to the guitar." *Sort of.*

She said, "Buddy Griffen. That lowlife. That sorry excuse for a man. I haven't thought of him for years, but I sure enough remember him."

"Did you ever have any dealings with him?"

"Oh, he wanted me to. He was after me to let him represent me. I didn't need an agent. I was a session singer, and I had a straightforward contract with Stax. I told him to go do something rude to himself."

"You knew about his reputation?"

"I certainly did. I didn't need any shit from him."

My eyebrows rose.

"Excuse me, but it's coming back. How mad I was at him. After all these years!" She shook her head. "I don't know why I'm feeling like this now."

I thought, *I do*. I asked, "But he left you alone."

"It wasn't just me," she said. "It was the other singers." She pursed her lips. For a moment she looked like Virgie Lee, righteously angry. "He hooked them, one after another. First with a promise of a career, which was bullshit, and then with the worst kind of codependency. 'I hit you because I love you.' A few of them got hooked on drugs, too, and they were wrecked. God, I hated him."

I thought, *Is this misplaced anger about Jeffrey, or is there something else?* I spoke softly. "Did you know someone he hurt?"

She said, "Every time I talk to you, I tell you something that's been tucked away for years."

There was. I felt a shiver of anticipation. "You know I'm not here to drag anything out of you."

She said, "You know when someone asks you about

something you're buried for a long time, and suddenly you can't wait to let it out? It's like that."

I nodded and I waited.

"It was my friend Yvonne. We went to school together, all the way through. We met in grade school, and we graduated in the same high school class. Yvonne Ballard." She took a deep breath. "I sang in the church choir, and I got the occasional solo, but she was a gospel star from the time she was eight years old. Her father was a preacher at one of the big Church of God in Christ churches in Memphis. You know about that? The Pentecostal churches?"

When I shook my head, she said, "They were big on singing for God's glory. Yvonne started early, and by the time she was in high school, she'd been on the road touring in Tennessee and Mississippi. Sending them for God. And under her father's thumb the whole time. The Pentecostals sing like crazy in church, but they're really strict outside of it. She didn't dance or drink or date. She hated it."

"I can imagine," I said. I thought of Virgie Lee's fierce, unyielding piety.

"She listened to the radio and to records, like we all did, and what she wanted was to sing secular music. Like Aretha. She was sure she could do as well as Aretha, putting the spirit into pop and soul music. When I went to work for Stax, she envied me something terrible. She was still singing for her daddy. Sending them to God every Sunday, and sick of it."

I waited.

"She wasn't Buddy's usual target. He liked them fresh

from the Delta, stupid about the music business. But he had a nose for someone's weakness. And he figured her out in ten seconds. She wanted to get away from her daddy so bad she'd do anything." Michelle shook her head. "Anything."

"What happened?" I said, remembering to keep my voice soft.

"She went from the frying pan into the fire. From her controlling daddy to an agent who was even worse. Her daddy had her in knots of guilt, but he never hit her. Buddy hit her." She shook her head again. "That bastard, he was smart enough to hit a woman where it wouldn't show."

"That's awful," I said.

She took a deep breath. "Thank God she pulled herself together. I'm glad Stax played a part in it. Stax had a distribution deal with Atlantic Records back then. With Jerry Wexler, who produced Aretha and made her a star. Jerry used to come to Memphis all the time to sit in on the Stax sessions. Yvonne got herself over to Stax and sang for Jerry. And the next thing we all knew, Jerry signed her to Atlantic and she left for New York."

She looked tired, and I remembered Joe Jordan, whose fatigue had cut our conversation short. "What happened to Buddy Griffen?"

"As much as I hated him, I don't know. One day he was gone, and I've got to say, no one missed him. I don't know if he ended up in the state pen or at the bottom of the Mississippi River."

I had to restrain myself from blurting out, "Was it after

Mo Raskin shot him?" Instead, I asked, "Did he have any arguments with my grandfather?"

Her expression changed. "I don't think Mo liked him much, but Mo never kept anyone out of the record shop. I don't think so."

Let it go. "Are you still in touch with Yvonne?"

"No, we lost touch years ago, when she went to New York."

Something was bothering me, but it was time to stop. "Michelle, I can't thank you enough. This has been really helpful."

She relaxed a little. "If you find out what happened to Buddy, be sure to tell me. If he's dead, I'd like to know." It was a joke, and it wasn't.

I said, "I shouldn't keep you." I rose to go. "Good luck with the Wiley. I hope you get it."

She rose too, smiling. "I can, if I pay for it."

WHEN I WALKED into the shop the next day, Gideon was behind the counter, even though it wasn't his duty day. "You don't have to be here today," I said.

"You don't want me here?" He was kidding.

"I'm always glad to have you here."

"Did we do all right yesterday?" he asked.

"I had to refuse to buy something because I was afraid it was hot."

"You call the cops?"

"No, it was a family problem between Jeffrey Swann and his mother. They worked it out."

"He's stealing from her?" He shook his head.

"I think it's a matter for a family therapist, not the police," I said. "And I really don't want to get between the two of them."

He shook his head again.

Jeffrey was trouble, and Gideon knew too much about that kind of trouble. I didn't want to go back there. I asked him, "You ever hear of a singer named Yvonne Ballard?"

"I have. She started out as a gospel singer in Memphis. Then she sang soul for a while. Trailed around after Aretha and never made it big. How did her name come up?"

"She was Michelle's best friend in high school."

Now I'd surprised him. "I'll be damned."

"Well, at least you've got a lot of good company down there."

I CALLED my father at his office during his business hours on Thursday, which were also mine, and he told me he was slammed and couldn't talk. "Do you have time early tomorrow morning? I can stop by the shop before you open."

"You don't have to drive in from Germantown."

"It's no trouble. I'd like to look around. And it's never too early to look for a birthday present for your mother."

When he arrived on Friday morning, he didn't hug me. There was still some awkwardness between us since my inquiry about the shooting. I didn't remind him. He looked around the shop and nodded in approval. "You've moved things around since you opened."

"We've sold some stuff. And gotten new stuff on consignment."

"That's good." He stopped before the photograph of Mo Raskin. "Is he behaving himself? Or is he haunting you?"

I said, "He keeps popping up."

The edge was back. "Nat, are you still looking into the record store? I thought you'd dropped it."

"No, this is something that came up while I was researching the guitar for Gideon."

"I thought you were done with that, too."

"Not yet."

He turned away from the photograph, upset again. "What is it now, Nat?"

"I wondered if you found a guitar when you went through Grandpa's stuff after he died."

He stared at me in surprise. "A guitar? Why would he have a guitar?"

"Why not? I was curious, that's all."

"What kind of guitar?"

"An electric guitar. Kind of hard to miss. Red finish."

"Nat, will you drop this?"

Why did he sound so uncomfortable? "Dad, is something the matter?"

He moderated his tone, as though he'd listened to himself and he didn't like the way he sounded. "Nat, sweetheart, I shouldn't be so sharp with you. But your grandfather's association with the music business is ancient history. I can't help you with it, and I wish you'd turn your attention elsewhere." He put his hand on my arm. "Please, Nat."

"Dad, are we all right?"

He gently squeezed my arm. "I hope you'd never think otherwise," he said.

THE PREACHER'S DAUGHTER

My grandmother called me, and suddenly I expected her to ask me why my father and I weren't getting along. Instead she invited me over for Friday night dinner. I breathed a sigh of relief. "Just us?"

"Why not?"

I bought a good bottle of California pinot and let the smell of chicken and honeycake envelop me when she opened the door. My grandmother had never been religious, but her Friday night comfort food was the cuisine she'd learned from her mother, Jewish and East European. She hugged me close and pressed her cheek to mine. "It must be cold out," she said.

"Cold for Memphis." I handed her the wine.

"Very nice. I'll open it. We'll find something to toast."

I was used to a whole family at the Sabbath table, and it was strange with just the two of us. When she poured me a second glass of wine, I asked her, "Nana, when you went through Grandpa's stuff, did you find a guitar?"

She laughed. "A guitar? You think he wanted to be Jimi Hendrix in his old age?"

I hadn't mentioned that it was electric. "If he still had it, it would be hard to miss. Electric guitar. A Fender Stratocaster. Deep red finish. Candy-apple red."

She laughed harder. "An old man with a guitar like that! No, of course not."

"Not in the storage unit, either?"

She said, "There was nothing in the storage unit but 45 records. I assumed they were leftovers from the shop's inventory. I didn't have any use for them, and that's why I sold them. I'm sorry I didn't ask you first. I had no idea you'd want them."

"It's all right. If I want 45s, I can buy them online."

She said, "You know, there was something strange about the storage unit. It was the most secure kind they had—he paid a premium for security—and it was climate controlled. It seemed like overkill to store old records. I wondered why he wanted a unit like that."

"You didn't know about it?"

"I knew about it. I didn't know how much he was paying for it. I was glad to cancel the lease." She asked, "Why do you think he had a guitar?"

"I know he had a guitar. He bought it in 1984. I'm curious about where it might have gone."

"If he sold it, he didn't mention it to me. Was it valuable?"

"At the time, probably worth a few thousand dollars."

"Well, not pennies on the street, but we were comfortable enough that he wouldn't have bothered me about selling it."

"I bet you didn't save his old receipts."

"No, we always cleaned that kind of thing out every year. Mo never wanted to be one of those people who left behind fifty years of Southern Bell phone bills." She looked away. Her voice was a little throaty. "I appreciated that. It helped me after he died." She looked up again. "I only had to get rid of the important things."

I touched her arm. "Nana, I'm sorry, I didn't mean to stir up your grief."

She covered my hand with her own. "I never know when it's going to come back to me. I don't even know what to tell people not to bring up."

I thought of myself, helpless with pain in Gideon's van. I nodded.

She said, "I'll go look in the attic again. If I stumble over a bright red electric guitar, I'll let you know."

THE NEXT DAY, Thomas Waverley came in carrying a manila envelope and set it on the counter. "I stopped by because I found something for you." He rested his hand on the envelope. Smiling, he said, "At Mr. Fairchild's request."

I turned to look at Gideon, who raised his eyebrow. I asked Thomas, "What is it?"

He carefully extricated something from the envelope, which he laid on the counter. "Yvonne Ballard."

I swiveled around to ask Gideon, "What did you tell him?"

"Just that her name came up while we were researching the guitar."

Thomas rested his hand on the photograph. "It's a publicity photo from Atlantic. With a signature."

She was darker-skinned than I'd expected, and her hair had been processed smooth and cut short to emphasize her cheekbones. Her lips, full and lipsticked pink, curved in a seductive smile. She wore a gold sequined dress that followed every curve of her body. Unlike Michelle, who was lithe and slender, Yvonne was voluptuous.

I said, "She's gorgeous and she knows it."

Thomas said, "Our very own queen of soul."

"Why don't I know about her? How could I miss someone like this?"

Thomas said, "She had a few hits in the 1970s as a soul singer. Then she fell from the public eye, and she isn't well remembered today. Which is a shame. A glorious voice to go with those glorious looks."

I touched the edge of the photo. "Is it for sale?"

"For you? Only ten dollars."

As I pulled the money from my wallet, I asked, "Where is she now? Does she still live in New York?"

Thomas said, "She's been back in Memphis for quite a while."

"She's here now?"

He nodded.

I handed him the ten-dollar bill. "Do you think she'd talk to me?"

Thomas smiled. "I know someone I can ask."

"Does this person have her phone number, too?"

Thomas winked. "It's quite likely."

WITH THE WAY smoothed and Yvonne Ballard's phone number in hand, I was suddenly hesitant to contact her. I knew what I wanted to ask her. It was the last thing I could say to a faded celebrity who was a stranger.

She was gracious on the phone, telling me that she had heard from Thomas and that she would be glad to fill me in on the old days. She had a lovely speaking voice, as though her singing voice was still intact. I wondered if she'd preserved her looks, too.

I presumed a little. I said, "A wise man told me that you get more interesting answers to questions when you ask them in person. May I come to see you?"

"I'm out of the way."

Not Cordova, I thought. "I don't mind."

"I'm in Collierville."

I was surprised. Collierville was a suburb that had blossomed as white Memphians fled a city where the neighborhoods and schools were increasingly Black. I didn't think they'd welcome a Black neighbor. "When is it convenient for you to talk?"

When I drove up her street, I was surprised to see that the houses were like those in Germantown, even though they were built a little closer together. And I was even more surprised when I saw a Black woman, dressed in designer jeans and a cashmere hoodie, pushing a stroller down the street. As I slowed, looking for Yvonne Ballard's address, she halted and bent down to adjust her child's hat. She didn't look up at me or smile. A neighbor, but not a friendly one.

The woman who opened the door to me had changed very little from her 1970s photograph. Her face was unlined, her hair was exquisitely straightened and styled, and she wore a conservative sheath dress and high-heeled pumps, much too formal for lounging around at home. I wondered if she'd misunderstood me for a journalist who would photograph her.

She welcomed me inside. In her home, she'd spent her money wisely. The furniture was new and of high quality. The room was tastefully and sparingly furnished. There was no etagere full of photographs. Had she married? Were there children? Perhaps she kept her photographs hidden away in albums. She must be well-used to scrutiny and to keeping things private.

The oil painting on the opposite wall caught my eye. "That's a lovely picture," I said. "Do my eyes deceive me, or is it a Jacob Lawrence?"

"Your eyes don't deceive you," she said. "It is."

Not all collectors of African American art knew each other, but I thought of Michelle in Cordova, and I began to wonder if she'd seen Yvonne more recently than 1968.

As we sat, I said, "This is a lovely home," hoping she'd open up.

She settled herself gracefully and smiled. "Thank you." There was a pause. I'd learned to let silence encourage people to talk, but she evidently knew that trick—of course, she'd been interviewed many times—and she set the pace herself. "I understand you have some questions for me. About the 1960s."

"I've been doing research on a guitar that belonged to

Bobby Swann. I recently talked to his widow, Michelle Montgomery. She mentioned your name."

"I think I heard something about that. Has it turned up?" Her voice stayed level. Did it really mean nothing to her?

"No, not yet," I said.

She inclined her head. "I knew Bobby, but only in passing," she said. "I'm afraid I can't tell you much."

"It's a bright red Fender Stratocaster, if that reminds you of anything."

She laughed. "They were all such peacocks, those Stax musicians. Bobby and the rest of them. Even their instruments were eye candy."

I waited, but so did she. I said, "I understand you were a gospel singer. How did you get your start singing non-religious music? Was it at Stax?"

"There was a Stax connection, but I never sang for them. Stax had a relationship with Atlantic Records. Atlantic distributed for Stax in the 1960s. Jerry Wexler, who produced all the soul artists at Atlantic, used to visit Stax to see what they were doing. I got a chance to sing for Jerry, and he liked what he heard."

"How did that come about?" I knew, but I wanted to hear her version.

"Well, I had a little help," she said. "There was a man named Morris Raskin who ran a record store, and he knew many of the Black musicians and singers at Stax and on Beale Street." She looked at me. "Raskin. Was he any relation to you?"

I said evenly, "He was my grandfather."

"Really? He was very encouraging to anyone who had

talent. I'm glad he thought of me that way. He knew Jerry Wexler, and he arranged for the audition. I'll always be grateful to him for that."

It would be the height of rudeness to mention the name of Buddy Griffen. I waited.

She smiled and said, "I was with Atlantic for fifteen years. I did very well there. But every record meant taking to the road, and there came a time when I got tired of touring. At that point, I came back to Memphis and settled down here."

"When you started out in Memphis, did you have an agent?"

There wasn't the slightest hesitation in her voice. "I started to work with an agent when I went to New York and signed with Atlantic. Beatrice Mackay. She represented just about every jazz and blues and soul act. She was really something. Smart and tough. I was in good hands with her."

I was silent. She'd obviously told this story many times. Beatrice Mackay may have acted as her publicist and written the script for her. She'd edited the past so carefully I couldn't reach it. I'd talked to many rich people who wanted to protect themselves, but never a celebrity who was so careful of her public persona. And if I asked her the questions I really wanted to ask, she'd never speak to me again.

I thanked her politely, but when I was on the road back to Memphis, I let myself feel furious. Her lies were the most egregious ones I'd heard, but everyone who had known Mo Raskin had lied to me. I was sick of being spared because I was white and a Raskin. I was ready to hear the truth.

<hr />

THE NEXT DAY, Gideon shared shop duty with me, and as we got ready to open, he asked me if I'd had a chance to talk to Miss Yvonne, queen of Memphis soul.

"I wasted my time driving out there. I could have read the bio on her website."

He said, "A celebrity who told you what her publicist told her to say. I'm shocked to hear it."

I was still angry, and I didn't care that I sounded petulant. "Why are all these people lying to me?"

He said, "In your long life at Sotheby's, talking to touchy rich folks about their treasured heirlooms, no one ever lied to you?"

"Not like this. And it never made me mad like this."

"Because this ain't business," he said.

I looked at him, and I didn't like the depth of understanding in his eyes.

"It's personal. You aren't doing business here, asking after your grandpa. You're just a nosy parker."

"I don't even dare ask them what I really want to know."

"And what do you think they'd say to you if you did? 'Sure, I knew Mo Raskin, and I know why he shot a man. Let me tell you how I know.'" He shook his head.

"This business has gotten under my skin. The shooting. Yvonne Ballard. I want to know what happened. My father is sitting on something, I know it."

His eyes were intensely blue. "He is, but this isn't about researching provenance. It's about your father's feelings. If I were you, I'd watch it."

I was still mad.

He said, "You're just itching to do something stupid, I can feel it. You're smarter than that, Miss Minerva. Don't."

WHEN I VISITED my parents for dinner on Friday night, my father was his usual self with me, as though there had never been any strain between us about the guitar. He asked after the business. "It's good," I said, as he always had when he didn't want to tell my mother he was worried about vendors or customers or monthly expenses.

"Did anything interesting walk in the door?" my father asked.

"Just the usual," I said. "Elvis collectors, interior designers, and Cordova matrons." I glanced at my mother. "Our bread and butter, thanks to you."

My mother said, "You look tired, Nat."

"Busy," I said, just as Dad would. "Nothing to worry about."

My mother reached out and patted my hand. "Don't overdo it," she said, just as she'd always reminded my father.

Don't do anything stupid. It's about his feelings. That didn't stop me. I took the tone of the bright kid I'd always been at this table, from toddlerhood through high school. I said, "I've been learning some interesting things about the history of music in Memphis, doing the research on the guitar."

My father stopped eating to listen, his fork in midair.

"Really?" my mother asked. "What did you find out?"

Leave it alone, my father had said. But Michelle's equivocation and Yvonne's outright lies had bothered me too much. "It turns out we had our own Aretha in Memphis. I didn't know."

My mother said, "Are you talking about Carla Thomas?"

My father set down his fork and gave up all pretense of being interested in his dinner.

I said, "No. She didn't record with Stax."

If Gideon were here, he'd tug on my elbow. And if Jude were here, she'd kick me under the table. "She got a contract with Atlantic, and she recorded for them."

My father pressed his hand harder against the edge of the table.

I went on. "Did you know that Jerry Wexler used to visit Stax? That's how she was discovered."

My mother's smile faded as my father curled his hand into a fist.

"Grandpa helped her out, like he helped out all the musicians he knew." I smiled at them both.

"Who was this, Nat?" my mother asked. Her tone was a warning.

I ignored it. "Her name was Yvonne Ballard."

My father's voice came out low and hoarse. "Never mention that name in this house. Not ever again in this house."

I was so surprised that I said, "What?"

My father slammed the palm of his hand on the table so hard the flatware rattled. "I don't need to tell you why," he said, and he rose roughly from the table and stomped from the room.

At that my surprise turned to shock. I stared at my mother. "What was that about?" I asked.

She rose, too, and threw her napkin on the table. "I have to talk to him."

From the kitchen, their voices rose in argument. I couldn't hear the words, but the tone was clear. My father was angrier than he'd ever been as my mother tried—and failed—to calm him.

I sat alone at the dinner table, my appetite gone. I no longer heard the anger in the other room. I heard Gideon's voice, full of regret: *Didn't I tell you?*

Early on Sunday morning, Nana called me. At the sound of her voice, I wanted to spill out my worry and my confusion. I hoped she had heard. I hoped she would say, "What's wrong between you and your father?"

As a kid, I'd gone to Nana when I was upset with my mother or my father. She'd listen, give me something to eat, and smooth things over. She'd tactfully told me I was in the wrong to ask for a low-cut dress for my bat mitzvah party, and she'd sided with me when my parents held me to a ten o'clock curfew on weekends in high school. She'd negotiated with my father more than once. She'd even talked to my mother, although she felt on shakier ground with a Beardsley than with her own flesh and blood. In high school, and even into college, it had been natural to ask Nana for her point of view and her assistance.

This was different.

This was about my grandfather. This was about the shooting that no one in the family wanted to admit to. This was about Buddy Griffen, who had a pimp's hold on Yvonne Ballard.

My grandmother's love for me had always been unconditional. But I couldn't ask her for an explanation. Or an intercession. She had loyalties I'd never bothered to understand when I was younger. Now that I was an adult, her relationships with my father and my grandfather had subtleties that she was unlikely to share with me.

And secrets that she was unlikely to share with me. I hadn't liked it when Michelle, a recent acquaintance, and Yvonne, a stranger, had lied to me. I hated the thought that my grandmother would lie to me, too. As much as I longed to, I couldn't ask her.

Now she said, "Nat, I remembered something about the storage unit. I'd forgotten about it, because it came at such a terrible time for us. Mo had just gotten bad news from his doctor. His heart condition wasn't responding well to treatment, and he was worse. The only thing I remember vividly from that time is how upset and worried I was."

"If it's too hard to talk about—" I said. At the sound of her voice, I wanted to spare her, as I hadn't cared to spare my father.

"No, what I called about isn't. It's just that I had to work to remember it. The storage locker was broken into, and Mo got very upset. I couldn't imagine why. 'What's in there that's worth this kind of tzuris?' I asked him. 'Don't get agitated! The doctor told you not to!' But he was beside himself. He wanted to sue the owner of the storage facility."

"Did he?"

"Of course not. I talked him out of it. God knows we didn't have the Hope diamond in there. I didn't care about whatever was stolen. I wanted him to take care of himself."

"Did he file an insurance claim?"

"I don't know. I don't even know if the stuff in the storage locker was insured. I wasn't thinking about insurance."

"Nana, would you mind if I checked with your insurance company?"

"You could. I never changed our insurance. I still work with the same agent. I can give you his name."

"I'll call him. In my role as an appraiser, not as your granddaughter."

"Tell him you're my granddaughter."

"Is he Jewish?"

"No, just an old-fashioned Southern gentleman. He'll talk to you."

"Thank you, Nana. This is really helpful."

"Sweetheart, you know I'd do anything to help you."

I wanted to tell her everything. It hurt to keep my mouth shut.

She said, "I heard that you and your father had some kind of disagreement. What's the matter, Nat? That isn't like either of you."

"Who told you?"

"Your mother called me."

Careful. I gave her part of the truth. "I don't know what happened," I said. "I just mentioned something from the old days."

She hesitated. She was censoring herself with me, too. "What was it?"

"I mentioned that I'd been doing some research and I'd found out that Grandpa knew a singer named Yvonne Ballard. Helped her get a recording contract. Dad got furious, and he wouldn't say why."

That hesitation again. Her tone was still warm, but her words were not. "Nat, I'll do anything to help you research this guitar. That's your business, as an antique dealer. But this business with Mo is different. It's past. Leave it alone."

I'd been right. She was keeping the truth from me, and I hated it.

1 2

LIE TO ME

I CALLED MY GRANDMOTHER'S INSURANCE AGENT, A courtly and old-fashioned Southern gentleman who offered belated condolences on the death of my grandfather. "He was a fine man, Ms. Raskin." He praised my grandmother. "It's a pleasure to do business with her." He asked after my parents, my business, and complimented me on my experience at Sotheby's. It was the conversational equivalent of sweet tea, and the New Yorker in me itched to get to the point. I hadn't been back in Memphis long enough.

Finally I got the chance to explain the official reason for my call. "I wondered if my grandfather filed an insurance claim for the guitar."

"When was it stolen?"

I told him.

"Let me take a look. It's all online these days, but sometimes it takes a moment to find something."

"That's quite all right." I waited.

189

He said, "Well, Ms. Raskin, I don't see any claim filed in that year. Do you know if he insured it?"

"No, I don't."

"There is a homeowner's policy. Let me check to see if the guitar is mentioned in it."

I waited again.

"No, I don't see any mention of it."

"That's not unusual. I'm an antique dealer, and I don't insure my personal collection."

He chided me gently. "If you don't have a security system, you should look into one."

I asked, "Would he have filed a police report?"

"We don't have a copy of it, since he didn't file a claim with us, but he might have."

"Is there a way I can get a copy?"

"I believe you can request one from the Memphis Police Department."

"I'll give that a try. You've been very helpful."

"Give my regards to your grandmother the next time you talk to her."

"Of course I will."

When I called the police department, I hit a snag. I discovered that being the granddaughter of the victim wasn't good enough. Neither was being a licensed antique appraiser. It wasn't like requesting military records from the National Archives, where "historical research" was a legitimate enough reason for them to search the records and bill for copying the pages. The clerk, a woman with a Black Delta accent, was friendly and cheerful. But she was insistent. I couldn't get a copy of the report.

I knew someone who could.

I called Detective Ivey, who was pleased to hear from me. He asked if I'd learned anything more about the shooting in my grandfather's shop.

"No, just that my father doesn't want to talk about it. I was calling about something else."

His voice was cheerful. "What now?"

I explained about the appraisal and the guitar. "The guitar was stolen. I'm hoping to get my hands on a police report."

"They said no to you?"

"They did, and I wondered if you knew how I might persuade them I'm official enough."

He said, "I can make a call and get you an incident report. I have friends on the force, and my son's an officer in the Burglary Unit."

"I'd be indebted to you."

"You won't be. I'm happy to keep a hand in." He chuckled. "I can get you an electronic copy and email it to you, easy as pie."

The report came that afternoon. The description of the incident was brief, but the description of the missing item was spot on. A 1964 Fender Stratocaster electric guitar, candy-apple red finish. My grandfather had given them photographs. He'd also given them the serial number.

I called Gideon to tell him, and he said, "Email me the report. I want to check the serial number against the one on Justin's guitar."

"It's wending its way."

"How did you get it? They don't usually give them out to distant family members."

"I know a retired cop."

He laughed.

"The one I interviewed about the shooting."

"I just got your email. Okay, I'm looking. Serial number. I'm looking at a picture of Justin's guitar."

Of course he'd taken a picture of the serial number.

"Is it a match?" I asked.

"It sure is."

I said slowly, "Justin bought my grandfather's guitar."

"It seems so."

"And we don't know where it was between the time it was stolen and the time Justin bought it."

Gideon said, "If it came to me with a history like that, I wouldn't buy it."

I sighed. "To sell it, the provenance needs to account for the gap."

"Nat, if it's been stolen, Justin has more trouble coming than being able to give an auction house a provenance."

"Let's fill in the gap first. Does he have any documentation? A receipt or a canceled check?"

"He said he'd look."

"I know how tired and distracted he is, with Jasmine, but remind him. Tell him it's important."

"Yes, ma'am."

It began to sink in. "We found Bobby Swann's guitar," I said.

"And we found a problem. I'll lean on Justin."

THE NEXT DAY, Gideon came into the shop to tell me, "Justin told me that he'll find the check if we come over and babysit for fifteen minutes."

"Okay," I said.

"You all right with that?" he asked me.

"I really want to see that check."

"You mean it? About the babysitting?"

"I'll live."

When Justin let us in, he wasn't holding the baby. He whispered, "She's sleeping."

Gideon whispered, "We won't wake her." I nodded.

Justin continued to whisper. "I'll just be a moment."

He disappeared into a back room, and when he returned, he held a printed page in his hand. "I emailed it to the shop's address, but I thought you'd like to see a hard copy." He handed it to Gideon, who glanced at it, then folded it up and tucked it into his jacket pocket.

We all heard the thin wail from the baby's room. "That's my cue," Justin said.

And that was ours.

On the sidewalk, Gideon asked, "Will you sit in the truck for a minute?"

"I'm not even faint."

"That's good. There's something I want to talk over with you."

I got into the truck, and Gideon pulled the page from his pocket. I asked, "Do you recognize the name of the seller?"

"Yes, I do," he said. "He's a local dealer."

"So you've done business with him."

"I've never bought a thing from him. He's always had a reputation for being shady."

"What do you mean?"

"Let's say that he doesn't always ask a seller for a receipt."

"That's a big red flag."

"No kidding. I don't know about this guitar, not for sure. But I want to talk to him. I want both of us to talk to him."

I WAS INTRIGUED to meet a dealer that Gideon called shady. Even at Sotheby's, I'd dealt with dealers who operated in a gray area. They were slapdash in their attributions and sloppy in their record-keeping. I'd also run into dealers and buyers—primarily museum directors and curators—who were guilty of handling stolen Nazi art or looted artifacts, however far in the past. But to my knowledge, I'd never met a dealer who received and sold stolen goods in the here and now. I'd never met a fence.

Denny Barnett agreed to meet us at the shop on a day we were closed. He didn't look shady. He was a white version of Justin, youthful and slender, with a ready smile and big brown eyes that added to his air of innocence. He looked around with appreciation. "I saw the photos on your website, but it's nicer in person," he said as Gideon introduced me. He found Gideon's case. "This is your stuff, I can tell."

Gideon said, "I have three cases and some floor space."

Denny's eyes traveled to the far wall. "And some wall space, I see."

Gideon said, "There's a spot in back where we can talk in private."

I led him into our back room, which he liked. "Break room," he said. "Nice to have in a shop."

I told him that this used to be my grandfather's clothing store until the 1980s.

After we sat, he said, "So, Gid, what's up? Why did you want to talk to me?"

"We're researching a guitar. Nat is the provenance expert, after fifteen years at Sotheby's, and she's working with me on establishing the history of ownership. The current owner told us he bought it from you, and we had some questions about it."

"Fire away," he said, not the least bit worried.

"Do you remember a '64 Strat? Red finish?"

"I've handled a few Strats over the years. Do you have a picture? To jog my memory?"

Gideon found the image on his phone and slid it across the table. Denny's face lit up. "I remember that one," he said. "What a beauty it was. Everyone who owned it took good care of it. And the sound! Lovely, just lovely." He sighed. "It was hard to let it go. But I wouldn't be in business long if I kept everything I liked."

"You remember who you sold it to?"

"I do. Young guy. Blues musician. Justin Taylor. I've heard him play. He's good. Does that guitar justice."

Gideon sounded nonchalant. "You remember where you got it?"

"Off the top of my head, I don't remember."

Gideon said, "Well, I'm wondering because we're trying to pin down the history of ownership." He leaned against the table, diminishing the space between Denny and himself.

Denny nodded.

Gideon said, "If you have the receipt with the seller's name on it, that would help us a lot."

"I'd have to dig around for it."

Gideon said, "Do you have it?"

Unruffled, he said, "Like I said, I'd have to look for it."

I said, "It was stolen in 2004. Did you know that?"

"Stolen?" He arched his eyebrows, overdoing his surprise.

"Denny," Gideon said, "both Nat and I have seen the police report."

Denny shook his head.

Gideon never raised his voice. "It would help us a lot if you could tell us who you bought it from."

Denny smiled. "I can't tell you that," he said. "You understand. You have clients you want to protect, too."

I looked at Gideon, who said, "Look, we have a client who wants to sell it. You know he can't if it has a gap in ownership. Especially if there's a theft on the record."

"Oh, I know," Denny said, his face serene.

Gideon said, "Will you excuse us for a moment?"

"Sure."

Gideon walked back into the shop, where we were out of Denny's earshot. "That's what I expected," he said.

"He's a mighty cool customer."

Gideon allowed himself the annoyance he hadn't shown as we talked to Denny. "He's a liar."

I dropped my voice. "You suspect or you know?"

"You know how I feel. I don't guess. I want to hear him tell us who he bought it from."

"Will he?"

"Maybe, if we try a little harder."

"What do you mean?"

"You'll see."

We returned to the back room. Denny, still unruffled, was checking something on his phone. He looked up. "Email," he said.

Gideon remained unruffled, too. "We can do this the easy way or the hard way," he said. "You go home and look through your files and send me a copy of the receipt. Or email me the name of your buyer. That's the easy way." He paused for emphasis. "The hard way involves telling the cops about it."

Denny said, "There's nothing for them to find."

"Then you can tell them that."

"Gid, there's no reason to bring the cops into this. It's hard enough making a living as an antique dealer without having the cops looking into your business." He threw a look at me. "You wouldn't want that, either."

I thought of Jeffrey. I said, "I don't buy stolen goods. I won't risk my dealer's license."

He ignored me. "Gid, you don't want to ruin my business, do you?"

"I want to know if you bought a hot guitar."

"I can't tell you that. Confidentiality."

Gideon said, "I know all about that."

I said, "We don't need a name. We just need confirmation that it was stolen."

Denny's voice rose, just a little. "And if that gets out? That's as bad as giving you a name."

Gideon said, "What about this? Can you answer this? It was a 'no questions asked' transaction, wasn't it? A no-receipt transaction?"

Denny crossed his arms and didn't reply.

"Was it?"

Denny was silent.

I said, "As an appraiser, I draft documents that have to stand up in court. Sometimes I have to go to court myself. If I had to swear, under oath in court, that this guitar was stolen, would I be lying?"

All the boyish innocence left his expression. He was as sullen and gray as a mug shot. "It's not my worry if you perjure yourself."

Gideon said, "All right, that's enough bullshit. I'm calling the cops. We know someone in the Burglary Unit." He picked up his phone.

"You won't," Denny said.

Gideon began to tap on the keypad, then turned on the speaker so that we could all hear, "Memphis Police. How can I direct your call?"

Denny shouted, "Hang up, damn it. Hang up!"

Gideon hesitated.

Denny glared at me, and his expression clearly said "damn it" to me as well. "No!"

"No to what?" I asked.

"Perjury. Your question about perjury. No."

He said to Gideon, "Fuck you and fuck your mother. Hang up."

Gideon broke the connection. "Nice doing business with you too, Denny."

He rose. "The hell with you, and your girlfriend over there, too."

Gideon looked at me. "Just business, Denny." I watched as Gideon escorted him out as though he didn't trust him to leave by himself.

When Denny was gone, I leaned against the counter. "We'll have to tell Justin he bought something hot. I don't look forward to doing that."

"I don't either," Gideon said.

I had a disturbing thought. "Is he guilty of anything? Buying something that was stolen?"

"Anyone who unwittingly buys stolen goods is in the clear. He's fine."

"That doesn't make me feel any better," I said.

13

WHO IT BELONGS TO

I'd had to tell clients that their treasures were fakes. That wasn't great news, but at least they had something in their hands, even if it wasn't worth what they expected. What I had to tell Justin was much worse. The guitar in Justin's hands had belonged to Bobby Swann, and its market value reflected its association with a Memphis music legend, but it didn't belong to Justin Taylor. He couldn't keep it, and he couldn't sell it.

Gideon felt as bad as I did, and he had no words of consolation for me. I wished I could invite myself to my parents' house for dinner to tell them about my dilemma and hear what they had to say. My father still wasn't talking to me. And how could I raise the subject of the guitar associated with his father, who had done something that offended him so much he couldn't explain it to me?

I called Josh, who said, "Mama told me that you and Dad had a fight. She said he's still upset with you. It that right? The two of you never fight."

I tried to joke. "You obviously don't remember my high school days. Clothes? Curfew? The car?"

"This seems different. More serious. Is it about Grandpa?"

"I wish I knew."

"How can I help?"

I hadn't realized how his professional life had sharpened his natural ability to listen for the problem and the pain beneath the words. "I did call you about some family stuff, but it's estate related, if you don't mind my asking."

"Is it about the guitar?"

"Yes, it is."

"Did you find out where it went?"

"Yes, I did, between the time it was stolen and the time the current owner bought it." I took a deep breath. "The current owner bought it from a guitar dealer, but the dealer bought it from the thief."

"So the current owner isn't the legal owner."

"No."

"If Grandpa owned it when it was stolen—"

"We own it."

"Is it worth anything?"

"Yes."

He said, "You sound like hell. This isn't about the guitar, or the money. What's wrong?"

"You should see the guy who owns it now. Young guy. Struggling musician. He and his wife just had a baby. He wanted to sell it to start the baby's college fund. And now I have to tell him it isn't his."

"Nat, can this sit for a while?"

"It's not an emergency, no. But I should talk to the current owner soon."

"Nana's the legal owner, since it belonged to Grandpa. Have you talked to her?"

"Not yet. I'm not up for more family drama right now."

"No one will hear it from me, unless you tell me it's all right."

"Thanks."

"It's the least I can do."

"Did you ever have a situation like this? Telling a client they didn't get what they expected?"

"I'm an estate attorney. I've had angry family members threaten to kill me because they didn't get what they expected. There's always a solution. We just don't know what it is yet."

"I hope so."

"I know so."

I still didn't feel any better.

ON THE DAY Gideon and I visited Justin, the weather finally promised spring. The air smelled green, and I could imagine the fragrance of magnolia that would fill the air in a few weeks when everything began to bud. I felt worse than if the day were dark and cold. Despite the mild temperature, I stood outside Justin's house shivering.

Gideon tapped me on the shoulder.

I said, "Don't tell me it will be all right."

"It won't. But you'll get through it. We'll get through it."

Justin opened the door, a quiet Jasmine in his arms. He burped her and whispered, "She's full. She should be quiet."

We walked into the living room, still untidy, still smelling of milk, baby powder, and diapers. Jasmine cooed, and Justin kissed the top of her head. He pointed to two chairs, which we cleared before we sat. On the sofa, still cradling Jasmine, he said, "So you have some news for me." His eyes were bright.

I felt like hell. "We've been able to establish the history of ownership."

He patted Jasmine on the back. Eager and excited, he asked, "Is it Bobby Swann's guitar?"

"Yes, it is."

"We add a zero." A bright smile spread over his face. "Do you hear that, Jasmine?"

I felt miserable. "There's a problem."

"What? What kind of problem?"

"With the ownership."

"What are you talking about?"

I took a deep breath. "At some point, the guitar was stolen."

He looked at me in puzzlement. "When?"

"In 2004."

"But I bought it from Denny Barnett two years after that."

"Denny bought it from the man who stole it."

"Did he know it was stolen?"

I couldn't even look at him.

Gideon said, "Yes, he did."

"How do you know?"

"We got Denny to confirm that he knew it was stolen."

"What does that mean?" His voice rose. "That I bought something stolen? Am I in trouble for buying a hot guitar?"

Even more miserable, I said, "You were what the law calls an unwitting buyer. You didn't know. Denny made sure you didn't know. An unwitting buyer isn't guilty of any wrongdoing."

Thoroughly angry, he said, "Only of being a fucking idiot!"

Gideon said, "Denny's a goddamn con artist. Don't you dare blame yourself for believing him."

"I'll kill him, the bastard!" He startled Jasmine, who began to cry. Justin ignored her.

I said, "He owes you restitution for the cost of the guitar. You can sue him."

"As though that does me any good!" At the sound of his fury, Jasmine wailed. "If I don't own it, who does?"

I wished I were anywhere but here. I'd rather be at my parents' dining room table, facing my father. "When it was stolen, it belonged to a man named Morris Raskin. He was my grandfather. He died four years ago. Now it's part of his estate, which passed to my grandmother."

"You own it?"

"Legally, personally, I don't."

"Did you know about this?"

"Believe me, when I started researching, I had no idea. I was as surprised as you are."

"Jesus. It's yours. So you can just take it from me?"

I said, "If you brought this to the attention of the

police, or to a lawyer, they'd tell you that you had to return it to the legal owner."

"You."

"Justin, I am so sorry to tell you this."

Jasmine was screaming. It hurt me to listen to her.

"No, you aren't. You own Bobby Swann's guitar. Worth fifty thousand. And I don't. That money was for my child's education. Her future. Now it's gone."

Gideon said, "Justin, would you like me to hold Jasmine?"

Justin glared at both of us. "Don't you touch my baby," he said. "Get out, both of you. I don't want to see you or talk to you, either of you."

Gideon said, "If you want to talk to a lawyer—"

He was furious as he held Jasmine, who was still screaming. "I'll get my own lawyer. You get the hell out of my house."

THAT NIGHT, at home, I sat in my low-lit living room, too dispirited to listen to music. I didn't deserve to listen to Otis. I should be listening to the Temptations singing "Smiling Faces," about deceit and betrayal. I poured myself a glass of wine and stared at it, because I saw no comfort there.

The guitar's ownership was now settled. The question of who it really belonged to was not.

I should call Nana to tell her that she now owned Grandpa's guitar. Bobby Swann's guitar. Not Justin Taylor's guitar. I missed my father's advice and affection. I didn't know why he'd withdrawn from me, and I didn't know how to mend the rift. I'd call my mother. Maybe she'd help.

Maybe she'd lie to me, too.

If I called now, I'd sound low, but I doubted I'd do any better in the morning. My father was likely to be home, but it didn't matter. My mother wouldn't offer to hand the phone to him. Wouldn't risk asking, "Do you want to talk to Nat?" to hear him say, "No."

When I called, my mother asked, "Are you all right?"

"Tired. It's just a business problem."

"With the shop?"

"No, the shop is doing fine. It's about the appraisal I'm doing. It's not going so well."

"I'm sorry to hear it." Which is just what she'd say to my father when she didn't really want to know the details.

I couldn't keep the sadness out of my voice. "I wish I could talk to Dad about it."

"Oh, Nat."

"He still isn't talking to me, and I don't understand why."

My mother said, "I've asked him. More than once. It hasn't done any good."

"Do you have any idea what this is about?"

A silence, then a sigh. I'd learned to read these non-verbals. *I do, and I can't tell you.*

I said, "Do you want things to go on like this?"

Another silence. I could translate that one too. *Of course not.* I felt a profound exhaustion. "I shouldn't have called."

"No," my mother said, upset. "Don't feel that way."

I didn't want to hear her say, "I love you, and so does your father." I said, "I can't help it," and hung up.

THE NEXT MORNING, I sat in the big armchair in my living room, drinking coffee. I hadn't slept well, and I didn't feel much better than I had the night before. The phone rang. It was my mother.

What else was there to say? But if I didn't pick up, she'd leave a message that would make me feel guilty as well as sad. I answered.

"Nat?" she said, her voice tentative. "I didn't get you too early?"

"No, I've been up for hours," I said. "It's fine."

There was a brief silence. "Really?"

I said, "No, not really."

"Can I come to see you?" she said, in a tone I'd rarely heard, small and sad.

"Is there anything more to talk about? I don't really think so."

"Oh, Nat." Her voice was still small. "Let me come over."

I thought of Detective Ivey's advice. *You get better answers in person.* "If you stop by, I'll be here."

I ran to the local bakery and made more coffee. As I put the pastry on a plate, I thought of Michelle, giving me muffins to sweeten the story of her bitterest worries and fears.

My mother looked as though she hadn't slept well, either. Her eyes were puffy and red-rimmed. She sat heavily in the guest chair, without her usual grace, and let me bring out the refreshments. She took a bite of the croissant and put it back on the plate, then drank a sip of coffee and put it down, too.

I said, "I know you didn't come here to nosh."

"No, I didn't."

I said, "Is there really anything else to say?"

"Things changed," she said.

"What happened?"

She met my eyes, and I felt a stab of apprehension. "I had a fight with your father last night."

"You and Dad? A fight?" But I thought of the way they'd raised their voices after I'd mentioned Yvonne Ballard.

"Yes." She hesitated.

"What was it about?"

"About you," she said.

I shook my head.

"I've never disagreed with your father like this. But I decided I owe you an explanation."

I saw something I didn't recognize in her face. "The fight wasn't really about me."

"If I'm being honest—"

"Someone should be."

I waited as she braced herself. As Michelle had. She nodded. "It's been a secret too long. And it hasn't been worth keeping a secret."

As a daughter, I was full of apprehension. But as a researcher, I was thinking: *Here it is*. As with the strangers I'd talked to, I held back. Like Joe Jordan, like Michelle

Montgomery, like Detective Ivey, my mother had a story to tell. I'd let her tell it at her own pace.

Unlike all the other griots I'd listened to, she didn't start at the beginning.

"I was in the shop when your grandfather shot Buddy Griffen."

I sat up straight in my too-big chair.

"To understand why, I need to back up a little. More than a little. Back to 1967, when St. Mary's Church began to get the youth group involved in the civil rights movement. I was just about to be confirmed, but I was on the side of the angels, with the Reverend Martin Luther King. It didn't hurt a bit that it made my mother furious. She was so angry about political activism at St. Mary's that she nearly went looking for another Episcopal church."

My mother smiled. To this day, it cheered her to needle her mother, the patrician in Cordova who had never stopped using the term "Negro." My mother said, "It turned out that Temple Israel was on the side of the angels, too, and the church youth group and the synagogue youth group got together to plan some activities. That's how I met your father, I had a crush on him from the moment I saw him. So handsome, with those soulful brown eyes. A good listener. Warm. Affectionate. Not like my family at all. The first time he touched me, he put his hand on my back. Like a brother, but neither of my brothers had ever touched me like that. I was already serious about being an activist, but once I met Mike Raskin, I told myself I'd go anywhere and do anything for civil rights if he was there with me."

She smiled again at the memory. "The youth groups

started out by socializing, but by 1968, we were a lot bolder. We demonstrated in support of the sanitation workers' strike. And we went to the Masonic Temple to hear Dr. King speak. I heard him, Nat. I heard him say, 'I've been to the mountaintop.' And your father was standing beside me." She looked up and added, "We were holding hands."

It startled me to think of my parents as idealistic, love-struck teenagers.

"If it wasn't church business, I had a hell of a time getting into Memphis. Mike invited me to come to his father's record shop, but I couldn't get a ride from Cordova. Then Dr. King was assassinated and South Main was on fire and I really couldn't get a ride in from Cordova. If I told my mother the truth, I'd never get to Memphis to see the inside of Raskin's Records. But a few months after things quieted down, I begged and wheedled a ride with the brother of a friend who was old enough to drive, and I told my mother I was going to a youth group meeting at St. Mary's. Two years before, at thirteen, Mike told me, he'd become a man, at least in the synagogue, and since then, he'd been responsible for his own sins. I'd just turned fifteen myself, old enough to get confirmed at St. Mary's, and I figured I was old enough to sin on my own account, too."

She picked up her coffee cup and set it down again. "So I walked into Raskin's Records, that den of iniquity, and I was a little disappointed. It was a record store. Mike was already there, looking through the newest 45s from Stax, and he grinned and waved, and I joined him. He knew all the groups and the singers. He showed me Otis

Redding's posthumous release. 'It's really sad,' he said. 'And really good. There's a record player in back if you want to listen to it.'"

"'Sitting on the Dock of the Bay,'" I murmured.

My mother nodded. "We were flipping through the records, laughing and kidding around, when a woman walked into the store. I just stared. I'd never seen anyone who looked like that. Black and absolutely gorgeous. Big almond eyes. Full pink lips. Straight shiny hair. And her shape! She could have been wearing a flour sack and she'd still have that shape, but she was in a sheath dress, and it showed every asset she had. I knew I'd never grow up to look like her, but right then, right there, I prayed to God for a miracle."

She shook her head. "She walked up to the counter, and Mike's dad smiled at her. He'd smiled at me when I walked in, but this was something else. She leaned against the counter to talk to him, and he leaned toward her. I was just old enough to feel desire. Just old enough to know that I could feel that way about Mike. And I could tell that the air between Mike's dad and this woman was electric. I knew it."

Let her talk, I thought. *Let her tell it.*

"And then the door flew open, and a man came in. A Black man. He was shouting. 'Yvonne! Yvonne!' He raised his arm, and he had a pistol in his hand. 'You bitch! You whore!' Mike's dad stayed calm as can be. 'Put the gun down, Buddy.' Buddy pointed it right at him. 'You bastard. You Jew bastard. She's mine. Stay away from her, or I'll kill you.' Mike's dad reached under the counter and brought out his own gun. He didn't say anything. He just shot. He hit Buddy in the arm, and Buddy began to yell. Mike grabbed me by the hand and dragged me in back, and he called the police."

I wondered if she'd remember Detective Ivey.

"Buddy went to the hospital, but the rest of us had to stay there for hours while the detective talked to everyone. I remember that he was a big man, light-skinned, with freckles on his nose. He even wanted to talk to Mike and me. As he was finishing up, Mike's dad said to him, 'Leave Miss Ballard's name out of it.' The detective said, 'I have to write up a report.' Mike's dad took some money from his pocket and tried to slip it into the detective's hand. He looked disgusted. 'I can't take that,' he said. 'But I'll see what I can do.'"

That explained why the *Appeal* hadn't mentioned Yvonne Ballard of Orange Mound. Or fifteen-year-old Barbara Jean Beardsley of Cordova.

My mother looked exhausted, and she stared down at her hands.

Very softly, I said, "So that's why Mo Raskin shot Buddy Griffen."

My mother looked up. "Now you know."

Because of Yvonne Ballard.

14

ASK LILLIAN RASKIN

WHEN GIDEON CAME INTO THE SHOP ON SUNDAY, HE looked tired. "I heard something you should know about."

"Someone found Robert Johnson's guitar?"

"No, closer to home. The word's out that I've found Bobby Swann's guitar."

"Who told you that?"

Before he could answer, our electronic bell jangled, and Joe Jordan strolled into the shop. He was especially debonair today, a handkerchief folded into his jacket pocket, his fedora set at a jaunty angle on his head.

"How are you feeling, Joe?" I asked.

"All recovered, Miss Natalie."

"You were sick?" Gideon asked.

"Just a little cold. Don't you fuss over me, too." He leaned against the counter, not for support but in a nonchalant posture that echoed Morris Raskin's stance in the shop photo.

I asked, "Can we sell you something today, Joe? Add to your Beale Street collection?"

He shook his head. "No, thanks. Heard something I thought you two might want to know about."

I glanced at Gideon, feeling a prickle of apprehension. "What?"

"Friend of mine told me about Justin Taylor, said he was worth listening to. I was in a club last night. Enjoyed myself. He's good. Knows what to do with that guitar."

"His red Strat?" Gideon asked.

Joe said, "He was telling people it was Bobby Swann's guitar. The one Bobby played on all those hits for Stax."

I sighed.

"And he was also telling anyone who'd listen that it wasn't his. Had quite an attitude about it." He leaned forward and rested his elbows on the counter. "Miss Natalie, he said that it belongs to you."

Gideon expelled a breath. If we'd been alone, he would have expelled a curse word, too.

I asked him, "Did you hear that?"

He nodded.

Joe said, "Every musician in that place went home to tell his friends and relatives. All those folks talk to each other. They go to church together. I reckon everyone in Orange Mound knows by now."

After Joe left, Gideon said, "Shit."

"My sentiments exactly. So that's what Justin's been doing? Blabbing all over town?"

"Seems so."

"I thought he'd act better than this."

"After the way we let him down? Are you surprised?"

"I can understand why he's mad. I just thought he'd keep his mouth shut."

"You want me to call him?" Gideon asked.

I said, "I'd offer, but I don't think he'll speak to me."

"I'll do it."

We had desultory business all afternoon—we even sold a few things—and Gideon didn't get a chance to call Justin until just after we closed. Once he got Justin on the phone, he said to me, "He wants to talk to you, too."

"So he can yell at me?"

"I'll referee."

Gideon put me on speaker. I said, "Hi there, Justin."

"You're on my shit list."

"Nice day to you too, Justin."

Gideon said, "All right, you have something to say to both of us, go ahead and say it."

"What the hell am I supposed to do with the guitar now?"

I said, "Just hang on to it. Use it."

"Is that all right?" His voice dripped sarcasm. "Since it isn't mine? You won't call the cops to get it back?"

I said, "My family has to make a decision about it, and they aren't in a hurry."

"Thanks a lot."

Gideon said, "Nat wants to be gracious about this. You be gracious, too."

Sullen silence.

Gideon said, "Look, I know you're mad, but you've put both of us in a bad spot, telling everyone that Nat owns it. Which she doesn't, by the way."

"Too late for that."

I thought, *Now that every guitar collector, dealer, and thief in the southeast knows about it.*

Gideon asked, "Have you thought about putting it somewhere secure?"

"I need it. I play it."

"Storing it somewhere secure?"

"It's never out of my sight."

"It's at home, where your family lives. Your baby. Think about it."

Justin said, "I've got to go. Jasmine just woke up." He hung up.

We looked at each other. Gideon said, "He really needs to get that thing under lock and key."

"What a mess," I said. "On top of the other mess."

"The family stuff?" Gideon asked.

"And how."

"Is it about your grandfather?"

I looked at the photograph of Mo Raskin from his suave postwar days. "I think so."

"Is it related?"

"I don't know yet."

"What do you know?"

That had always been the question at Sotheby's when the provenance was tangled and messy. I took a deep breath. "After I talked to Yvonne, I heard from my mother. She had a different story. She was an eyewitness. She was in the store the day Mo Raskin shot Buddy Griffen."

He nodded.

"Her version is a lot different from Yvonne's. Or Michelle's." I recounted what my mother had told me.

He said, "Mo did a lot more than mentor Yvonne in her career as a singer."

"I'm guessing that's true. But it's like you said once. You don't like to guess. You like to know." I met his eyes.

He said, "You want to know, and you don't."

I nodded.

"You talk to your grandmother yet?"

"No."

"You should."

"I can't," I said.

THE NEXT WEEK, late in the day, the bell jangled, and Jeffrey Swann walked into the shop. He looked better than the last time I saw him, not so wan and not so haggard. His nose wasn't running, either. He smiled as he approached the counter. I greeted him.

"Hi, Nat. I see Gideon's here, too." He held up his hands to show me they were empty.

Great, I thought. *You didn't boost your mother's silver before you came to see us.* "Is there something I can do for you?"

"Yes, there is." He leaned against the counter and rested his hands on the glass, splaying out his long agile fingers. "I heard you found my father's guitar."

"Where did you hear that?"

"Every blues musician in town knows," he said.

"I guess so," I said.

He lowered his voice. "I heard that Justin Taylor doesn't own it."

"Did he tell you himself?"

He broke into a big smile. "I heard that you do."

"That's not quite right."

"But I bet you know who does."

I said, "And you know I can't tell you."

"Why not? Aren't you finished with the appraisal? Not held to confidentiality?"

"It's still confidential."

"Could you pass a message along to the person who owns it?"

"What kind of message?"

"I want to buy it."

"The owner hasn't decided what to do with it yet."

"That's all right. Just let the owner know I'm interested and I'm serious."

I said, "You're aware that it's not going to be cheap."

"I understand. I'm not looking for a bargain."

I wondered if Michelle knew that Jeffrey was planning to tap her for it. Of course, I couldn't ask. "Well, it's up to the owner, not me."

He was still smiling. "Will you talk to the owner? And let me know what the owner says?"

"When I talk to the owner," I said, feeling stubborn and angry at the interior voice that repeated, *Have you told your grandmother yet?*

"Is there some kind of problem?"

"No. It's just that it's valuable and the owner needs time to think it over. That's all."

He looked at me and laughed. "You're holding out on me. I know, because I know how it's done. And I'm much better at it than you are."

"I have your number, Jeffrey."

"Don't you," he said, smiling as he turned to go.

"Gideon!" he said on his way out. "Great job on finding the guitar!"

After he left, I said to Gideon, "I've never seen him so cheerful."

Smarting from Jeffrey's comment, Gideon said, "Maybe his birthday is coming up and he thinks his mother is going to give him a hell of a birthday present."

I sighed. "I should call her."

"Go ahead. And after that, call your grandmother."

"Lay off," I said, sharp with irritation.

———

I TALKED to Michelle that evening. Her first words were, "I heard you found Bobby's guitar."

"Who told you?"

"It's out on the street," she said.

So she got the word from the street in her aerie in Cordova. "Don't tell me you want to buy it."

"Me? I got rid of it years ago. Why would I want it back?"

I said, "Jeffrey was in the shop today. He offered to buy it. He said he'd pay whatever we valued it at."

"Really? And how does he expect to find the money?"

"That's why I thought you should know. Because you'll be hearing from him soon, if you haven't already."

She said, "I'll be prepared, then." She paused. "I heard that you own it now."

"Not really. It belongs to my grandfather's estate. We'll have to figure out who owns it."

"Your grandfather? Are you telling me that Mo bought it?"

I'd forgotten she didn't know. "He did. In fact, he bought it from Ike Levy the moment you walked out of Diamond Pawn."

She said slowly, "So he helped me out, like he always helped Bobby out."

My questions about Yvonne were burning my tongue, but this wasn't the moment to ask.

She said, "What's going on with it now?"

"Until my family figures out what to do, the current owner can keep it and use it. He's a musician. He needs it."

"I'm beginning to think no one needs that guitar."

"Hold on to that thought when Jeffrey bugs you about buying it."

She sighed. "Life's been good lately," she said, her tone ironic. "I just found out I didn't get the Wiley."

It was a relief to talk about art. "Oh, that's too bad. What happened?"

"I bid stupid money, but someone else bid stupider money."

"Well, his work doesn't come up every day, but it does come up. You'll have another chance. And maybe you'll get the next one for a better price."

"Maybe, maybe not."

"You never know at auction," I said.

"Kind of like the rest of life," she said.

CALL YOUR GRANDMOTHER. The thought nagged at me and bothered me at odd times. When I sat at a stoplight. When I poured myself a cup of coffee in the morning. When I woke in the middle of the night and couldn't get back to sleep.

In the shop, every time I glanced at the photo of Grandpa.

I was in the shop with Jude and Gideon on a Friday afternoon when Nana walked in. She didn't have the usual look of a customer, of anticipation or pleased surprise. She was clearly unhappy.

I put on my best retail mien. "Nana, it's so nice to see you in the shop."

She glanced around. "It's different." As she walked up to the counter, her eyes rested on the photograph of Grandpa.

I said, "Let me introduce you to my dealers." I made the introductions, and she nodded to them without speaking.

She asked, "Can we talk privately? Is there still a room in back?"

Behind the woodshed. "That's not different."

Once we sat down in back, she spoke without any preliminary. "A young man named Jeffrey Swann turned up on my doorstep to ask if I'd sell him a guitar. Do you know anything about this?"

Why had he visited her? "He came to see you? Did he say why?"

"He thinks I own it. That's news to me. Do I?"

I looked down at my hands. I'd refreshed my nail

polish this morning, and my nails gleamed pale pink in the fluorescent light of the back room.

"Nat?" Her voice was sharp.

My face flushed. I looked up. "I should have told you sooner."

"Yes, you should have, if it means that strangers are going to bother me about selling something I don't realize I own. It must be worth something. He insisted he'd pay market value for it. How much is market value?"

I am in so much trouble, I thought, and realized how adolescent I sounded. How much like an adolescent I'd behaved. "Nana, I'm sorry, I should have told you. But it's about Grandpa, and I think it's related to whatever is bothering my father so much. I didn't want to make things worse."

"Natalie, I don't know what's wrong with your father, but that doesn't excuse your behavior. You're both adults, not children."

I felt sheepish. Foolish. Childish. "You're reading me the riot act."

"Yes, I am."

"I can explain."

"Please do."

I hadn't hurt her—she was too tough to feel slighted because I hadn't told her—but she was irritated with me. And rightly so. I explained that Grandpa had bought the guitar and kept it in storage all those years.

She said, "So that was the reason Mo got upset about the theft from the storage locker. Someone stole the guitar."

I nodded.

"And now this young musician, the one with the new baby, has the guitar, but it isn't really his. And he's very unhappy about it."

I nodded.

"What are you planning to do?"

"I don't know." I felt very small.

"Neither do I." She gave me a stern look. "It's not just up to me."

"Dad won't talk to me. But he'll listen to you."

"He's still not talking to you?" she asked.

"No."

She gripped the edge of the table, and for a moment I was afraid she'd slam it down as my father had. "Nat, I don't want any more tzuris about this guitar. Not from your father or from you." She rose.

"It won't go away," I said, but she only shook her head.

I followed her onto the shop floor. She threw a glance at the photo of her husband. The electronic bell jangled as she left. I had never heard it sound so gloomy.

After Nana left, Jude rolled her eyes and Gideon shook his head. "Behind the woodshed?" he asked.

"Shut up," I said, still feeling small and petulant.

Jude said, "Gideon, what do you say we take Nat out for a drink after we close up?"

The bar she chose was big and dark and noisy, and we sat in a booth for further anonymity. It wasn't a place to order white wine, and even if it had been, I was too upset. I ordered a shot of bourbon and gulped enough to make me sputter and cough.

"So," Jude said. "Justin's got it. Jeffrey wants it. Your grandmother owns it. Am I missing something?"

"I haven't heard from Brenda yet," I said, taking another gulp of bourbon.

"Is she the one who hired that slimy guy who said he was an investigator?"

Gideon said, "We don't know, and she won't say."

I lifted the glass again, and Jude put her hand on my arm. "Sip it, please. It makes me crazy to hear you cough."

I put the glass down. "I don't even like bourbon," I said.

Jude said, "What I don't get is how Jeffrey Swann knew to talk to your grandmother."

How did he? I doubted that Michelle had told him. Justin believed I owned it. Maybe Jeffrey had decided to work his way through every member of the Raskin family, and I was lucky that he'd talked to Nana first and not Josh. Or worse yet, Dad. "I don't know."

Gideon said, "If he could find out, then anyone can. I don't like the idea that Brenda can."

"If she hasn't already," I said. My grandmother was alert and vigorous, but she was nearly eighty, and she lived alone in the house she had shared with my grandfather.

What was the real reason for my father's fury at me and for my grandmother's refusal to talk about the past? Was it worth risking a burglary—or worse?

I suddenly felt too sick to drink any more bourbon. I pushed the glass away. "I have to go home," I said.

As I drove to Evergreen, I felt increasingly angry. It hurt to admit how much in the wrong I was. I let myself feel furious with Jeffrey. This mess was his fault. I knew who I'd call and who I'd yell at.

But as soon as I punched in Michelle's number, I lost

heart. It wasn't her fault. She wasn't any happier with her errant son than I was. She was more than a client but less than a friend, and I couldn't raise my voice at her. "Have I called at a bad time?"

"No, it's fine. Jim's out of town, and I have an evening to myself for a change." Her voice was slow and a little slurred. Had she been drinking, too? "What is it? You find a stray Wiley?"

"Oh, I wish," I said, and I put too much longing into it.

"Trouble?" She was drunk.

"Yes." Again, I put too much emotion into it.

"Is it Jeffrey again?"

"Yes."

She expelled a breath. "What now? Is it worse than last time?"

My fury drained away. I wanted to spare her. "I think so."

She sighed, a sound with a lot of pain in it. "What did he do?"

I forced myself to breathe deeply, and I told her.

"You didn't make a deal with him, so he showed up on your grandmother's doorstep to harass her about selling him the guitar?"

I thought of Brenda showing up on my grandmother's doorstep. "I'm afraid so."

Her voice was low and hoarse. "He plays me all the time. I'm used to it. He's played you, and you know how he works. But to play your grandmother! That's low, even for him."

"She can deal with a little manipulation. I don't like that he found her address."

"Oh, Lord," she said, a curse and an appeal. "The manipulation. The lying. The stealing. And now this. I've run out of people to call. The doctor. The psychiatrist. The rehab director. I should just call the cops."

I thought of my contact in the Burglary Unit, who was Detective Ivey's son. Michelle would never call the cops on Jeffrey. I knew that. I let her feel guilty because I needed something from her today. "There's no reason to."

Her voice was thick. "Nat, you're kinder than we deserve."

"I don't know about that."

I heard the sound of her gulping. Was she drinking bourbon? She must be a pro, she didn't cough. Her voice was as blue as Otis Redding's. "Now is there anything I can do for you?"

I was upset and she was drunk, and it wasn't a situation for a fair fight. But I said it anyway. "Actually, there is."

"You want a Wiley?"

As though she could pull it from her bottom dresser drawer and make things right between us. "I just want to ask you a question."

"Is that all? Sure. What is it?"

"It's about Yvonne."

"Yvonne? What does she have to do with any of this?"

"Something. After I talked to her, I mentioned her to my parents, and my father blew up just to hear her name. Now he won't talk to me. And no one in my family will explain why."

Her voice cooled. She sobered, a little. "Why ask me?"

I said, "If I were inclined to bet—which I'm not—I'd

bet you've talked to Yvonne more recently than forty years ago."

She was silent.

Jeffrey had taught me something. I knew how to play his mother. "Yvonne was very gracious to me. She had nothing but good things to say about my grandfather. And she didn't say a word about Buddy Griffen."

"You asked her?"

"No, I didn't. But after I talked to her, I heard a different version of the story from my mother."

"What would your mother know about it?"

"She was there."

"And what did you hear from her?"

I told her about Buddy's rage and his ugly words. About Buddy brandishing a gun, and Mo shooting him.

Michelle took a while to compose herself. She didn't sound completely sober, and I knew it bothered her. "Buddy was crazy jealous. I can see how he'd misinterpret Mo's encouragement."

"I had the impression—my mother had the impression —that Yvonne and Mo were much more than friends."

She didn't reply.

Go for it, Natalie Minerva, I told myself. "Why is it that whenever I talk to someone in the Black community who knew Mo Raskin in the 1960s, I get the feeling that that person is sitting on something?"

Michelle sighed. I heard her take another slug. "Do you really think you're going to hear anything ugly about your grandfather from us? A man who's revered in Memphis for being an ally to Black people?"

Even if you're blotto, you can do better than that. I gave her the credo I'd lived by when I worked for Sotheby's. Did I still believe it? I hoped so. "I'm a researcher by profession. And it turns out I'm a researcher by nature, too. I'm willing to hear the truth if anyone is willing to tell me."

In the ensuing silence, I wished we could return to the pleasanter, safer topic of collecting art that cost too much. But I'd pushed her hard, and I'd declared myself a truth seeker. I didn't temper my voice. "Were Yvonne and Mo Raskin lovers?"

The long pause told me what I wanted to know. Michelle's voice dropped to a whisper. "That isn't my secret to tell."

"Should I ask Yvonne?"

"Don't," she pleaded.

AFTER I TALKED TO MICHELLE, I was wrung out. I crawled into bed early and fell into a heavy sleep. When the phone woke me, I was so befuddled that I didn't know what time it was. I didn't recognize the number, but I answered anyway.

It was Yvonne, and her voice was icy. "I don't appreciate your poking into something of mine that's private."

I sat up in the dark, fully awake, my heart pounding and my head aching. "You heard from Michelle."

"Yes, I did."

Evidently my secrets, unlike Yvonne's, were Michelle's to tell.

She said, "Mo's gone. All that's left is his good name. I

don't want anyone—and I mean anyone—digging up the past like this. It's over. It's finished. Leave it alone."

As my father had said, and my mother. My head felt heavy, and my tongue felt thick. "I don't want to hurt anyone," I said. "But I want to know the truth. This is my business, too, because it's my family's history."

Her voice became even icier. That cold rage was worse than a hot one. "Well, you aren't going to get anything from me. If you want to know the truth, I suggest you talk to someone else. To Mo Raskin's wife. Talk to Lillian Raskin. See what she'll tell you."

15

WHERE'S THE GUITAR?

A FEW DAYS LATER, DURING THE AFTERNOON LULL AT THE shop, Gideon picked up his phone. "Justin? What is it?"

As he listened, his mouth tightened and the crow's feet around his eyes deepened. "Hey, Justin, can you wait a minute? Nat's here. I want to put you on speaker."

"What is it?" I whispered.

Gideon turned on the speaker. "Justin? You there?"

"Yes," Justin said. He sounded badly shaken. "Nat?"

How could I stay angry at him? "Hi, Justin. What's going on? Is something wrong?"

"My place was broken into this morning."

Just like we warned him, I thought, but I said, "That's awful! Are you okay? Is Jasmine okay?"

"We were out. I was running errands, and I had her with me. When I got home, I found the door unlocked. The place had been tossed." He sounded even shakier.

"Is anything missing?"

"No. Just a mess. Someone was looking for the guitar and got mad that it wasn't there to find."

Gideon said, "Where the hell is it?"

"It's locked up at a club I play at."

"That ain't secure, and you know it," Gideon said.

"Of course I know it," Justin said, too upset to be angry.

I asked, "And this happened in broad daylight?"

"Most of our neighbors are at work at that hour. No one's around."

Gideon asked, "Did you call the cops?"

"They've already been here, looking around and asking questions. They said they'd file a report, and if anything was missing, they could send out the info to the pawnshops." He took a deep breath, and I heard how ragged he sounded. "It wasn't a punk on a casual B&E. There's a brand-new big-screen TV in the living room, and they didn't touch it. Whoever was here was looking for the guitar."

Jasmine let out a powerful wail. Justin tried to comfort her. "She's tired," he said. "Late for her nap."

"Are you really all right?" I asked.

"Just shook up." Jasmine was still wailing. "I've got to go," he said.

"You really can't leave the guitar at home," Gideon told him.

"Man, they looked everywhere. They know it's not here. I don't think they'll come back."

"You know that's not good enough. And you can't keep it at a club, either. You have to put it somewhere secure."

"Storage? Can't afford it."

"Let me help you out. I can store it for you."

"Where?"

"It's better if you don't know." Gideon looked at me, telling me: *Neither should you.*

I thought of Nana, not of myself, and I felt a chill.

Sounding plaintive, Justin said, "What am I going to do for a guitar?"

"I'll can lend you one of mine. Something good but not so good you'd be afraid to carry it around." Before Justin could object, Gideon said, "Sit tight. I'm coming over there right now."

Jasmine wailed louder than before. "Okay, I'm not going anywhere," Justin said, and he hung up.

"Do you want me to go over there with you?" I asked him.

"No. Once he starts feeling better, he'll remember that you're still on his shit list."

After Gideon left, I asked Jude, "Do you know where his storage unit is?"

"God no. He doesn't tell anyone."

"Is he paranoid?"

"Realistic," she said, gesturing toward the beautiful, expensive instruments arrayed on the back wall.

I DIDN'T FEEL BETTER NOW that the guitar was in an undisclosed safe location. I knew the power of gossip among musicians, and they'd know right away that Justin was no longer playing Bobby Swann's guitar. They'd ask him where it was, and when he refused to tell them, they'd speculate. I thought of the buzz going from Beale Street to Orange Mound and Whitehaven, and I worried about its path from Black Memphis to white.

And before the week was over, I found out I'd been right.

After we closed the shop, I drove home, now in daylight as spring approached. We'd had a good day, steady sales, and the strangers, the tourists, were interspersed with the regulars who wanted to chat, show us their most recent acquisitions, and let us know what they were looking for. Retail regulars were different from Sotheby's clients. They were like neighbors, casual friends who renewed the relationship every few weeks. I hadn't realized how much I would enjoy having customers like that.

I was tired, and as I turned onto my street, I looked forward to the comfort of being home. On my block, the flowering shrubs had just begun to bud, and the air was faintly fragrant. In a few weeks, the scent of magnolia would be overpowering in the air. Our urban birds, wrens and sparrows and robins, called before they settled for the night. My block was a haven, where I could let myself feel my fatigue, knowing I'd soon be wrapped in the comfort of my big armchair with a glass of wine at my elbow. I saw an unfamiliar vehicle parked outside Val and Emmy's house. We all knew each other's cars, and Val and Emmy kept theirs in back. They must have a visitor.

As I trudged up my front steps, someone leaped from the car and slammed the door. A trim woman in a navy-blue pantsuit, her stride controlled even as she hurried.

Brenda.

She caught up with me on the porch. Her shoulders

were rigid, and her eyes were so wide her stare disconcerted me. "I have to talk to you."

Not here. Not now. "Can't this wait, Brenda? Can't you call me tomorrow at the shop?"

She demanded, "Where's the guitar?"

"What do you mean?"

"Justin isn't playing it anymore. Where is it?"

"I don't know."

"Don't kid me. You own it and you don't know?"

"I don't own it." Exhaustion surged through me.

"Don't lie to me," she said.

That's good, coming from you. "I'm not. It's somewhere secure. I don't know where."

"Gideon. Does he know?"

"I can't tell you."

Brenda came closer. She reached for my shoulder. She raised her voice. "Don't bullshit me," she said, the vulgarity doubly shocking coming from her. "Where's the guitar?"

"Don't touch me."

She grabbed me by the shoulder. "Where's the guitar?"

I pulled back and raised my voice, too. "You let go of me. You leave me alone. It's not mine, and I don't know where it is."

Her voice dropped to a growl. "Don't lie to me."

She wasn't hysterical. I thought of Justin's break-in, and I felt afraid and angry to be afraid. I said, "You let go of me, or I'll call the police. They already know about Justin's break-in."

She tightened her grip on me. "Don't you threaten me."

"Was that you?"

Her face twisted in rage, and she looked just like Virgie Lee.

Val opened her front door, and as soon as she saw Brenda, she sprinted down the sidewalk, calling out, "Everything all right here?"

Brenda pulled back, letting me go. "Who the hell are you?"

Val bounded up my front steps. "I live next door to Nat. And I'm the block captain. I keep an eye on things on the block."

"This is none of your business," Brenda said. She edged away from Val, who towered over her by a head.

"Nat? What's going on?" Val asked.

I said, "Disgruntled customer."

Val regarded Brenda, her calm, level gaze as heavy as a hand on the shoulder. "Sister, the shop is open four days a week. Why don't you talk to Nat there?"

"I'm not your sister," Brenda snarled.

"In a manner of speaking," Val said.

"I'm not doing anything wrong," Brenda said, her tone low and mean.

Val moved closer. I had never been so grateful for her height and her broad shoulders. "Why don't you go home quietly before you do?"

Brenda's eyes glittered. "What are you going to do? Arrest me?"

"I've been known to call the cops."

Brenda said, "She says she doesn't know a thing." She turned to me. "But her grandmother might."

Nana. "If you bother her—"

Val took out her phone as calmly as if she were

ordering a pizza. Her finger poised over the keypad, she said, "Get in your car and go home."

This again.

Brenda pivoted to stare at Val, then back to Nat to glare at her. "That guitar is mine," she said, her face ugly. "And I'll find it." She threw Val one last furious look before she tramped down the steps to her car.

Val watched until Brenda drove down the block and turned at the corner. "What's going on, Nat?"

"I'm handling a big expensive item that a lot of people want." I was trembling. "Some of them are pretty worked up about it."

Val shook her head. "Over a thing? I don't get it. No thing is worth getting that worked up over."

I laughed, a wobbly sound. "If they weren't, I couldn't make a living."

"Emmy and I will keep our eyes open. If she comes back, we'll call the cops."

I was trembling. I wasn't worried for myself, between Gideon's presence at the shop and Val's next door. I was worried about Nana.

I CALLED Nana to tell her to keep an eye out. "If anyone else calls you or appears on your doorstep to ask about the guitar, call me right away."

Nana said, "Someone bothered you about this guitar? Who was it?"

"Jeffrey's half-sister, Brenda Sawyer. She's not as suave

as Jeffrey. And she wants the guitar a lot more than he does."

She sighed. "More tzuris, even though I didn't want it. How worried should I be?"

"Don't let any angry strangers in the house."

"As though I usually do. If one turns up, you'll be the first to know."

"Promise me you'll call me right away if someone does."

"Before or after I call the police?"

I hesitated. I thought of the so-called PI in the cowboy hat. I was sure Brenda had hired him before, and she might hire him again. God help me, I decided not to tell Nana to watch for him. I decided not to alarm her. "I don't think it will come to that."

ON FRIDAY, after we closed up, neither Jude nor I wanted to go home. We went to dinner down the street and lingered over it. By the time we left the restaurant, it was around eight and completely dark. Jude offered to drive me back to the shop, where I'd left my car, but I told her I felt safe walking down South Main.

At the shop, I glanced at the displays in the windows, then walked through the yard. I heard the owl's call and stopped at the foot of the overgrown live oak. The bird, who flew soundlessly, alit on a lower branch, and she swiveled her head so that she could gaze right at me. She hooted softly, her call high and sweet, then flew away.

As I looked upward, someone grabbed my arm.

It was the man in the cowboy hat. "You be quiet," he said.

The flicker of anger was drowned by a flood of fear.

He gripped my arm hard enough to leave a bruise. "I've got a question for you, little lady."

He knew how much I hated to hear that. And there was nothing I could do or say to stop him.

"Where's that damn guitar?"

I shook my head.

"Where is it?"

"I don't know," I said. "Gideon is the one who knows."

"I ain't asking your boyfriend. I'm asking you."

It wasn't the time to remind him that Gideon was my partner in business. "I don't know."

He rested his free hand on my shoulder. "I bet you can find out."

I didn't reply.

He tightened his hand around my shoulder, putting enough pressure to bruise there too. I was so afraid it was hard to talk, but I got the words out. "You think it's going to help you to hurt me?"

He moved close, as though he wanted to embrace me. He smelled of cigarettes, Old Spice, and sweat, and the smell nauseated me. He whispered into my ear, "If you don't tell me where that guitar is, I know who will. Because I know who owns it." He tightened his grip on my shoulder, making it hurt worse, and when I gasped with pain, he released me.

He turned away and walked through the parking lot. He walked past my car, giving it a once-over as he'd looked at Jude and the shop.

He'd broken into Justin's house. I was sure of it.

I waited until he was down the alley and out of sight. I shook as I walked to my car. I opened the door, fell into the driver's seat, and locked all four doors.

I leaned against the steering wheel, my arm and shoulder hurting, shaking so badly I could barely lift my phone from my handbag. I fished it out and stared at it as though I'd forgotten how to use it.

I know who owns it.

I should call the cops. But I was too worried about Nana to wait at the shop until they got here and talked to me. I called Nana from the parking lot, thinking, *Pick up, pick up.* When she didn't, I left her a message, not bothering to disguise my worry or my fear. Then I took a deep breath and called Gideon.

But I got his voicemail, too, and I tried to sound only slightly upset. I told him I was driving out to Germantown, and why.

Before I left, I called Nana and got voicemail again. I told myself she had an active social life. For all I knew, she was having dinner with some friends from the women's group at Temple. But I couldn't stop panicking. I left another message. "Nana, it doesn't matter when you pick this up, call me."

I pulled out of the parking lot. I wasn't thinking clearly. I felt too much alarm.

Nana's street was dark and quiet. When I pulled up to her house, the lights were out. Was she home and asleep? Or not here at all? I called once more, and the call went to voicemail.

I ran to the front door and rang the bell, not caring if I

woke her for nothing. If I dragged her from sleep, it would take her a few minutes to put on her bathrobe and make her way downstairs.

But after ten minutes, she hadn't answered the door.

Then it struck me. *Check the garage.* She kept it locked, I knew, but there was a window I could look into. I didn't care what the neighbors thought. I peered inside.

The garage was empty. She wasn't home.

At midnight? Where was she?

A polite voice behind me scared the bejeezus out of me. "Excuse me? Are you looking for something?" He wore a T-shirt and sweatpants, the clothes he slept in, and in the faint light I could see that he was in his forties and clean-cut when his hair wasn't mussed by sleep.

I asked, "Are you a neighbor?"

"I am. Who are you?" Still polite.

"I'm sorry. Did I wake you?"

"My wife saw you out the window and insisted I take a look."

"I'm Lillian Raskin's granddaughter. Nat Raskin."

"She's mentioned you. You have that antique shop."

"Yes, I do." This wasn't the moment to tell him when we were open. "She hasn't been answering her phone tonight. I wanted to make sure she was all right. I may be overreacting, but I'm worried."

His expression clearly said, *Yes, you are.* "I saw her leave at six," he said. "She was fine. She waved at me as she drove off. She's probably having a late night with some friends."

I saw myself through his eyes. Overreacting. I forced myself to sound calmer. "You're probably right," I said. "I'll leave her a note. I'll slip it under the door, and I'll go. I'm sorry I disturbed you."

He ran his hand through his unkempt hair. "No, it's all right. We all like Lillian. The kids adore her. They call her their third grandma."

I pulled a card from my purse and wrote my cell number on it. "If you see anything suspicious, call me right away."

He took the card and yawned.

"I'm really sorry I woke you up."

He laughed. "My fault for falling asleep so early," he said.

He watched as I wrote my note and slipped it under Nana's front door. He kept an eye on me, Lillian's granddaughter, as I got in my car and drove away.

IN THE MORNING, as soon as I dared, I called her.

"Nat?" she said, sounding distracted. There was a commotion in the background, as though she was in a crowd. "This isn't a good time. The police are here."

"The police? Are you all right?"

"Don't worry, I'm fine."

"I'm coming out there right now."

She said, "Excuse me, Officer, it's my granddaughter, and she's worried about me" To me, she said, "Nat, I have to go."

I tore out of the house and arrived in Germantown in record time. Nana's cul-de-sac, so quiet last night, was abuzz with activity. A patrol car was parked outside her house, the lights flashing, and on her front lawn, a crowd had gathered. I parked, got out of the car, and pushed my way through the crowd. Someone I'd never met said, "Don't push me, young lady," and I snapped, "I'm her granddaughter! Is she all right?"

Nana was talking to a police officer, a tall, lanky white man whose navy uniform and holstered gun were doubly anomalous among the leisured women of Germantown who had gathered before her house, well-dressed, well-coiffed, and upset.

"Nana!" I cried out. "Are you all right?"

The police officer said, "Excuse me, ma'am."

Nana said, "It's all right, Officer, this is my granddaughter, and she's been worried about me."

"What happened, Nana?"

"Let me finish talking to the police."

A blond woman in her forties said to me, "Were you here last night? Are you the one who talked to my husband when I sent him next door to see what was going on?"

I said, "I'm sorry I woke anyone up. What's happening?"

"I got the jitters after you showed up last night. When I saw that man talking to Lillian, looking threatening, I called the police. Maybe I overreacted."

"Or not." I glanced at my grandmother. "Is she all right?"

"Shook up, I'd guess. The police are real interested in this guy. I heard he called himself an investigator, but he's not."

"Did you see him? Was he a stocky guy in a cowboy hat?"

She shook her head. "No cowboy hat. Stocky? Maybe."

Nana called to me, "Nat, it's all right, they're finished with me."

I rushed to her. "You're all right? What happened?"

She said, "A very unpleasant man showed up at my door and tried to push his way into my house. I locked the door behind me and told him to speak his piece in the front yard."

"What did he want?"

"He wanted to know where the guitar is. When I told him I didn't know, he threatened me."

"Did he hurt you?"

"Grabbed my arm. He had quite a grip." She rubbed her upper arm. "I think I'll have a bruise."

"You're sure you're all right?"

"Natalie, it's never good when the day starts with someone telling you he'll get the truth out of you the hard way. I'm glad my next-door neighbor called the police."

I wanted to burst into tears. "That's why I called you last night, Nana. I know who this guy is. He calls himself a private investigator, and last night he threatened me."

Indignant, she said, "He threatened you too? Are you all right?"

"Don't worry about me. He's not an investigator, Nana."

"I didn't think so."

"He's a thug." Now that I knew she was all right, I was upset enough to let her have it. "Why didn't you call me back last night?"

"I was busy last night."

"Too busy to answer the phone? What were you doing?"

She blushed. "Natalie, that's a question I wouldn't ask you, now that you're an adult."

Suddenly I got it. "You're seeing someone?"

Nana was as embarrassed as a teenager. "That's none of your business, ziskeyt."

I said, "I feel awful, Nana. This mess is all my fault."

"I've seen worse."

"I wish not."

She put her hand on my arm, on the bruise that matched hers, and when I winced, she asked, "What's wrong?"

"He grabbed me, too."

She stroked the sore spot and sighed. "When we were having trouble with the Klan at the store, we were having trouble at home, too. They put a brick through our living room window. Compared to that, this is nothing."

"Is that what you'll tell Dad?"

She looked tired and shaken. "For that, I'll wait," she said. "I don't need tzuris from him, too."

Once in my car, I slumped over the steering wheel. Now I had an even worse call to make. I had to call Gideon.

16

NEVER BEEN SO ANGRY

ON SATURDAY AFTERNOON, THE BELL JANGLED AND THE pneumatic hinge on the door sighed. My father stood in the doorway. We had about ten customers on the floor, browsing, and I stood behind the counter, running a credit card for a woman who'd just bought a mid-century wooden elephant for her grandson.

My father strode to the counter, crowding the customer. He gave me an order. "Nat, I have to talk to you. Now."

I was stunned. In my entire life I had never seen him interfere with a sale. As pleasantly as I could, more for the customer than for him, I said, "Just let me finish up this transaction, and I'll be right with you."

His eyes were unnaturally bright. "No, right now. In back, Nat."

Gideon, who stood beside me as he kept an eye on the front cases, said to me, "I can finish up here. It's all right."

I was furious, but I didn't want to show it to the

customer. "Will you excuse me, please? My father is here, and it seems to be urgent."

"Not at all," she said, but she was flustered to be caught in the middle of a family crisis.

I followed my father into the back, where I said, "What do you think you're doing? I was in the middle of making a sale."

His whole body was stiff. His hands were curled into fists at his sides. Not bothering to modulate his voice, he said, "You put Nana in danger."

What had he heard? "What are you talking about?"

"I heard all about it from a neighbor I ran into this morning at the bakery. She asked me, 'How is your mother?' I said, 'Fine, as far as I know.' She said, "You didn't hear?' And I said, 'Hear what?' And she told me what."

Oh no.

"Some thug showed up in her front yard and threatened her. Tried to assault her. Her neighbor was so worried, she called the cops. They sent two squad cars. They blocked off the street." His voice rose. I was sure they could hear him in front.

"Dad, keep your voice down—"

He moved closer. His cheeks were flushed with anger. "This guy is wanted all over Tennessee. Warrants out for him as far away as Nashville. He's dangerous. He could have really hurt her. And you sent him right to her doorstep."

I thought, *Yes, he's right, I did.* "Dad! I was there on Saturday morning. I saw her just after the police arrived." My own arm still ached. "She was shook up. But she was all right."

"This is all because of you. You and that damn guitar. How many times did I tell you to leave it alone?"

"Dad, listen to me."

"No, you listen to me." He ran his hands through his hair, tugging on it in his ire until it stood up in wild curls. "I've had it. This is enough. I'm going to break your lease. I want you out of this building. I want you out of the antique business. I want you out of Memphis."

How dare you, I thought. I raised my voice to get his attention. "Do you think you can punish me like I'm a kid? Give me a timeout, send me to my room? You can't break the lease. We haven't done a thing to warrant it. Shut down my business? Throw me out of Memphis? Are you crazy?"

"You'll see how crazy. I'm calling my lawyer this afternoon."

"I can get a lawyer too. You want a lawsuit? You want to go to court? You want all of Memphis watching the Raskin family rip itself to shreds? Raskin vs. Raskin, the best show in town!"

"Yes, if that's what it takes to keep Nana safe. Didn't you think? Don't you care?"

"I love Nana. I would never do anything to hurt her." I grabbed his arm and forced him to face me. "Look at me. This isn't about Nana. It isn't about the guitar. It's about your father, Mo Raskin, and Yvonne Ballard. Don't tell me I can't mention her name. That's what this is about."

He yanked his arm from my grasp. "You'll be hearing from my lawyer. I want you out."

"Dad—"

But he was already stomping away, and all I could do

was trail after him. He pushed past my customers, who stared at him in surprise. On the floor, Gideon waylaid him, trying to slow him down.

He glared at Gideon, and he didn't bother to lower his voice. "You're responsible, too. You dragged her into this mess." He yelled at me: "Who the hell is he, anyway? What do you know about him? I bet you never ran a background check. Maybe he's got a criminal record himself."

"Get out of my shop," I said, too upset to care that a dozen customers could overhear.

My father yanked the door open, and when it didn't slam behind him, he stood on the sidewalk, glaring at it in reproach.

My voice shaking, I said to the nearest customers, a middle-aged couple and their adult daughter, "Sorry about that."

The older woman said, "I'm sure you'll get it figured out."

I nodded. I couldn't bear to stay in the shop. My voice thick, I said to Gideon, "I have to get out for a while." I fled through the yard to my car and started it without any idea of where I might go.

THE MISSISSIPPI RIVER was the reason Memphis existed in the first place, and all our weather was the result of the water. As a student at Columbia, I'd spent a lot of time in Riverside Park, looking out at the Hudson, and I liked to watch its gray-green span in every kind of weather. But I rarely went down to my hometown river. Now, troubled, torn up, I drove toward the Mississippi.

In the park at River Crossing, which allowed a vista across the watery boundary between Tennessee and Arkansas, I stopped to walk as close as I could to the river's edge. The Mississippi had a warm, swampy, muddy smell, the odor of the alluvial delta. I watched the boats on the river, a combination of steamboats for tourists and working boats that hauled cargo north and east, and I let the breeze from the water ruffle my hair. I envied anyone on a boat today, going upriver from Memphis. Somewhere else. Anywhere else.

"Hey, Nat." I felt a light hand on my shoulder, a gentle touch on the bruised spot.

I turned. It was Gideon. "How did you know I was here?"

"I followed you."

"Why?"

He gestured toward the muddy, roiling water. "You thinking about jumping in?"

"Not really."

He moved a little closer. "Thinking about going back to New York?"

"Maybe."

He faced me, and I saw all the wear on his face and all the concern in his expression. "I know your father is mad as a hornet. But I doubt he's going to break your lease and put you out of business."

"There's a first time for everything."

"I've seen families who hate each other, and believe me, yours isn't even close."

"Yours?"

"Why do you think I hightailed it to Nashville when I was eighteen and never looked back?"

I thought of a life without my family in it. For the first time, I wondered if distance had helped us get along so well. "I might give that a try. Does it work when you're all grown up?"

He laid his hand on my arm, another gentle touch. I didn't mind when Gideon touched me. "You can do different when you're grown up."

"You can," I said, staring out at the water. "That doesn't mean you will."

"I overheard what you said in back, and you're right. This isn't about the guitar."

I nodded.

"It's not really about your grandmother, either. That's just a reason to get mad and yell at you."

"Well, it is. He loves Nana and worries about her, like I do."

"You're spot on that it's about your grandfather."

I met his eyes. "Not just about my grandfather. It's about Yvonne Ballard." I took a deep breath. "I can't fix what's wrong between my father and me until I know what happened between Mo and Yvonne."

"Time to pry the truth out."

"Yes. Yvonne was the one who told me how."

"Yvonne? What did she say to you?"

"Ask Lillian Raskin."

THAT EVENING, I got a call from Josh. I wished I didn't have to answer it. When I picked up, he said, "Dad called me."

"Was it about Nana or about suing me?"

Josh sounded very weary. "I told him I can't get involved in this as a lawyer."

I said, "I didn't think so." And to my shame, I began to sob.

"Oh, Nat."

"This is awful, Josh."

"I know."

"Do you remember when you offered to run interference for me?"

"As a brother? Sure. That still stands. I need to run some interference as a son, too." He sighed. "Let me think about how."

MY MOTHER CALLED ME, too, but all I could say was, "Please, Mama. I can't talk about it right now." I let her demur, but I repeated, "Not now," before I hung up.

Nana called me before I could call her.

"Did you hear that Dad and I had a terrible fight?" I asked.

"Yes, but I wanted you to know that I heard from the police. The Germantown police."

"They arrested the guy?"

"No, but he has a record, the officer told me. He's a thief, and he's been stealing guitars all over Tennessee. He has a reputation in Nashville, too."

"Oh, God."

"Nat? Is there something you're not telling me?"

I groaned. "I feel guilty enough already."

"There's enough of that to go around. Your father called me. I already got an earful from him."

"Did he tell you that he wants to shut down my business because I put you in danger?"

"Yes, and there was no reasoning with him, not a bit."

"I've never seen him like this. I don't know if we can fix it."

She didn't contradict me.

"Nana, this isn't about me. It's about Grandpa." I took a deep breath. "It's about his relationship with Yvonne Ballard."

Now she was the one to say, "Oh God."

And I was the one to ask, "Nana, is there something you haven't told me?"

She hesitated. "And now I'm the one who feels guilty."

"I can make a guess, but I don't want to guess. I want to know."

She was silent.

"Not over the phone. I'll come to see you."

She sighed.

I said, "Don't bother to give me babka. This isn't a time for sugar. Just talk to me."

I drove to her house, full of trepidation that I was going to hurt her. Hadn't I already done enough damage?

I got out of my car, relieved to see the street was quiet and the lawn had recovered from being trampled by a crowd of cops and neighbors. The magnolia in the front yard had recently budded and now perfumed the air.

At the door, she shook her head and put her arms around me in a tentative hug. I pulled her close, my trepidation worse.

"Nana, if this is too hard, if this is too painful, tell me, and I'll shut up and never mention it again."

She sighed. "We're both grown women, and we're not made of glass. Come in."

She'd kept her promise about the babka, but she'd made coffee, which I accepted, even though I set the cup on the coaster without drinking from it.

"So," I said. "Grandpa and Yvonne Ballard."

She said, "When you were a child, you didn't need to know, but you're not a child anymore."

I wanted to speak, but she raised her hand in the gesture the Supremes had made famous. Stop. "Let me start from the beginning," she said.

"After the war, Mo and I got married—we were eager, like everyone else, to get married and to start a family. It wasn't easy for me. It took a while for me to get pregnant with Mike. Once I was pregnant, we were so happy. And when he arrived, we were even happier. You'd think no one had ever had a baby before, he seemed so wonderful to us."

My gaze fell on the photograph of my grandfather holding my father as an infant.

"Well, when he was a little over a year old, we looked at each other and said, 'This one needs some brothers and sisters!' We got busy, and right away I was pregnant again. Excited. I got through the first three months, when you're supposed to wait, and in my fourth month I told everyone so they could be happy for me. And two weeks later, I miscarried."

My midsection began to ache.

"I was terribly disappointed. Discouraged. The doctor told us it would be all right, that most women who miscarried once went on to carry babies to term, and we shouldn't worry. We waited until we both felt ready, and then we got busy again."

She didn't look happy with this memory.

"This time I wasn't excited. I was worried all the time. Not just for the first three months, but into the fourth month. And I had good reason. Because I miscarried again."

I keenly felt the ache. I wanted to press my hand against it for relief.

"And this time I wasn't just discouraged. I was depressed. I was sure I'd never be able to have another baby and give Mo the family he wanted so much. That we wanted so much. I wasn't one of those depressed women who gets into bed and stares at the ceiling. I couldn't, with Mikey to take care of. But I went numb. I couldn't bear the thought of letting Mo back into bed with me. I couldn't stand the thought that I might get pregnant and miscarry again."

I remembered feeling that way, all too well.

"I pushed him away. I knew I shouldn't, because he was hurting too. He was grieving too. But I couldn't manage to put out my hand to him so we could be together again. We were in that house, far away from each other, terribly alone."

She put her hand to her forehead to rub it. "I didn't

blame him for going down to Beale Street to spend time with the musicians who came into his store. He wanted company as much as anything. I didn't think he might meet singers, too. Or other women." She hesitated. "At a certain point, I knew something was wrong. We were as far apart as ever, but he wasn't lonely anymore. Deep down, I knew why."

This was familiar, too.

"And one day he sat me down and he said, 'Lillian, I have something terrible to tell you.'

"I said, 'Are you sick?'

"'No.'

"'You want a divorce.'

"He shook his head.

"'Then what?'

"'I've done something very wrong,' he said.

"I knew before he said it.

"'I've had an affair.'

"'Who is she?'

"'No one you know.'

"'Who is she?' I insisted.

"He looked at me with anguish, and he said, 'A singer. A Black woman.'

"'Tell me her name.'"

She took a deep breath. "He said, 'Her name is Yvonne Ballard.'"

I let out a breath.

"And I said the first thing that came into my head. 'You don't want to marry her?'

"'How can I? Marry her and live in Memphis? Marry her and live anywhere?'

"I couldn't reply. He said, 'I love you, and I love Mike. I want us to stay a family.'

I thought, *What does Mike know? It will kill him to find out about this.*

"He said, 'I'm not stupid enough to ask you to forgive me. It isn't a matter of one day of atonement and we're finished. It's going to be many more days of atonement than that. If you want to try.'

"I said, 'I'll have to think about it.'

"'That's as much as I deserve,' he said, and hearing that, tears came to my eyes. I was angry at myself for wanting to cry.

"He reached for my hands. "I am so sorry,' he said.

"'You had better be.'

"'I need your help.'

"'For forgiveness?'

"'For more than that.'

"'There's more?' And at that, the tears dried up and I was furious.

"'She's pregnant.'

"'It's yours?' That was mean, but I felt mean.

"'Yes. I'm sure of it.'

"'Why are you telling me this?'

"He tried to reach for my hands again, and I yanked them away. He said, 'I've made a terrible mistake here, but I want to do what's right.'

"'What is that?'

"'I want to take care of the child.'

"'Money?'

"'Mostly. But I want to be a father, as much as I can.'

"I looked away, because I was hurt and angry at the same time, and it was coming out as tears.

"He said, 'I don't want to do this behind your back. I want you to know about it.'

"'You don't think I'll be happy about it!'

"'I wouldn't ask you to be. Just to let me follow my conscience. Allow me that.'

"I should have said, 'Maybe.' Or, 'I'll think about it.' But instead, I asked him, 'Can we afford it?'

"He said, 'We'll go over the accounts together so you can see. But I'm sure we can afford it.'

"And that's how I agreed to it."

She swiped her hand over her eyes and waited a moment. I waited too.

She said, "She went to New York—Mo told me she got a job there—and he didn't see her anymore. He wrote a check every month, and when the boy got big enough, Mo would write him a letter, too. The boy started to write letters back. The mother stayed in New York, and Mo asked if I minded visiting his relatives there. Once a year, we'd go to New York to see them. And one afternoon, he'd excuse himself, saying he had an errand. He was going to take the boy out for an excursion. The zoo or the museum. The first time he did that, I excused myself and I went to Bergdorf Goodman. I was furious. I told myself I'd buy the most expensive thing I could put my hands on, just to show Mo how angry I was. I walked around the store. I'd pick up something—a purse, say—and look at the price tag. Then I'd ask myself, 'Do I really want this?' The same with the dresses. I even looked at the fur coats. 'Do I want this?' Every time I put something down, I felt less angry. Finally, I picked up a scarf. It was pretty, and it wasn't cheap, but it wasn't crazy expensive, either. I said to myself, 'This I'd wear.' And I bought it." She shook her head. "Every year, when Mo took the boy out for their excursion, I'd go back to Bergdorf Goodman. I was less angry every time. Finally, I just walked around and realized I didn't need or want a thing. I wasn't angry anymore."

I was disturbed that she called him "the boy." "What's his name?"

"His mother named him Kevin. And he took her surname. Kevin Ballard."

"You never met him?"

"No. I heard about him, a bit at a time, from Mo. That he did well in school. That he played baseball. That he couldn't sing, which Mo thought was funny. Well, when it came time for him to apply to college, Mo said to me, 'I want to pay his tuition.' And just like last time, before I could stop myself, I said, 'Can we afford it?' As it turned out, he was smart and talented, and his background didn't hurt him. He got into Columbia with a full scholarship. Mo paid for the luxuries and the vacations."

"When was he there?"

"He started in the late eighties. He graduated in '92."

"I started there in '94. We just missed each other." I asked her, "Did my father ever meet Kevin?"

"No. You know Mike idolized his father. He couldn't be mad at Mo, so he was mad at the mother and the son."

"Evidently he still is."

"Natalie, do you know what a shande this was in the Jewish community back then? That Mo Raskin, known as a beacon for civil rights at Temple Israel, was an adulterer with a son who was half Black?"

"Nana, do you want to know something ironic? Everyone I've talked to in the Black community—everyone who knew Grandpa—knew about this. It's an open secret in the Black community. And they all sat on it when I asked them, because they didn't want to be the one to tell a white woman and a Raskin that her grandpa had an affair with a Black woman and fathered a half Black child."

"It had to be a secret in the Jewish community. We couldn't get a divorce. That was another shande all by itself. It was better to stay in a marriage in those days, no matter how bad it was."

"I wish it hadn't been such a painful secret in the family."

Like every other person who'd confessed to me, my grandmother now sighed. "I thought I'd feel better, telling you. But all I feel is tired and sad. It's still a burden."

I took her hand and pressed it between both of my own. "I know."

"The guitar," she said. "We still have to figure out what to do with it."

"You could make that decision yourself," I said.

"No, it wouldn't be right. And it wouldn't help things between you and your father."

I felt as tired as she did. "Do you think anything will?"

17

LET IT GO

Shortly after I talked to Nana, Josh called me. I knew this conversation wasn't going to be pleasant, but I worked hard to kid him. "Calling me during the day? Sacrificing billable time? This must be serious."

"They let me eat lunch, take bathroom breaks, and fill out my timesheet," he said, kidding back. "I can't bill for any of that."

"What's up?"

"Dad's lawyer called me. It was about Dad's snit over the lease."

Great. Now another stranger knew. "Why did he call you?"

"Lawyer to lawyer. And his kids are in religious school with ours."

I could never forget how small a town Memphis was. "What did he have to say?"

"There are no grounds for breaking the lease. Like I told you, you can sue over anything. But it's not worth the bother."

"Did he tell you it was a family problem instead of a legal one?"

"Yes, he did, and he probed a little. I told him about the guitar, how it's surfaced and drawn a lot of unwanted attention, not to mention caused a lot of family conflict. Was that okay?"

"Yes, because it's all true, even if it isn't the whole story. Did he recommend we get some family therapy?"

Josh actually laughed. "Well, he thought of an arbitrator first, then a consultant who works with family businesses. After that, he suggested a therapist."

I debated telling him the secret that Nana had shared with me. I decided against it for the time being. "Nana wants the family to make a joint decision about the guitar. That might be a good way to hash this out."

"Maybe. If we need an outsider's perspective, we know where to get it. I can bring that up and take the heat for mentioning it."

"You'll talk to Dad?"

"Not just yet. Is that all right with you?"

I'd have to live with my father's fury for a while, as much as it hurt. "I guess it will have to be."

"Nat, I know I've said this before, but there's a way through this, I'm sure. We just don't see it yet."

"I hope you're right."

I WAS reluctant to tell Gideon about my conversation with Nana, even though he'd appreciate the confirmation that his hunch had been right. How could I pretend that this salacious revelation was a business issue?

At Sotheby's, we'd unearthed family secrets all the time, either by dealing with angry families or digging out provenance. How often had I gossiped about a client family's infidelities or illegitimate progeny and called it "research"?

It was different when the secret, and its stain, was in my own family.

Gideon didn't insist. As we closed one night, he said to me, "Would you like to hear Eli Hunter play?"

Eli Hunter was a national draw among blues singers and guitarists, but he'd gotten his start in Memphis. "He's going to be in town?"

"Playing at the Blues Bar."

"How did you hear about that?"

"Local guys are going to back him up. One of them is a friend of mine."

"Do you play there?"

"Sometimes."

My shoulder ached, a psychosomatic twinge. I'd used up Gideon's sympathy for my emotional symptoms. "Okay."

"The bourbon's on me," he said.

"Thanks."

"The ribs, too."

I brightened. "Even better."

He laughed. "The way to a Jewish girl's heart. Dinner."

"How many Jewish girls have you dated?"

"In Nashville?"

I caught myself. "This isn't a date."

"Of course not. Just a friendly evening out between business associates." But he winked at me as he had when he was wooing me to bring him in as a dealer.

I rested my hands on the glass countertop. "I had a talk with my grandmother. About Mo and Yvonne." I sighed. "You were right."

He waited for more, but I shook my head. "And that's all I can manage to tell you."

He touched my sore shoulder, and the pain went away. "It's not going anywhere," he said.

THE BLUES BAR was bigger than E&H, but not by much, with small wooden tables crowded onto the floor. Old concert posters plastered the walls, and neon signs punctuated the darkness. The air smelled smoky with barbecue and bourbon. The bartenders and waitstaff here were all Black, smiling and a little too servile for my taste. As a teenager, I hadn't come here, since we considered it hokey and touristy, and as a replanted native, I'd avoided it for the same reason. In Gideon's company, I felt like an insider. We were locals, here to put on a show for the visitors.

The stage, which ran the length of the back wall, was full of equipment, amps and speakers, a drum kit and a keyboard, but empty of musicians. This early, the music came over the sound system, a familiar song sung by an unfamiliar artist. "Who's singing 'Love in Vain'?" I asked Gideon.

He laughed. "You don't recognize Robert Johnson?"

"Is he playing that mythical guitar of his?"

"Sure enough."

When we ordered, I declined bourbon, opting for beer instead, and ate the ribs with pleasure, licking the grease and sauce off my fingers. Gideon laughed softly as I wiped my hands with a towelette. "You can take the girl out of Memphis, but you can't take Memphis out of the girl," he said.

As we ate, the bar began to fill up. The crowd was mostly white, like the tourists who came to the shop, casually dressed in jeans and T-shirts, eager for a taste of the Black Memphis that didn't have a painful history attached to it. As they drank, they talked louder and laughed more, trying to make themselves heard above the sound system, which had switched to John Lee Hooker.

"Hey, Gid," said a stranger, who pulled a stray chair from a neighboring table to sit with us. He was a short, chunky man who laid his guitar case over his lap.

"Hey, Tyrone," Gideon said.

Tyrone said, "Who's your friend?"

"This is Nat Raskin. We're friends, but we do business together," Gideon said. "Nat owns an antique shop on South Main, and I rent space from her."

I said, "He's too modest. He keeps us in business because he can sell anything to anyone, and he does."

Tyrone laughed. "That's the man I know," he said. "Charm the birdies out of the trees." He nodded to me. "Enjoy the show."

"Planning on it," Gideon said. As Tyrone walked onto the stage, Gideon said, "We've played together a lot."

I asked, "Why aren't you backing up Eli Hunter?"

"As a bluesman, I'm not in Eli Hunter's league," Gideon said.

As Tyrone plugged in his guitar, a familiar figure made his way to the stage. A slender, willowy man in a white shirt that was too big for him. He carried a guitar case, but I knew what was inside. I knew that starburst pattern. When he saw us, he stopped at our table and stared at us in surprise. "Imagine meeting you guys here," he said.

"Hi, Jeffrey," I said. "You're playing?"

"Eli invited me."

Gideon said, "Good for you, backing up Eli Hunter."

Jeffrey lifted the guitar case. "I wish I was playing my dad's guitar."

"Don't start," I said.

He gave us his best beguiling smile. "Enjoy the show."

The noise level rose as the waiting crowd drank another round. "I need another beer. You want anything?" Gideon asked me.

"I'm fine."

He slipped through the tables to the bar, where he chatted with the bartender and exchanged a few words with a big, muscular man who stood with his back to the bar and his face to the room.

When he returned, beer in hand, I asked, "Who's the big guy?"

"Oscar? He's the bouncer."

"Will there be trouble?"

Gideon laughed, and I remembered he'd worked as a bouncer himself. "Oscar's insurance."

The crowd began to clap, and I saw why. Even I knew what Eli Hunter looked like: a compact, smiling man with a snub nose and close-cropped hair, his hand resting easily on the guitar slung over his shoulder. He nodded and smiled as he made his way to the stage, at ease with the cheers, the whistles, and the shouts of "Eli!"

As he walked onto the stage, I whispered to Gideon, "What's the guitar?"

"Fender. A sweet one."

"Old?"

"Not as old as Bobby Swann's."

Eli surveyed the crowd, which was still clapping and cheering for him. He raised his arms in greeting, an amiable smile on his face, and said, "It's good to see you too, Memphis!" They quieted down. "I was born and raised up here, and I played every bar and club on Beale Street. It's great to come back." A broad smile, and more cheering. "And great to play with two local bluesmen with big reputations in Memphis. Tyrone Wilson, my man!"

Tyrone nodded and raised a fist in solidarity with Eli.

"And we have something really special for you tonight. I'm playing with a bluesman who's the son of a legend. Bobby Swann, the best guitarist who ever played for Stax. Jeffrey Swann is carrying on his father's legacy. A big hand for Jeffrey!"

Jeffrey nodded and gave the audience his seductive smile. They were in the mood to cheer and whistle, so they gave it up for Jeffrey, too.

Eli said, "Let's play some music!"

Gideon nudged me. "Look who's here," he said, his voice low.

She'd come right from work. She wore a navy pantsuit and a white blouse, out of place among the tourists in their jeans and the locals in their clubwear. The place was too crowded even for a stool at the bar, and she stood against the counter, angling her body to watch the stage.

It was Brenda.

"What is she doing here?" I asked.

"She likes blues music?"

"She's not here for Eli," I said.

"You don't know that."

Brenda turned her head in our direction. She stared at us both, but she didn't acknowledge either of us.

Now I sighed. "Should we tell Oscar there might be trouble?"

"If there is, he'll handle it."

I began to feel nervous. I leaned toward Gideon. "Are you going to tell me you've seen a situation a lot worse in a bar?"

"No," he said.

As Eli played, I couldn't stop feeling Brenda's presence. She wasn't here for Eli. She was here for Jeffrey, and her focus on him bothered me.

Like Brenda, I didn't watch Eli. I watched Jeffrey. I'd heard him play, but I'd never seen him perform. I'd watched video from Wattstax, and I knew what Bobby Swann looked like onstage. He was confident. Proud. Sexy. It gave me a chill to watch Jeffrey but to see Bobby Swann.

Brenda shifted uncomfortably against the bar, but her eyes never left Jeffrey. I whispered to Gideon, "I'm worried about Brenda."

"Let Oscar handle it."

When the set ended, the crowd clapped and cheered. Many people rose to their feet. They called out, "Eli! Eli!"

Eli raised his arms and said, "Thank you, Memphis! God bless you, Memphis!" He ran down the stairs to the main floor, and as he made his way through the crowd, he pressed hands and beamed at them like a politician.

Tyrone unplugged his guitar and laid it back in the case. He shook Jeffrey's hand and he, too, left the stage. Jeffrey took his time. He stayed on the stage as though he savored standing there. He surveyed the room, even though the crowd wasn't his today.

Brenda picked up her bag and walked quickly to the stage, intent and in a hurry, as she must walk to her meetings at the hospital.

I threw a glance in Oscar's direction. He turned to watch Brenda.

Brenda stopped at the stage and called out, "Jeffrey!"

Oscar moved swiftly, in a fluid motion for such a big man, and rested his hand on her shoulder. "Ma'am?" he asked, his voice polite but firm.

Brenda said, "I'm not bothering anyone."

"I'd feel better if you stepped away from the stage," he said.

Brenda snapped, "I'm not here to make you feel better."

Jeffrey turned. "Hey, Oscar, it's okay. It's my sister Brenda."

"She got herself an attitude," Oscar said.

Jeffrey laughed. "Yeah, that's Brenda," he said. He unslung his guitar and laid it on the keyboardist's bench. He wiped the sweat from his face with the sleeve of his shirt. He walked to the edge of the stage, where he squatted down to talk to Brenda. Smiling, he said, "How did you like the show?"

"I didn't come here for the show."

Still smiling, he asked, "Then why did you come here? Is there something you want?"

She leaned forward, too close to him. "I want the guitar," she said, her voice low and hoarse.

He sat back on his heels. "Hey, Brenda, I can't help you with that."

Her voice rose. "You think you can have whatever you want because you can buy it."

"Oh, Brenda," he said, his voice dropping low.

"But you can't." She balled her hands into fists. "That guitar isn't yours. Your mother never should have sold it. It should have come to me. It's mine."

Jeffrey reached for Brenda's hands. "Brenda. Calm down."

"Don't tell me to calm down." Her voice rose alarmingly.

Oscar was ready. He reached for Brenda's shoulder again. "Get off me," she growled at him, and she tried to grab Jeffrey's arm. He rocked back on his heels, trying to get out of her way, but she flailed at him. "Why should I?" She was shouting now. "It's not yours. It's mine, and I'll get it."

The crowd, which had thinned a lot after Eli finished the set, now gazed at the altercation. A few people edged closer, not to help but to watch.

Jeffrey said, "It's okay, Oscar, I'll handle it." He gripped her wrists. "Brenda, quiet, quiet down."

"Don't you try to shut me up!" she shouted. She yanked

her arms back and pulled hard, and before I could cry out, before Oscar could stop it, I saw it happen.

I saw Jeffrey rock back and forth. I saw him try to steady himself. I saw him lose his balance, and then he couldn't right himself. Before Oscar could pull Brenda away or catch Jeffrey, Jeffrey fell. He tumbled from the stage face first, hitting the floor with a terrible thud, and he lay still.

Brenda began to scream.

Oscar grabbed Brenda by the arm and said, "You come with me." As he pulled her in back, he said to the bartender, "Call 911."

The crowd now backed away. I heard a man mutter, "I didn't come on vacation to talk to the cops," as he pushed his way to the door.

Gideon didn't rise to go. He didn't even look particularly perturbed. I felt sick. I whispered to him, "Is Jeffrey all right?"

"I don't know."

"Is there anything we can do?"

"Stay put. The cops will want to talk to us. If you want to throw the book at Brenda, this is your chance."

I could hear screaming. Brenda must be somewhere in back.

I was shaking. "How can you be so calm?" I asked Gideon.

"It don't help to get worked up."

Jeffrey hadn't stirred. "How can we leave him like that?" I asked.

"Don't try to move someone with a concussion. Let the EMTs handle it."

I sat at the table, my hands on the sticky surface, every nerve tense for the sound of a siren. Somewhere in back, Brenda was still screaming.

When I heard the familiar wail outside, I felt sick with relief. The EMTs came in first, followed by the police. I hoped Val was on duty, but the EMT team consisted of two men, one white and one Black, muscular and calm like Val. I jumped up, but Gideon pulled me back. A few of the remaining patrons had gathered, but the EMTs moved them aside with a practiced hand, and the police stopped at the bar for their inquiry.

"Excuse me," I asked the Black EMT.

"Ma'am, please don't get in the way."

"I have an emergency contact for you. His mother is a friend of mine. Do you want me to call her?"

"Hang on. We'll take the name and number from you."

"How is he?"

"Ma'am, please sit down, and we'll get to you."

Sitting, shaking, I wrote Michelle's name and number on a cocktail napkin. When the EMT came to the table, I handed it to him.

I saw Jeffrey's face as they removed him onto the stretcher: bruised and bloody. He was still unconscious.

The screaming had stopped.

"Sit down," Gideon said to me. "I'm going to get you something to drink."

"No whiskey."

He brought me cola. "It's full octane, but don't argue with me about it. You need some sugar."

"This is a hell of a time to flirt with me."

"It's for shock," he said.

<hr>

THE NEXT MORNING, Gideon and I stood in the lobby of Baptist Memorial. The doctors, clad in blue scrubs, were in a hurry, but the nurses, whose scrubs were floral, strolled down the corridors as though they were on break. A woman in a black pantsuit, clipboard pressed to her chest, hurried past us, and I remembered that Brenda worked here. The air had the scent of air freshener and very faintly, of flowers. The smell of sickness was far away. I watched as a nurse wheeled a young woman toward the front door. She looked dazed and exhausted, but she bent over the bundle in her arms with a big smile on her face.

In a hospital full of gunshot wounds, concussions, heart surgery, and cancer, I was painfully reminded of the reason for my two visits to Mount Sinai in New York. I put my hand on my midsection. "I hate hospitals," I said.

Gideon rested his hand on my arm. "Let's go find Jeffrey," he said.

I forced myself to stand up straight. "And Michelle."

Gideon tapped on the door of Jeffrey's room, where the air smelled more aggressively of air freshener, and a heart monitor beeped every few seconds. Jeffrey lay on the hospital bed, his eyes closed, looking even worse than he had in the dim light of the bar. Both his eyes were ringed with black bruises, and his left cheek, where he'd hit the ground, was purple and badly swollen. His lip was split and just starting to scab over.

Michelle sat at his bedside, accompanied by a man who must be her husband, Jim. All the makeup had worn off Michelle's face, and every mark of strain, every line of age, showed beneath her eyes and around her mouth. Jim, a handsome man in better moments, now looked exhausted and ashen. Michelle introduced us, never letting go of Jim's hand.

"How is he?" I asked.

Jeffrey hoisted himself up. "He can talk for himself," he said.

Gideon turned to look at Jeffrey. "How are you?"

He brightened a little. "I look like hell, and I feel like hell, but nothing serious is wrong," he said. He peeled back his blanket and flexed his fingers. "My hands are fine."

Michelle made a sound between a snort and a sob. Jim put his arm around her shoulders.

Nothing like a senseless assault to bring a family together, I thought. "We won't stay long."

Jeffrey lay back and closed his eyes. The bruising looked worse.

There was another tap on the door. "Yes?" Michelle said. She said to me, "The nurses have been fussing over him all morning."

Virgie Lee stepped into the room, and Michelle stared at her in surprise. "What the hell are you doing here?"

"I ain't here for my own pleasure, that's for sure," Virgie Lee said. She tugged on someone's arm, and Brenda stumbled into the room.

Brenda looked like hell, too. The woman who prided herself on being crisp, clean, and color-coordinated was a mess. Her suit was rumpled, as though she'd slept in it, and her white shirt was creased and stained. Her hair was badly mussed. Her face was gray and lined. An unpleasant odor rose from her. A harsh disinfectant and a rank smell of sweat.

She'd walked through the hospital, her workplace, full of people who knew her, looking and stinking like that.

Virgie Lee said, "She insist on coming right here."

Jeffrey asked, "What happened to you?"

"I was arrested."

Virgie Lee said, "She called me from the jail. And I told her she could spend the night there to think about her sins."

Confused, I said, "Why didn't you call Edwin?"

Virgie Lee said, "He's out of town on business. Or so he says."

Brenda's eyes were darkly shadowed, and her skin had an ashen cast. She edged toward Jeffrey's bed, opposite Jim and Michelle.

Michelle asked, "Why the hell are you here?" just as Jim said, "I don't really want you here."

Her arms helplessly at her sides, she said, "Jeffrey, I am so sorry. I never meant for this to happen."

He sat up a little.

"If you want to press charges, you should. I deserve it." Tears began to slide down her face.

"Jim?" Jeffrey asked. "Can we scare up a chair for Brenda?"

Jim said, "You should throw her out," but he rose and carried his own chair to the other side of the bed. Then he went back to Michelle and put his hands on the back of her chair, too tired to keep himself upright.

Jeffrey patted the seat. "Brenda?"

She fell heavily into the chair, letting tears slip down her face. "I am so, so sorry," she repeated. "I never meant to hurt you. I just wanted—I just wanted—"

Jeffrey said softly, "It was never about the guitar, was it?"

"I just wanted to know that Daddy loved me. I wanted something I could hang on to—something to prove it—" The tears came faster.

Jeffrey reached for Brenda's hand. "Oh, Brenda," he said. "Of course he loved you." He cradled her hand in his own.

No inkstains, I thought. *How do people get fingerprinted these days?*

"He loved all of us," he said, his blackened eyes taking in his mother and Virgie Lee, who stood in the doorway, her arms crossed over her chest. "He hurt all of us. He damaged every one of us. That's his legacy for us, and believe me, it isn't a legacy to be proud of."

"I am so, so sorry, Jeffrey," she said, the words muffled by sobs.

"Oh, Brenda," he said, and he sat up, extending his arms to her. "Come here." As she sobbed, he gathered her into his embrace. The injured half brother held the lawbreaking half sister in his arms as she wept and wept. He stroked her disheveled hair. "Let it go, Brenda," he said softly. "It's all right. All of it. Just let it go."

1 8

MO'S LEGACY

On the sidewalk outside the hospital, where the air smelled of magnolia and car exhaust instead of air freshener, Gideon asked me, "Do you really think Brenda's going to let it go?"

I punched him lightly on the arm, like Jude punched me. "You're a Baptist, aren't you? You just saw them come to Jesus. Have a little faith!"

A middle-aged woman, pushing her elderly father in a wheelchair, threw a surprised glance at me.

Gideon nodded at her and smiled. To me, he said, "Has your grandmother decided what she wants to do with the guitar?"

I said, "First my family has to come to Jesus, too."

He laughed. "Lots of luck with that."

I called Nana. After I asked after the bruise on her arm ("It's gone") and her general mental health ("Also fine, now that the police are after that no-goodnik"), she said, "You didn't call me to ask about my arm. Spit it out, Natalie."

I spat it out as though it were a cherry pit. "Dad is still furious with me, and I feel like hell."

"I know. I don't blame you."

"I want to get the family together to talk things through. The real problem. Not just Dad and me. The truth about Grandpa."

She didn't hesitate. "Ask everyone to come here."

"You'd do that?"

"For you? Of course. And don't forget, I'm Mikey's mother. I can say and do things no one else can."

"Josh doesn't know the whole story yet. I want to talk to him before we get together."

"You do that."

"Nana, are you up for this?"

"No, but I can't stand to watch you and your father hurt each other. Whatever happens when we get together, it can't be worse than that."

I MET Josh in his office after the shop closed. The last time I'd been here, I hadn't admired the view, but the river was visible from here, and at sunset, the last of the light was reflected in the dark water of the Mississippi.

As I stared out the window, he asked me if I wanted anything to drink.

"Do you keep whiskey in your credenza?"

"Ha-ha. I have ice water."

"That will have to do."

He dispensed with further courtesies. "Nat, what is this about?"

"Why Dad is so angry with me," I said.

"Has he sicced his lawyer on you yet?"

"No. It was a bluff, like you thought. But he's still mad at me." I sighed. "I want to tell you the real reason why. This is going to be difficult for you to hear."

He steepled his fingers, his lawyer's gesture, using the professional veneer to brace himself for whatever I had to tell him. "Go ahead."

"It isn't about the guitar, even though that started it. It isn't about the shooting, but that leads to it. Have you ever heard of a singer named Yvonne Ballard?"

"No, never."

"She was our local Aretha before she signed with Atlantic and had a moment in the 1970s as a soul singer."

"Okay," he said. "What's the connection?"

"Grandpa had an affair with her back in the 1960s."

Despite his professional cool, he was surprised enough to drop his hands to the table. "Is that true? How did you find out?"

"Nana told me. Believe me, she's in a position to know."

"Jesus, Nat."

"That's not all of it."

"There's more?"

I took a deep breath. I was breaking the family faith, and I was disillusioning Josh, who had loved and respected Grandpa. "She had a child by him."

"Grandpa? The civil rights beacon at Temple Israel?"

"If you don't want to take my word for it, you can ask

Nana."

"What happened to the kid?"

"His mother moved to New York, and he grew up there. He went to Columbia University, a few years before I did. I looked him up online. He's a senior marketing exec at J.Crew. He's in the rag trade, like Dad is."

"Is he a Raskin?"

"No, he took his mother's name. His name is Kevin Ballard."

"Nat, I see why it had to be a secret back in the day. It was a scandal, wasn't it? Especially at Temple Israel. And I see why they didn't tell us when we were younger and while Grandpa was still alive. But why have they kept it a secret? Why didn't they trust us with it?"

"I don't know."

"Nat, who knows about this?"

"Mama and Daddy. Nana. Me. And now you."

"Should I tell Celia? Or should I keep it quiet?"

"No, you should tell her. That's the whole point here," I said. "To let the secret out. That's why I want us to get together to talk about it."

He stared down at the table. "As a lawyer, I can't tell you how many family secrets I've heard in this room. I've never known a family that was any happier for keeping a secret. But now I know exactly why they sit on this stuff until it makes them crazy."

I WAS the first to arrive, as Nana and I had planned. I looked around the living room, the scene of so many holiday and birthday celebrations over the years, and tried to imagine this discussion in it.

I sniffed the air. "You baked something."

"I couldn't help it. If we're still speaking to each other afterwards, I'll bring it out."

The doorbell rang. It was Josh, who had come alone.

Nana asked, "Celia didn't come with you?"

"No, she decided not to insert herself into a Raskin family fight."

So Celia had more tact than I gave her credit for.

Nana asked, "Did you tell her about Mo?"

"Yes, I did, after Nat told me. I hope that was all right."

Nana said, "Of course it was all right. Come in."

"Babka?" he asked, his voice hopeful.

"Later."

By the time my parents arrived, Josh and I were in the living room. Josh got up and hugged Dad, then Mama.

I didn't.

Nana seated us at her table. She didn't offer anything, even coffee.

My father said, "I don't think I've ever come to this house without being offered something to eat or drink."

Nana said, "I didn't know what to serve for a family fight."

Both he and Josh laughed, a nervous sound.

I asked my father, "Do you really want to shut my business down?"

"No. I was sorry for that as soon as it came out of my mouth."

"Can we talk about why you're really mad at me?"

"I asked you to leave it alone," he said to me. "You see

all the trouble it's caused."

"I didn't go looking for it," I said. "I found Mo Raskin. And I found Yvonne Ballard."

"It's something I never wanted you to know."

"Well, I do now. Josh knows, too. I told him."

"She told you?"

Josh said, "I'm not planning to spread it around. As far as I'm concerned, it's like any family secret I hear from a client. It's private, and it's confidential."

Except for Celia.

"You had better mean that," my father said, and it wasn't a joke.

Josh said, "Dad, I understand why it was so shameful forty years ago. I don't understand why it's still so shameful."

"Do you really have to ask? You really don't understand why it had to be a secret and stay a secret?"

"Why couldn't you tell us? Nat and me?"

My father said, "Do you think we liked keeping it?"

I asked, "Why did you?"

My mother echoed me. "Mike, why did we?"

"You know better than anyone," he said to her, his face shadowed.

"And what a burden it's been, all these years," she said, and I saw the weight of it in her expression. "Hiding it. Keeping it close. Lying to our kids about it. It wasn't worth hanging on to anymore, Mike. That's why I told Nat."

My father hesitated. When he spoke, his voice was low and halting. "You don't know what it was like back in the sixties in Memphis," he said. "How bad segregation was.

How ugly the hatred was. My father was a hero. He fought Jim Crow. He stood up to the Klan." His eyes settled on Josh, then on me. "I never told you how the Klan intimidated us at home, too. That didn't stop him. He wouldn't be moved." He looked down at his hands, clutching the edge of the table. "When I watched the Reverend King speak, I thought of my father."

He continued to stare at his hands. "I was in the record shop the day my father shot Buddy Griffen. I saw the whole thing, and I understood what I was seeing. The shame was bad enough, but the shock was worse. He wasn't a hero anymore."

I said softly, "You were just a boy."

Nana said, "And you're not a boy anymore."

I thought of myself, a grown woman of more than thirty, loving and adoring my father, thinking he could do no wrong and he would never hurt me.

Nana said, "Mike, look at me."

My father raised his head. He looked as stricken as he had after Grandpa died.

Nana said, "I forgave Mo. I did such a good job of it that Nat never knew. She thought we had the perfect marriage. When hers fell apart, she blamed herself because she hadn't created a marriage as perfect as Mo's and mine."

When I winced, she said, "I'm sorry, ziskeyt, I know that hurts you. But this is for my son to hear. Mike, what possessed you to hurt Nat when she found out? To push her away when she mentioned Yvonne Ballard's name? Is your love for her, and hers for you, really worth so little to you?"

My father looked away, and I felt my eyes sting.

Nana said, "When Mo told me what happened, he asked for my forgiveness. He said, 'It will take more than one day of atonement to make things right.'"

How old was I today? Was I thirteen, proud of being a woman in my body as well as by Jewish law? Was I eighteen, happy to run away from Memphis to New York? Or was I thirty-two, old enough to know better?

I said, "Dad, listen to me."

He shook his head.

"No, Dad. Listen to me. Your father stood up for civil rights. He stood up against the Klan. That's what we're all proud of. But it's only part of who he was."

My father raised his eyes to mine. I couldn't meet them, not yet.

"He was flawed, too. He made a mistake, a big mistake. He was unfaithful to Nana. He had an affair with Yvonne Ballard. He had a child with her. And then he did his best to make it right."

My father didn't look up.

I asked, "Why can't we see him for all of what he was? The good and the bad, the right and the wrong?" I looked around the table, and I heard what I was saying. Really heard it and let it sink in. Why couldn't I see my father the same way—as the good man who loved me and the flawed man who hurt me?

Long after I'd grown up, I'd still loved my father like a child. Now I knew better. He'd made a big mistake with me, and now I had to learn to love him like an adult. I didn't know what that would look like, or how long it would take.

More than one day of atonement, that was for sure.

My father said, "What a legacy."

Jeffrey Swann's words. I said, "That's what we have. The good and the bad together. That's Mo Raskin's legacy."

Nana said, "And the guitar."

My father said, "I don't care about the guitar."

"I know you don't," Nana said. "But I do."

My father said, "For my money, you can burn it."

"Don't worry," Nana said. "It's not your guitar or your money." She looked at me. "By the way, it's worth a lot of money these days."

That was my cue. "As much as fifty thousand at auction."

"It's not about the money," she said. "I don't need the money." She surveyed us, one after another. "That guitar was Mo's heartfelt way to help a struggling musician. He didn't know Bobby Swann would become a Memphis legend. That didn't matter to him. He just wanted to do the right thing. And now there's another musician who needs it. He bought it to play it, not knowing it was stolen."

Now I was glad to chime in. "He's a blues guitarist. He and his wife just had a baby. He was planning to sell the guitar to put away money for the baby's future. A struggling musician, just like the people Grandpa used to help."

Josh said softly, "That's the legacy."

Nana said, "You're exactly right. I want to use the guitar to honor Mo's memory. I don't want to sell it. I want this young man to have it. I want to give it to him." She looked at Josh. "Can we do that?"

Relief washed over Josh's face. "Yes, we certainly can."

Now Nana surveyed the room, her gaze settling on us, one after another, as though she were taking a vote. No one objected. "Then that's what we'll do. We'll give it away. We'll let it go."

I felt a jolt of satisfaction to hear those words in the Raskin family, too.

Let it go.

NANA, Josh, Gideon, and I assembled on the sidewalk outside Justin's house on a bright spring day, when the magnolia was in full bloom and perfumed neighborhoods even as urban as Justin's. I was surprised to realize that neither Josh nor Nana had met Gideon. I made the introductions.

Nana asked, "You have it with you?"

Gideon lifted the guitar case. "Right here."

I rang the bell, and Justin answered. "Come on in," he said. "My wife, Kim, is here. You can meet finally her, too."

Kim sat on the sofa, Jasmine in her arms. She was a smiling, rounded woman who held her daughter with an ease that must have come from raising little brothers and sisters. She said softly, "Excuse me if I don't get up. I just got her settled." She kissed Jasmine's head.

I made more introductions.

Justin's eyes went to the guitar case as Gideon and the rest of us sat.

My grandmother said, "Mr. Taylor—"

"Call me Justin, please."

"I don't know if Nat has told you much about her grandfather, my late husband, Morris Raskin."

"I know that he owned the guitar."

"He did. He bought it from Bobby Swann's widow to help her out, and he was the one who loaned Bobby the money to buy it in the first place. He knew all the musicians on Beale Street and all the musicians at Stax, and he was glad to help them when they needed it. He'd lend them money to cut a record, and he'd stock the records in his shop. He put up flyers for their gigs, and if they needed cash to go on the road, he'd help. He loved the music, and he cared about the people who made it. He was happy to make their careers and their lives a little easier."

Justin nodded. As far as he was concerned, this was ancient history.

"We Jews don't believe in Heaven, but we believe in memorials. I've decided that I want to make a gift of the guitar to you. It's what Mo would have done if he were still with us. Mo's here in spirit, believe me. This is our memorial for him."

Justin looked at her in surprise.

Josh said, "I'm an estate attorney, and I handle property transfers all the time. I've drawn up what's called a deed of gift to transfer the guitar from my grandmother to you. We want to give you undisputed legal ownership of the guitar. It would stand up in any court and in any auction house to prove that the guitar belongs to you. It's what's called an irrevocable deed. That means we can never ask for it back."

Nana said, "It's yours forever."

Justin's eyes widened. "You mean that?"

"I've never meant anything more in my life," Nana said.

Gideon picked up the guitar case. "You'll probably want to keep it somewhere secure, but I took it out of storage for you. I thought you'd want to feel it in your hands."

Justin laid the case on his lap, touching it as though he needed reassurance that it was real. He opened the case, and the brilliant finish caught the light. He looked around the room at all the expectant faces and carefully lifted up the guitar. He slung it over his shoulder and rested his hands on it. "Oh, man," he said, and when he smiled, his eyes were wet. He looked at Nana, who was also smiling and blinking back tears. Then his gaze rested on Kim and Jasmine, and we all could see how passion for the guitar and love for his child warred within him.

Gideon said softly, "You want to play something for us?"

Justin shook his head. "For once in my life, I can't."

THOMAS WAVERLEY CAME into the shop with his usual box of new merch. Atop the carefully wrapped items rested a manila folder.

"What's in there?" I asked.

"Memphis history," he said.

"May I see?"

"It's the most ephemeral of ephemera," he said. "Handle it carefully."

I did, even though it was encased in a plastic sleeve. "This is really something," I said.

Thomas smiled. "Priced accordingly."

Not long after that, my father came into the shop, letting the door close quietly behind him. He saw that I had a customer at the counter, and he pretended to look in Gideon's case as he waited. When he stepped to the counter, he said genially, "You've changed it up again."

"We sold more stuff."

"It looks great."

"Can I help you with something, Dad?"

He leaned against the counter, like any customer who wanted something. His voice was calm, tinged with its usual warmth. "I still haven't found a present for your mother's birthday. Look around with me? Help me find something she'll really like?"

Jude, who was on duty with me, was her irrepressible self. "Are you in the doghouse, Mr. Raskin? Jewelry is always good."

He laughed. "I am so deep in the doghouse I need more than jewelry," he said. "But it would be a start."

I thought of Thomas Waverley's precious, ephemeral find. A few months ago, I wouldn't have dared to show it to my father, but now I decided that I'd let him make up his own mind about it.

"Dad, there's something I want to show you." I took it from the case.

"What is it?"

"It's the program from a church service."

He took it from me, his face asking a question.

"At Mason Temple in Memphis. On April 3, 1968. The

Reverend Martin Luther King gave a sermon that day. He said, 'I've been to the mountaintop.'"

He looked down. "I know," he said. "I was there."

"Mama told me. You were there together."

He shook his head. "I can't look at this," he said. "I can't give her this."

"Maybe someday."

He was silent, and the look on his face told me he was far away.

Keep telling him the truth. "Dad, I've been in touch with Kevin Ballard."

As a fellow Columbia alum, Kevin Ballard had been easy to find. His contributions to the class notes were chatty, telling his friends about his recent promotion, his house renovations, his kids' success in school and athletics, and the antics of the new dog. He invited his fellow grads to contact him and included an email address.

I'd worded my email carefully, mentioning the Columbia connection and saying only that our families were acquainted. If he knew, the name "Raskin" would tell him the rest. To my surprise, his response was warm, as though he'd always known. "I'm surprised to hear from you," he wrote, "but I'm glad you contacted me."

I said, "He's going to be in Memphis in a month to visit his mother. I'm going to meet him."

My father returned to the present, and to me. He handed the program back to me. "I can't see him," he said. "But I won't stop you."

"You couldn't," I said. I put the program back in the case and turned the key in the lock.

He met my eyes. "Let's look at the jewelry."

That was easier. We were easier together. I tried on the rings to show him how they looked and how they fit. He picked out a pair of earrings. "Let me see them on you." He held one up to my earlobe, and his hand brushed my cheek with the old affection.

The first day of atonement, I thought. *The first of many*. I looked in the mirror. "Give her these," I said.

ON A BRIGHT, fragrant Sunday, Joe Jordan strolled into the shop. In honor of the spring season, he'd switched from a fedora to a straw boater. He touched his finger to the brim as he greeted us. He had a pleased, sly smile on his face.

"You have good news, Joe?" Gideon asked.

"I surely do."

"You getting married?"

Joe spluttered with laughter. "Now that wouldn't be good news, Mr. Fairchild. No, it ain't even about me. It's about that young man who's playing Bobby Swann's guitar. Justin Taylor."

"I see he's been playing around town a lot."

"Better than that. He's got himself a contract for an album. They're up in New York, but they're coming down to Memphis to make the record. He's all excited about it. 'New Memphis music sensation plays Stax legend's guitar!'"

I said, "Don't tell me Bobby Swann's ghost got him a record contract."

Joe's eyes slid to the photograph of Mo Raskin. He

leaned closer to me. "Don't think young Mr. Taylor will be selling that guitar anytime soon."

I asked, "Will he be all right?"

Joe said, "Maybe he'll get rich and famous. Maybe he'll go crazy like Bobby did. Maybe he'll be in to see the two of you, wanting to sell the guitar. Could go any direction, and there ain't no way to tell." He winked at Gideon. "As you well know."

"Too well," Gideon said. "Well, give him our best when you see him."

"No hard feelings?"

"Of course not. It's great news."

The rest of the day was surprisingly busy, and it wasn't until we closed that we could stand beneath the live oak in the backyard and talk. The weather was full of the promise of summer, swampy humidity.

I said to Gideon, "So he's going to keep it."

"I thought he might."

"Why didn't he come to tell us himself?"

"Embarrassed, probably. After being so self-righteous about Jasmine's future."

"Maybe this will be the way to assure it," I said.

Gideon shook his head. "All that time and trouble, we won't make a dime on that damn thing."

We both heard the call before we saw her. She sat low enough in the tree to regard us both with her yellow eyes.

"We have to appraise or sell something we can make money on," I said.

"No argument from me."

The owl called again.

I said to Gideon, "Business associates forever?" I held

up my pinkie like we were kids, and he hooked his pinkie through mine. The touch of his finger made me unreasonably happy. Our eyes met, and I smiled at him. "I've got a question for you."

"What is it?"

I moved closer. "Where the hell in Tennessee are you from?"

He laughed and let go of my finger. "You ain't getting that from me so easy."

The owl hooted, and we both looked upward as she spread her wings and flew away.

THE END

Want more of Nat? *Secret of Memphis*, the second book in the Memphis series, is in the works!

When Nat is hired to appraise a valuable set of eleven chairs from the 1770s, her search for the missing twelfth chair embroils her in a family feud that goes back to the days of the Civil War. And she revisits her own past by trying again—with the high school sweetheart whose heart she broke fifteen years ago…

It's coming out later this year!

Want to know when? Sign up for my newsletter for updates at https://www.sabrawaldfogel.com/sign-up. And in the meantime, visit my website to learn more about my other books at https://www.sabrawaldfogel.com/.

HISTORICAL NOTE

It's a little strange to write a historical note for a story that takes place at a time in my own recent memory (although I had to remind myself that phone technology and music streaming technology were a little different when President Obama first took office). But this story has a historical context, and of course you readers want to know what's from the record and what isn't.

While the guitarist Bobby Swann and the singer Yvonne Ballard in this story are fictitious, the music scene centered on Stax Records is not. Stax was founded in 1957 by a brother and sister team, Jim Stewart and Estelle Axton. While their first recordings were country and pop music, they had shifted to rhythm and blues by the early 1960s. Their earliest stars were Rufus Thomas and his daughter Carla; a few years later, they added Otis Redding to their roster. He would become their biggest and best-known star, the voice of Memphis soul.

Stax had a distribution relationship with Atlantic Records, and Jerry Wexler, who produced Aretha Franklin, was a frequent visitor to the Stax studio. The connection with Atlantic would prove to be a near-disaster for Stax. In 1967, Atlantic was sold to Warner Bros.-Seven Arts, and Stax's master recordings became the property of the new company. As Stax lost its back catalog, the label suffered another disaster: the death of Otis Redding in the same year.

Stax was so well-regarded in the Black community that the unrest of 1968, which ravaged the city after the Reverend Martin Luther King's assassination, left the studio building untouched.

Despite business setback and civic tragedy, Stax survived. Al Bell, the company's chief marketing executive, became vice-president and co-owner. The interracial partnership of Bell and Stewart operated with a courtesy and respect unusual in Memphis at the time: they used the same telephone.

Under Al Bell's leadership, Stax rebounded, adding the sound of funk to its roster. Isaac Hayes, who produced in addition to recording and performing, was the star of the early 1970s. He was a well-known figure around Memphis, and he did buy a house in Cordova, the toniest suburb in the Memphis area.

Stax went bankrupt in 1974, but the music lives on.

ABOUT THE AUTHOR

Sabra Waldfogel, who is not from anywhere in the South, studied history at Harvard University and got a PhD in American history from the University of Minnesota. Since then, she has been fascinated by the drama of slavery and its long shadow in American history.

Her first novel, *Sister of Mine*, published by Lake Union, was named the winner of the 2017 Audio Publishers Association Audie Award for fiction. The sequel, *Let Me Fly*, was published in 2018. Since then, she has written a duology about South Carolina at the time of the Civil War. Her most recent work is a trilogy about the war at home, set between 1942 and 1944 in Detroit.

www.ingramcontent.com/pod-product-compliance
Lightning Source LLC
Chambersburg PA
CBHW050801190726
48285CB00005B/1751